Worried anew that I was losing my ability to use white magic, I began to pace around the yard, holding my flame hand well away from my body.

"You should try to get some rest," Pal said.

"I will, in a little while." I was absolutely bone-tired, and wanted nothing more than to lie down and sleep for the next sixteen hours, but I was afraid of what might happen once I drifted off. *If* I drifted off.

My flame hand seemed to catch on something. I looked down, puzzled. I was out in the middle of the yard; there wasn't so much as a tall dandelion nearby. I waved my hand through the empty air. And there it was again, the sensation of an invisible seam.

"Hey, there's something weird over here," I said to Pal. "Can you see or feel anything?"

He came over to investigate. "No, I don't sense anything . . . What is it?"

"I'm not sure." I blinked through several views with my enchanted stone eye. One showed a faint blue rectangular outline in the air, just barely perceptible.

Acting on a hunch, I dug my flame fingers into the seam and pulled. A small door swung open midair, revealing the inside of a wooden shipping crate. It was a little bigger than a school gym locker, maybe three feet tall and two feet wide, and perhaps as many deep. Stacked inside were several plastic-wrapped bricks of white powder and compressed plant matter. The air inside was musty with a familiar sweetly weedy odor.

ALSO BY LUCY A. SNYDER

Spellbent

shotgun
Sorceress

LUCY A. SNYDER

BALLANTINE BOOKS • NEW YORK

2010 Ballantine Books Mass Market Original

Copyright © 2010 by Lucy Snyder

All rights reserved.

Published in the United States by Ballantine Books, an imprint of The Random House Publishing Group, a division of Random House, Inc., New York.

BALLANTINE and colophon are registered trademarks of Random House, Inc.

978-0-345-51210-9

Cover illustration © Dan Dos Santos

Printed in the United States of America

www.ballantinebooks.com

9 8 7 6 5 4 3 2 1

For Sara Larson,
who, it should be noted,
bears absolutely no resemblance
to the Sara you'll find in this book.

Well, okay, there's one resemblance:
her kitten Fred is indeed a little devil.

Acknowledgments

I'd like to thank the people who helped bring this book into the world: my agent, Robert L. Fleck; my editor, Shauna Summers; and her assistant, Jessica Sebor. I'd also like to thank my publicist, April Flores, and my deepest gratitude goes to my first readers: Dan, Trista, and my ever-patient husband, Gary.

And finally, I must express my appreciation to the following molecule for helping me make my deadlines:

Image of caffeine structure courtesy of Wikimedia Commons.

part one

Suburban Outlaws

A Kick in the Head

The festering mob of meat puppets in their tattered Sunday best shambled aside as I rode Pal down Main Street toward the stark white columns and broad marble steps of the Saguaro Hotel. There had to be a thousand bodies in the stinking brown sea parting before us. My skull was pounding, the July heat and hard West Texas sun nearly unbearable. I tipped my straw cowboy hat forward in a futile attempt to get some of the weak breeze on the back of my head.

And in a blink, Miko was suddenly *there* on the steps, Cooper and the Warlock strung up naked and sunburned on rough-hewn mesquite crosses to either side of her. As a small mercy, their limbs had been tied, not nailed, to the twisted branches. Their heads hung forward, insensible, as their chests shuddered to pull in shallow breaths.

The devil kitten in my saddlebag was purring loudly. It could sense the impending carnage.

You ready for this? I asked Pal.

"Ready for a slow, bloody, excruciating death followed by eternal damnation? Of *course*. What fun."

Ignoring his sarcasm, I drew my pistol-grip Mossberg shotgun and racked a cartridge into the chamber.

"Give 'em back, Miko!" My voice was tight, shaky, a mouse's outraged squeak at a lion.

She smiled at me, and all at once her beauty and power hit me like a velvet sledgehammer. If I'd been standing I would have fallen to my knees. I hoped I wasn't getting wet; Pal would know and it would be a sprinkle of embarrassment on top of the disaster sundae I'd brought to our table.

"You know what I want," she whispered, her voice floating easily over the distance between us. "Give yourself to me, and your men shall go free."

A tiny part of me—the part that was exhausted, weary of fighting, weary of running—wondered if giving my body and soul to her would really be such a bad thing.

Oh, fuck that noise, the rest of me replied. *Fuck that long and hard.*

But wait.

I'm getting ahead of myself . . . as usual.

I should have known my life would keep going merrily to shit. The previous Friday had been busier than a dam full of beavers on crystal meth. I'd run police roadblocks, battled dragons, and literally gone to hell and back as I rescued my boyfriend, Cooper, and his little brothers from a fate considerably worse than death. Every muscle in my body ached, and I was looking forward to getting some rest, if perhaps not much actual sleep. I'd seen some things that evening that would probably give me insomnia for, oh, the next decade or so. And there was the little detail that I'd put our city's head wizard into a coma and killed a major guardian spirit. They both richly deserved it, but I'd broken about infinity-plus-one laws and surely the authorities were going to hunt me down with extreme prejudice. So I had prison and perhaps execution to look forward to as well. Yay, go me.

But, so far, it appeared I was safe for the night. I was definitely looking forward to the late dinner my witch friend Mother Karen was making for me and the other Talents who'd helped in the rescue. Whatever she had cooking in her kitchen smelled wonderful. And I knew my familiar, Pal, was plenty hungry.

I carried a platter of savory, steaming ham and a wooden bucket of water down Karen's back steps out into the moonlit yard. It probably looked the same as most other backyards in the neighborhood: rattan furniture and a shiny steel gas barbecue on the brick patio, a wooden picnic table on the lawn, a scattering of oak and buckeye trees bordering the tall dog-eared plank fence ringed by softly glowing solar-charged lights. However, I suspected this was the only place in the entire state of Ohio sheltering a shaggy, six-foot-tall spider monster.

Who, based on the circles his clawed legs had torn in the turf, had spent the past half hour stalking his own posterior.

"Hey, Pal, I got your dinner," I called.

He stopped going around in circles and blinked his four eyes at me, licking his whiskered muzzle uncertainly.

At least, I *thought* Palimpsest looked uncertain; as a ferret his emotions had been pretty easy to read. But now that his familiar form had become magically blended with his true arachnoid body . . . well, I didn't exactly know what "happy" or "sad" or "puzzled" was supposed to look like on such an alien face.

"Having troubles over there?" I asked, setting the platter and bucket down on the picnic table.

"I . . . have an itch," he replied gravely, his voice strange and muffled in my mind. Our telepathic connection was slowly improving, but that, too, was taking some getting used to.

"I could reach every part of my Quamo body and my ferret body," Pal continued, "but oddly these new rear legs aren't very flexible. I can reach my underside, but not my back."

"Maybe you just need to do some yoga."

Through the valved spiracles on his abdomen, he blew noisy chords that sounded like a child randomly banging on the keys of an organ. Laughter? Oh-please snorts? I'd only known Pal for a week, and already I had to get to know him all over again.

"That doesn't help me at the moment," he said.

"Horses back into trees and fence posts to scratch themselves," I replied. "You're tall enough to stand on tippytoes and scratch yourself on the low limbs of that oak over there."

"How dreadfully undignified."

"Or you could just roll around on the grass."

"And that's more dignified how?"

"Oh, hush. It's not like anybody can see you back here," I pointed out. "Otherwise you'd have flipped out the neighbors already and the cops would probably be here."

Long ago, Mother Karen had put her house and its yards under a camouflage charm to keep her foster children's magical practice sessions out of sight of the neighbors. So at least there would be no panicked suburbanites dialing 911 to report a monster prowling through Worthington.

I glanced up at the sky, half expecting to see a Virtus silently descending, ready to smite me like a curse from Heaven. One of the huge guardian spirits had already tried to do a little smiting earlier that evening. Mr. Jordan, the aforementioned now-comatose head of the local Governing Circle, had convinced the Virtus that I was committing some kind of grand necromancy instead of simply trying to rescue Cooper. I'd defended myself, not expecting to win the battle, but win I did.

It was still hard to believe: I had killed a Virtus. *Nobody* was supposed to be able to do that. Not with magic or luck or nuclear weapons or *anything*. It was as if I'd thrown myself naked in front of a speeding freight train in a desperate, stupid attempt to halt hundreds of hurtling tons of iron . . . and had somehow stopped it cold.

Miracles had abounded that evening. But I doubted the Virtus Regnum would see me as anything but a threat. They'd be coming for me, and from what I'd seen so far, they were as merciful as black holes.

I squinted up at the dark spaces between the stars, wondering what lurked there.

"Speaking of things that shouldn't be seen by mundanes, how is that working for you?" Pal asked.

"Huh?" I looked at him, confused.

He nodded toward the gray satin opera glove on my left arm. "The gauntlet. Is it keeping your flames contained?"

"Yes, Karen and the Warlock did a good job enchanting this," I replied, looking at the thin curls of smoke that were trailing from the cuff of the glove, as if I'd used it as a place to stash a still-smoldering cigarette. So far, that was the only sign that the lower half of my arm was a torch of hellfire, courtesy of my having to plunge my arm into the burning heart of the Goad, the pain-devouring devil that had imprisoned Cooper and his family.

"It slips down a little sometimes—I might have to find some double-sided tape or superglue to hold it in place."

Sheathed in the glove, my arm functioned more or less normally, but still had a squishy unreliability. Fine finger movements were still difficult. And that wasn't surprising, considering that my hand was boneless, fleshless, nothing but diabolic flame. I'd had to rely on a natural talent for spiritual extension to give it any kind of solidity; Pal had referred to the ability as "reflexive parakinesis."

And it was pretty close to true reflex. My crysoberyl ocularis—a replacement for my left eye, which I'd lost the week before in a battle with a demon—still hurt a bit, and I was constantly aware that I had a piece of polished rock stuck in my head. But a couple of times that evening, I had completely forgotten that my left arm was no longer entirely flesh. And fortunately I hadn't dropped anything important as a consequence.

"With luck we may be able to find someone to remove the underlying curse, and you'll have your regular arm back," Pal said.

I frowned. Everyone was treating my flame hand—and its power—like a curse. If I were an evil person, somebody bent on destruction and domination, my hand would have seemed almost purely a gift from the gods. With that kind of power literally at my fingertips, so what if having a fiery hand presented a few practical problems? That would be like complaining that you had to move a few boxes out of your garage to make way for the new Porsche. Or in my case, the new tank with a seemingly unlimited supply of surface-to-air missiles.

I was pretty sure I wasn't an evil person. Though I'd certainly made some decisions I regretted—crushing a couple of Mr. Jordan's men under the Warlock's Land Rover was currently at the top of my growing list—I'd been trying to do the right thing at the time. Evil, certainly, was bad. But the power in my hand had saved us all from the Virtus, hadn't it? I was getting pretty annoyed that everyone seemed to think I ought to be in a hurry to get rid of it.

"I should go back inside before they all start dinner without me," I said. "And anyway, your ham's getting cold over here . . . Did you want anything else for dinner? Karen's got pie."

"Let me start with the ham and see how it sits first," he replied. "Wanting to eat something and being able to digest it are two different things."

I looked up at him; surely he'd get bored or lonely staying out in the yard all by himself. "I could see if one of the others knows a shrinking spell so you could come inside with me and have dinner at the table."

"Thank you, but I'm quite all right."

"You sure? I mean, *someone* in the house has to know a good spell."

He blew another chord and reared up on his back

legs. In his ferret days the motion would have meant slight indignance, but in his new form it made him seem monstrously threatening. I had to stifle my prey-monkey instinct to run.

"*I* know a good spell, actually," Pal told me. "The only silver lining to my current situation is that I am finally the proper size. I'd rather not be . . . *diminished* again unless it's necessary."

"Okay, suit yourself. Let me know if you change your mind." I left Pal to his dinner and went back inside to the guest bedroom.

Cooper lay thin and pale under the covers, dead to the world. Dark curly bangs obscured his eyes. He'd lost a scary amount of weight during his time trapped in the hell; he'd always been on the wiry side, but now I could see every rib, every bump on his sternum. I wanted to crawl into bed with him and hold him close.

Instead, I gently shook his bony shoulder. "Wake up, time to eat."

He grunted and pushed away my hand. "Don' wanna. Wanna sleep."

"C'mon. Potions only go so far—we gotta get some real food into you. We can sleep after."

"Where's Smoky?" he mumbled. "I can't feel him."

My stomach dropped. I hadn't yet told him that his white terrier familiar died the night he was pulled into the hell. Smoky had been with him for years. And the loss of a familiar wasn't just the loss of a steadfast companion—Cooper's magical power had taken a hit, too. Even if my boyfriend was so heartless as to want to run right out and find a new familiar, he wouldn't be able to do any better than a dumb toad or mute alley cat. It would be another set of eyes, but nothing more: no intelligent advice, no friendship, no boost to his Talent. The Regnum controlled all access to the modern, intelligent familiars. And we were now outlaws.

I just didn't know how to break the bad news. "He, um . . . he's not with us."

Cooper seemed confused. "You left him at the apartment?"

I took a deep breath. "He didn't make it. The night you disappeared . . . he got killed. It was quick. I don't think he suffered."

A bit of a lie, that; being torn apart by a demon was quick but certainly not easy. I felt horrible about Smoky dying, because it was my own damn fault for not knowing what to do.

Cooper's features twisted in pain and sorrow, and he covered his face in his hands, pressing the heels against his eyes, I guessed to try to keep himself from crying. "Dammit. Poor little guy."

I wanted to weep, too, but if we both started with the waterworks we probably wouldn't stop for a while.

"Hey, everyone's waiting on us; we better get to the dining room." I hauled him up into a sitting position and helped him pull on a black Deathmobile T-shirt.

"This isn't mine," Cooper said, staring down at the flaming death's-head-motor band logo.

"It's Jimmy's," I replied, referring to Mother Karen's eldest foster son. There are spells to create clothing, but fewer and fewer Talents have bothered with that kind of magic since the Industrial Revolution made fabric cheap. "Your pajama pants are his, too. All our stuff is shrunk down in a safe-deposit box at the bank, so you may be wearing his hand-me-downs for a couple more days."

He blinked bloodshot eyes at me. "Why's our stuff at the bank?"

"The farmers wouldn't pay me for the rainstorm, so I missed rent and we were getting evicted. Also that rat-bastard Jordan bugged the apartment, so I figured it was best to pack up and go underground for a while."

"Benedict Jordan? He bugged our place? Why?" His eyelids were starting to droop again. Mother Karen's healing potions tended to put you right under until they'd done their work.

"He wanted you to stay gone in the hell. You're the secret half brother he was scared everyone would find out about. Because then everyone would find out that his father was a bat-shit crazy murdering son of a bitch and people would start questioning his family's authority or some crap like that."

"Whoa, wait . . . he's my *brother*?" Cooper suddenly looked wide-awake.

"Yep. Same mother, different father. Thank God. The Warlock, sadly, is his full brother."

"Huh." Cooper stared down at his knees, his eyes unfocused as if he was remembering something long forgotten. "Benny's . . . Benedict Jordan. Ain't that a kick in the head."

His expression abruptly changed, darkened; I could tell he'd remembered something else, whether from his childhood or hell I had no way of knowing. "That *fucker*."

He swung his legs over the edge of the bed, stood

up, and started to pace the room, agitated and furious. "Oh, this is just *great*. Ol' Benny knew what was going on right from the start. Could have kept me from going to hell, or tried to. Or he could have helped you and the Warlock out. But instead he tried to cover everything up. He screwed over my brothers and me to protect his family's reputation. As if *we* weren't his family, too."

I stepped toward him, concerned. "Calm down, honey—you'll make yourself sick. You need to rest."

Cooper looked at me. "Please, *please* tell me you kicked his ass. Otherwise I'm going to have to, and I'll probably end up killing him and anybody who tries to stop me."

I gently pulled his head down to mine and planted a kiss on his nose. His anger seemed to fade, his sudden burst of energy fading with it.

"Oh yes," I told him. "I'll probably go to prison for it, but his ass is well and thoroughly kicked."

My mind flashed on Jordan lying broken on his desk, his hand a horrible burned mess. My stomach twisted into a knot, but I angrily forced my guilt back down. I would *not* feel bad about giving that creep a taste of his own magic.

I helped Cooper down the hall toward Mother Karen's dining room. The scents of garlic steak, fresh rolls, and sweet potato pie wafted through the air. Cooper's stomach growled loudly.

The Talents who'd helped bring Cooper's infant brothers to Mother Karen's house were already seated at the long cherrywood dining table. Oakbrown and Mariette sat across from Paulie at the far end. Mother

Karen and Jimmy were ferrying plates of food in from the kitchen. The Warlock and Ginger sat across from each other at the near half of the table, arguing.

"I *am* tolerant," Ginger protested, twisting a lock of her red hair around her index finger. "But fundies get on my every last nerve. It's like they think the free expression of female sexuality is going to cause the Apocalypse or something. They're totally threatened by it, and it's stupid. I hate stupid."

"Ginger-pie, it doesn't matter what the mundanes believe, does it?" the Warlock replied. "How do their beliefs touch us? The fact is, they don't. It's been centuries since they were a real threat to us. We don't have to deal with them if we don't want to."

"But what about the Talented kids who get born into mundane families?" Ginger asked. "What about them? Are we just supposed to let them swing in the wind when their crazy stupid parents decide they're possessed by Satan and go all Spanish Inquisition on them?"

"We take care of our own," the Warlock said, looking up at me as I helped Cooper into the empty chair beside Ginger.

"Maybe," I replied, unable to keep the bitterness out of my voice. "Not all Talents are in a hurry to do the right thing, not even for their own kids." I moved around the table to sit across from Cooper in the chair to the Warlock's left.

"You were in a rough situation with your mundane family in Texas, right?" the Warlock said. "And your Talented relatives got you out of there, didn't they?"

"Yeah. My stepfather was going to have me locked

up in a mental institution, but my aunt Vicky found out and brought me to Columbus. She was really cool," I said, swallowing against a fresh swell of sorrow and guilt. No matter how much I told myself that Vicky's suicide wasn't my fault, my heart just wouldn't believe it. "But for what it's worth, my stepfather isn't religious."

Or at least he hadn't been when he sent me away; for all I knew my stepmother had finally converted him.

"See?" the Warlock said to Ginger. "Jackasses come in all faiths."

Mother Karen set a platter of halved, medium-rare flame-broiled rib-eye steaks down on the table beside Cooper, who immediately perked up.

"Oh, man, those look *so* good. Thanks, Karen!" He forked a half steak over onto his plate, waited for Ginger to get hers, then pushed the platter toward me and the Warlock. "Want one?"

"Of course!" I speared one of the garlicky, buttery slabs of meat for my own plate, cut off a perfectly cooked corner of the steak, and popped it into my mouth.

Suddenly, I was thrashing on a cold, wet floor, my mind filled with nothing but terror and the desperate desire to flee, but there was a rope around my hind leg, and a man lunged onto my head and rammed a steel restraint over my muzzle, pinning me to the concrete. The air stank of blood and offal. Oh God, I had to get up, I had to get out, but another man with a long knife brought his blade down on my exposed throat, and there was a hot, bright pain as my arteries poured out, steaming in the foul air, and the men on the other end of the rope heaved and grunted and jerked me flailing into the air as the bladesman slashed me again to finish the job—

I spat the meat back onto my plate, holding my forehead, my mind still humming from the horror of the steer's death. My skull felt as if the terrified beast had kicked me square between the eyes.

The Warlock stared at me. "What's the matter— whoa, dude, that's just *wrong*."

I looked down at my plate. The spat-out piece of steak was twitching like an epileptic slug. It reminded me of the dead animals the Wutganger demon had reanimated.

Ginger peered at the chunk. "Huh. Zombie cow. How'd you do *that*?"

"I—I don't know," I stammered, looking over at Cooper. He, too, had spat out his steak, but his was unmoving, nothing more than cooked muscle. Shuddering, I scooped my twitching piece off my plate and hid it under my napkin.

"Did you feel that?" I asked Cooper. "The men, and the knife?"

"Yeah," he croaked. "Anyone want the rest of this meat?"

"What are you talking about?" the Warlock asked. He hadn't yet started on his dinner.

"Try your steak," I said, then looked at Ginger. "You, too. Please."

They both cautiously cut off small pieces and tasted them.

"Seems fine. Great, in fact. Better than Peter Luger's," the Warlock said.

"Mine, too," said Ginger.

"Try mine," I said, pushing my plate toward the Warlock.

He cut off a piece, sniffed it experimentally, ate it. "It's the same. Delicious. What's the matter?"

"I . . . I felt the steer's death," I said. "So did Cooper, I think."

Cooper nodded, still looking gray.

"You what?" Mother Karen stepped out of the kitchen with a bowl of broccoli.

"You get your meat at a kosher butcher?" I asked.

Karen nodded. "Yes, there's a place on North High. Why?"

"Their slaughterhouse sucks . . . they need better workers," I said darkly. "That was *no* damn fun for the cow at *all*. In fact that was pretty fucking terrible."

Mother Karen looked horrified and helpless. "Kosher slaughter is supposed to be very quick and humane, just takes a few seconds—"

"Three seconds of getting your throat cut is a damn long time," I shot back. "Why the hell aren't they using magic? It's not like there aren't plenty of Jewish wizards. Any decent Talent could put 'em right to sleep, no pain at all."

"That would still be a really crap job," the Warlock said, sounding uncomfortable. "I don't know anyone who'd want to do that—"

"Moses on a moped! They could enchant the knives, the rope, the damn slaughterhouse itself!" I exclaimed, the pain in my head a buzzing sting like a wasp trapped behind my eyes. "This shit should *not* be going on in a world with magic. Period. The steer was born to be meat, fine, I get that, but his death shouldn't have been like that."

"Nobody's death is ever much fun," Cooper said, rubbing his temples. "But then nobody's birth is, either."

"So why did this happen? What's going on?" I asked him.

"We can't expect to do a resurrection without some lingering side effects," Cooper replied.

"A res— . . ." My voice failed for a moment when I realized what he meant. "No. That's *not* what we did. Your—your brothers, they were alive, we just, you know, brought them back from the hell . . ."

"They were alive when they went in, yes," Cooper said quietly. "But look at me. I was only in there a few days . . . they were in there for *years* . . ."

He trailed off.

Oh God, what had we done? A resurrection was considered one of the most taboo kinds of sorcery. The ritual demanded black magic that stained your soul like nobody's business; or at least that's what I'd always heard. Oh God.

"But they're fine now. Right?" Feeling my heart slamming in my chest, I looked from Cooper to Mother Karen. "The babies are fine now, right?"

"Well, yes," Mother Karen replied. "They seem fine. Ish."

"Ish? Fine-*ish*? What does that mean?" I demanded.

"Well, you know, they clearly have a few problems we'll need to deal with; nightmares and such—"

"But they're not demons, right?" I stared at the steak lump still twitching under the flower print napkin. "They're not . . . undead or something, right?"

"No, no, of course not," Mother Karen said. "All things considered, they seem very healthy."

"Getting the kids out of there was the right thing to do," Cooper said firmly. "And anyone who thinks it wasn't can lick my left one."

The Warlock cleared his throat nervously, as if he was trying to change the subject. "So, well, maybe this side effect is just temporary. Maybe it's something you just have to push through and then it'll be over. Try the steak again, Jessie."

"Uh-uh, I don't really—"

"C'mon, try it. Can't have your pudding if you don't have any meat," he wheedled.

Maybe he was right. I cut off a half-inch piece that was mostly crispy fat—I supposed fat wouldn't do much if it reanimated—and pressed it to my lips and tongue.

Immediately I was hit with the same kick-to-the-head overload of terror and pain. It was utterly horrifying . . . but also strangely exhilarating, like riding a roller coaster or downing a shot of strong whiskey.

No. No, no, *no*, I was *not* getting a thrill from the poor creature's death. I quickly spat the piece out into my hand and dropped it on top of the napkin. It shuddered weakly.

I stuck my fork in the rest of my steak and flipped it onto the Warlock's plate. "All yours. I'm not going there again."

"Well," Ginger said, "look on the bright side. You could help millions of kids with dead goldfish."

Something about Ginger's whimsy grated me to my core. I glared at her. "Very funny. I'm *so* glad this amuses you."

Ginger shrank back in her chair and said precisely the wrong thing: "Maybe you'll get used to it?"

A sudden fury took me. I stood up, whipped off the opera glove, and shoved my fiery hand toward Ginger. "Were you *asleep* earlier? Did you not *see* what I'm capable of?"

The others stared at me, shocked into silence.

"Did you see or didn't you?" I snarled.

"I saw," Ginger replied in a small, frightened voice, staring at the flames snapping inches from her face.

"So do you think it'd be *hilarious* if I got used to this horror and got a real taste for death? *Do you?*"

In my rage, my hand was losing shape, blossoming into a huge rose of fire. I could imagine scorching Ginger's pretty face right off, burning her down to teeth and charred bone. "I think I could learn to love eating all *kinds* of things if they really pissed me off."

Ginger was quaking in her seat, looked as if she was going to burst into tears.

"Jessie, for God's sake stop it!" Cooper rose from his chair.

The fire flared brighter along with my anger, the flames turning purple. I'd saved his life, and now he wouldn't back me in a fight?

"Set your skinny ass back down, *honey,*" I growled, my words thick with my long-buried Texas drawl.

The Warlock gripped my trembling flesh arm. "C'mon. Ginger didn't mean anything by it. We're all friends here."

"Please calm down," Mother Karen said, gripping the bowl so tightly it looked in danger of shattering.

I went cold at the fear in Karen's eyes.

What the hell am I doing? I quickly dropped down into my chair, my heart pounding and cheeks hot.

"Sorry about that . . . don't know what got into me," I muttered as I pulled on the glove.

Ginger stammered, "Excuse me," and fled the table, apparently heading toward the guest bathroom. Cooper shot me a look of mixed concern and irritation, then he and Mariette quickly followed the frightened girl.

The remaining Talents all sat in silence.

I completely jacked that up, I thought miserably. *The pooch done got screwed.* There didn't seem to be any way to recover from it. Maybe I should leave the table, too, and commiserate with Pal in the backyard.

"Well, *that* happened," the Warlock finally said. He nudged my elbow. "Want some potatoes?"

"Sure," I sighed, taking the bowl of buttered, parsley-speckled russets from him. I spooned a few spuds onto my plate, and then cautiously forked one up and bit into it. Instead of a punch of agony, there was a slow, alien discomfort: the sting of rootlets being torn from the soil, the ache of broken eye-sprouts, the dull pain of a knife slicing through cold white flesh.

"How is it?" Cooper emerged from the hallway and sat back down at the table, acting as if nothing had happened. Mariette and Ginger weren't with him.

"Unpleasant. Tolerable," I replied. "Who knew taters felt so much pain? Meals are just going to suck all the way around for a while, I guess."

"There's always fruit," Cooper said. "The plants *want* something to eat those."

"With our luck, we've probably been cursed with deadly strawberry allergies," I grumbled.

"Then consider the wide, wonderful world of tofu," the Warlock said. "Soybeans are fruit, too."

"Yay. Tofu." I mournfully eyed the platter of untouchable rib eyes. "Please pass the broccoli . . ."

Cursed

Ginger never came back to the table. I tried to find her after dinner to apologize, but she and Mariette were nowhere to be found. Paulie and Oakbrown made hasty good-byes after dinner and left as well. Mother Karen sent Jimmy off to check on Cooper's brothers, then gave me cheerful excuses as she pulled Cooper and the Warlock into her upstairs study for some kind of private chat.

Feeling frustrated and tired, I went into the guest bedroom and flopped face-first onto the homespun quilt. The "chat" was probably a prelude to Mother Karen telling me and Cooper that we had to go someplace else. Crap in a hat. We didn't *have* anyplace else to go, except perhaps the Warlock's bar, and the authorities would surely be waiting for us there.

Of course, the agents of the governing circle surely knew we were at Mother Karen's, yet they hadn't sent their goon squad after us again. What could the delay mean? It wasn't so much a matter of waiting for the second shoe to drop as waiting for a whole cargo plane full of combat boots to come crashing through the roof.

"Crappity crap crap," I muttered, pulling one of the poofy pillows over my head.

"You seem tense," Cooper said from the doorway.

"Lemme guess . . . Mother Karen's telling us to shove off, right?" I said from the darkness beneath the pillow.

"No, that's not it at all," he said. "She got a courier message from Riviera Jordan. Riviera is in charge of the Governing Circle now that her nephew Benedict's out of commission."

"What does she want? My severed head on a platter, I'm guessing."

"No, apparently not. Karen's supposed to open a mirror to Riviera's office tomorrow at noon, and we're all going to talk about arranging a neutral place to meet to discuss things."

"Things?"

"Like getting someone to help us take care of my brothers. And there's the trouble you and the Warlock and Pal got into on our behalf. Karen seems to think that Riviera is willing to listen to reason, even though you've apparently destroyed Benedict's mind."

I set the pillow aside and sat up on the bed. "So Karen isn't throwing us out?"

Cooper smiled at me; a bit of tea and food had seemed to do him a world of good. "Of course not; my brothers can't go anywhere right now, and if nothing else, she needs us for diaper duty."

He closed the door behind him and sat down beside me on the bed, an eyebrow cocked. "I thought the news would cheer you up more than this. What's the matter?"

"What's the *matter*?" I was incredulous. "I'm zombifying stuff with my *tongue*. I taste *death*. I went DEFCON 1 on poor Ginger for no good reason, and for the briefest second there I was thinking of killing her. For *real*."

Cooper scratched his goatee thoughtfully. "But if you killed her, then you could lick her . . . people would probably pay good money to see that."

I smacked his arm. "This is serious!"

"Honey, seriously, it's just garden-variety necromancy blowback. You absorbed a lot of spiritual energy from the Goad, even more from the Virtus, and it's bound to leak out in all kinds of weird ways. We'll figure it out, don't worry. And Ginger will forgive you, once she stops whimpering quietly in the corner, muttering '*Rosebud* . . . ' "

I laughed despite my worry. "Are you sure?"

"Yeah, it'll be fine. Ginger's cool, she knows you've been through a lot and you're not yourself right now."

"No, I mean about this being garden-variety stuff. Because . . ." I trailed off.

"Because what?" He butted my shoulder playfully with his forehead as if he were a big house cat. "C'mon, talk to me."

I took a deep breath. "I didn't lose my hand in your hell. I got the diabolic fire, yes—but I lost my hand the night you got sucked through the portal. Your little brother Blue sloughed all his bad emotions off into a soul-shard that turned into a demon when it escaped the hell and came to Earth—"

"Blue generated a Wutganger? Huh. Kid's got some issues."

"Gee, you think? Anyway, I took care of the Wutganger, but it bit my hand off and burned out my eye. It put some kind of poison in me. The zombie meat thing—the Wutganger could animate and control dead flesh. I'm a little freaked out that I'm showing some of its powers. I'm worried all this will . . . get worse. I'm worried that I'm becoming some kind of monster."

He gave me a hug. "Yes, it's a legitimate concern, *but*. Agonizing over this won't make it any better, will it? You're made of sterner stuff than . . . well, me, for instance. I don't know how you survived your fight with the Virtus. What you did to kill it—that should have killed *you*, too. I can't imagine how anyone could have survived absorbing its energy like you did, but here you are."

I gave him a look. "So basically, you're saying that I'm some kind of freak of nature? Am I supposed to find this news comforting?"

Cooper made an exasperated noise. "What I'm saying is, you'll survive this, too. *We'll* survive. We just have to stay calm, stay positive."

He touched my left hand. "Can I take a look at this?"

"Sure." I pulled off the satin glove and held my flame hand between us.

He held my arm by my elbow and frowned at the fire. "I . . . wow. This is really different. It's giving off a vibe like it's a curse, but not. I thought I could figure out something to do about this, but now that I'm looking at it, I'm kinda stumped. Er. No pun intended, there."

"Yeah, right." I gave a snort and slipped the glove back on.

"Hey, what did you do to your other hand?"

I looked down; my knuckles were bruised black and blue. They looked much worse than they felt.

"Oh. I, um, hit the Warlock. Kinda lost my temper with him earlier."

"He does have that effect on people." He took my flesh hand in his and whispered an ancient word for "heal."

"Is that better?" he asked, massaging my palm.

"Yes, much. Thanks, sweetie."

He kissed my knuckles and scooted around behind me on the bed and began to rub my shoulders. "You're still way too tense. You've got more knots back here than a ship's rigging."

"Arr," I replied, pirate style.

He slipped his hands up under the Hello Kitty T-shirt I'd borrowed from one of Karen's teenagers. His hands were like velvet on my skin. I felt my nipples go hard.

"Permission to come aboard?" he asked.

"Oh yeah. Just . . . just don't kiss me. On the mouth, I mean. I know we were kissing earlier, but I feel weird about that right now," I said. "And don't pull my shirt off—it might take the glove with it. Mother Karen would be really mad if we scorched her quilt."

"Aye, Cap'n."

Cooper gently pushed my T-shirt and sports bra up under my arms, planting small kisses across my back that made me shiver in delight. I sucked in my breath as he slid his hands around my sides and cupped my breasts in his hands, squeezing my nipples between his fingers. He pushed my hair to the side and began to kiss the sensitive spot behind my left ear. His goatee tickled my neck. Goose bumps rashed down my spine.

"It feels like it's been *years* since we did this." I pulled away so I could lie back and start to take off my khakis and undies. I wanted Cooper in me as quickly as possible, but in the back of my mind I was aware that the pants weren't mine, and I suspected I had only one other pair of clean underwear in my knapsack. So the fewer bodily fluids I got on either, the happier I'd be once the afterglow of our lovemaking had faded.

"Last week was work," he replied, meaning the erotomancy we'd used to call the rainstorm. He nudged my hands away from the front of my pants so he could finish unzipping them himself. "This is me showing my proper gratitude for you coming to rescue me."

I laughed as he tugged my khakis down my hips. "Honey, that still sounds a lot like work."

He tossed the pants into the corner and stripped my underwear down my legs. "I think you'll see the difference once I get started."

"Then I leave myself in your capable hands." I closed my eyes as Cooper gently spread my thighs and applied himself with all the dedication and enthusiasm of an Eagle Scout who'd just earned a merit badge in ear breathing.

My anxiety melted away as the sweet tension built and built, a hormonal freight train, fast even for me, but that was okay. Oh God was I ready—

—my thighs involuntarily clamped down on Cooper's head as the orgasm took me and I arched my back with a sudden gasp, my body rigid—

—a tiny part of me was aware of a sudden coolness on my left elbow and a faint *fwap!* that might be the sound of a satin opera glove hitting the wall—

"Mmmmph! Et oh, et oh!" Cooper frantically slapped my ass with his free hand.

I released him and opened my eyes. My flame hand

was jetting burning purple jelly all over the wall, all over the dresser, all over the ceiling, and the stuff was simultaneously corroding and igniting everything it touched. It looked like napalm from a particularly bad hell, and stank of sex and sulfur. The paint, plaster, studs, even the exterior bricks were flaring bright and burning down to noxious black ash with astonishing speed.

Cooper spoke an old word for "blizzard," a flurry of snow and ice bursting from his fingertips, but the spell fizzled against the flames. Parts of the wall were entirely gone, and I could see the neighbor's house through the smoke.

"Oh Jesus, make it stop!" he hollered.

My climax had well and thoroughly ended, but the arm wasn't stopping, and I couldn't even feel the jet. It wasn't part of me. I shook my head, frightened and baffled. "But I'm not doing this!"

"MAKE IT STOP!"

I closed my eyes, focused all my energy on the flames, trying to get them back under my control.

I heard the door bang open.

"What are you *doing* in here?" Mother Karen sounded like she was ready to kill someone.

"Why isn't this place fireproof?" Cooper yelled back.

"It *is*!" Karen protested. "This . . . this is insane, I've never—"

"Wow. Incendiary ectoplasm," I heard the Warlock comment from the hallway. "That's pretty unusual outside a hell."

I finally turned off whatever diabolic spigot had been opened in my flame hand, but I'd dripped enough in the process that now the bed was on fire, too, my ectoplasm eating huge holes right through the mattress and melting the steel springs. So much for the quilt. I scrambled to safety, then quickly used my flesh hand to pull my sports bra and shirt back down over my breasts, belatedly realizing it was a completely pointless gesture since I was naked from the waist down.

"I—I didn't mean to do this," I stammered. "I don't know how this happened."

Mother Karen's face had gone white. "The whole house will burn, we've got to get the kids out of here—"

"Try salt water, lots of it. All of you," the Warlock said.

We did as he suggested, and after a couple of false starts we were able to summon enough ocean water to douse the unholy fire.

The guest room lay in utter ruins; what had not burned was a sodden, stinking mess. Nobody said anything for a long time.

"Well." The Warlock broke the silence. "I wish Ginger was here to see this."

"Why?" Mother Karen asked.

"Because I think this illustrates *exactly* why ancient tribes came to fear the female freak-on."

Youthful Indiscretions

I stood in the backyard wearing what I'd already come to think of as the Itchy Plaid Wool Skirt of Abject Shame. An olive-drab sleeping roll and a pillow were tucked under my good arm. My left hand burned nakedly in the night air. The ectoplasmic emission had ripped open the seams on my glove, and at the moment Mother Karen and the Warlock were too busy with the guest room to fix it.

"Are they able to repair the damage to the house?" Pal stilted toward me on his rangy legs.

I nodded and tossed the sleeping bag and pillow onto the picnic table. "But it looks like I'm bunking with you tonight, out here where I'm less of a fire hazard."

He blinked at me. "But surely you and Cooper have enough self-control to avoid further carnal—"

"Wet dreams."

"Ah. Yes. Those."

"And probably any old nightmare would do it, too." I cleared my throat. "The others thought that you should stay up to watch me and wake me up if it looks like I'm having a bad dream. I mean, if you're up for that. I . . . I guess you're not really my familiar anymore, are you? So you're free to do what you want, but we'd all really appreciate it if you kept me from burning anything else down."

"Of course. I don't mind, and keeping Mother Karen's home safe certainly seems like a worthy cause."

I bit my lip. "What's going to happen to you now? It seems like maybe I'm not in as much trouble as I thought, but I don't know what kind of pull Riviera Jordan has with your jailers."

Pal scratched his shaggy thorax thoughtfully with one of his middle legs. "Honestly, I have no idea what will happen. I managed to break the binding spells my overseers placed on me, so I suppose the next logical thing for them would be to pursue me directly and take me back into custody. But so far there's been no sign they've implemented that plan. Even if I am exonerated for my actions over the past week, I still have several decades left on my sentence."

"So what did you do to get into trouble in the first place?"

Pal's face was still unreadable, but his voice sounded pained. "I was very young, and had an unfortunate interest in diabology, and some nefarious individuals discovered my interest and naïveté, and, well . . ."

I was dying to know what trouble Pal could've gotten into. "Well, what?"

"One thing led to another, and they convinced me to help them bring a manifestation of the ancient god you may know as Abraxas into the largest city of my home planet."

In the wake of all the chaos, my memory wasn't what it should have been. "Abraxas . . . I hate to sound dumb, but I can only remember that's the name of

an old Santana album Cooper's got in his vinyl collection."

Pal blinked at me. "The entity is also known as
Abrasax. Does the title 'Demon of the Great Year'
help you?"

My brain pinged on some of my Egyptian studies.
"Head of a rooster, snakes for legs, carries a whip and
shield?"

"That's one described manifestation, yes. Abraxas
has many recorded forms."

"But it's not really a demon, right? I mean, that's just
mundane confusion over the whole demon-versus-
devil-versus-god situation, right?"

"Indeed. Abraxas is no mere demon," Pal replied.

Demons are basically just supernatural servants.
Gods, devils, and powerful Talents can create them,
sometimes by accident, but usually intentionally.
They're often created from pieces of broken souls,
although some golem demons don't have any soul
elements at all (and consequently have all the person-
ality of your average vacuum cleaner). As a group,
demons are neither good nor evil, unlike devils, which
are typically selfish schemers at best and sadists of the
nastiest nature at worst. Devils poke and prod mortals
into action and feed off the resulting psychic energies;
the best of them are the muses, but even they rarely
have any qualms about driving their artists mad to
satisfy their own hunger.

Good servant demons—or daemons, as the more
intelligent ones would rather be called—normally go
about their tasks with quiet efficiency and are seldom
encountered by people they don't have business with.

Accidentally created demons, on the other hand, are usually uncontrolled, destructive, blatant incarnations of strong emotions like hate and anger. Their horrible natures taint the reputation of demonkind as a whole; even I carry a shoot-first prejudice against demons, and I should know better.

"But it's a telling detail that Abraxas is referred to as a demon," Pal continued. "It was once a god of creation and destruction, both good and evil, but as the aeons passed and other creators like Jehovah gained followers and power, Abraxas has become more associated with its darker nature. It's reclusive, mercurial, and nobody really knows what its true intentions might be these days."

"That doesn't sound good," I said.

"In fact, it was not. I am purely fortunate that I only got a few hundred years' sentence as a familiar. I suffer everlasting dismay that I was duped so very easily, when at the time I prided myself on what I supposed to be my superior intellect."

"So, why did you help them?"

"They were attractive and knew exactly what to say to me. In retrospect I was surely an easy mark; despite my aloofness I was desperate to belong. They preyed on my youthful conviction that democracy is fundamentally doomed to failure because the populace as a whole lacks sufficient intelligence and moral fiber to make good decisions. A god-emperor, they convinced me, would provide solutions to all our society's ills. And of course they promised that I'd have some important role in our brave new world under Abraxas."

"And then what happened?"

"They raised Abraxas—or what they claimed was Abraxas, at any rate—right in the middle of our capital city. To this day I don't know what it really was, but it was mainly interested in devouring as many of my people as possible. I realized my terrible mistake, of course, and went to the authorities with what I knew. The minions by then had staged a raid on the capital treasury and were long gone with a considerable number of priceless artifacts. Fortunately the authorities managed to banish the entity before the city was destroyed. And, as it turned out, I was one of a dozen youthful Talents they'd recruited for their scheme."

"Wow." I was silent for a moment. "Can you ever go back there?"

"Surely not like this." Pal gestured toward his hybrid body. "They don't have ferrets on my world, and even if they did, I'd still look nearly as monstrous to my own people as I seem to yours."

"Maybe Riviera can help you get your real body back, or find someone who can."

"Perhaps." Pal sounded supremely doubtful and a bit sad. "For all I know, the Fates have willed *this* unsightly mash-up to be my true form."

I didn't believe in Fate—or didn't want to, anyhow—but I didn't feel like arguing the point with Pal. As I pondered the frustrating nature of predestination, I let my flame hand drop too close to my leg. The fire bit right through the wool skirt into my skin.

"Ow!" I jerked my hand away from my scorched thigh. "Christ, I'm gonna have to start carrying a healing crystal like the Warlock. Dammit. Ow."

"It might be best if Riviera Jordan were to focus her resources on removing your curse," Pal said. "My current condition does not render me a danger to myself."

I no longer doubted that my flame hand was some kind of curse. I could barely eat, couldn't safely get off, and now it looked like decent sleep was definitely off the menu, too. "Well, I hope Riviera can do something about this. I hope she's not just lying to Mother Karen about wanting to talk things over reasonably."

The burn on my leg was roughly the size of a business card, and it stung like crazy. I placed my flesh palm over the wound and spoke an ancient word for "heal." It helped, but not as much as I'd hoped.

Worried anew that I was losing my ability to use white magic, I began to pace around the yard, holding my flame hand well away from my body.

"You should try to get some rest," Pal said.

"I will, in a little while." I was absolutely bone-tired, and wanted nothing more than to lie down and sleep for the next sixteen hours, but I was afraid of what might happen once I drifted off. *If* I drifted off.

My flame hand seemed to catch on something. I looked down, puzzled. I was out in the middle of the yard; there wasn't so much as a tall dandelion nearby. I waved my hand through the empty air. And there it was again, the sensation of an invisible seam.

"Hey, there's something weird over here," I said to Pal. "Can you see or feel anything?"

He came over to investigate. "No, I don't sense anything . . . What is it?"

"I'm not sure." I blinked through several views with my enchanted stone eye. One showed a faint blue rectangular outline in the air, just barely perceptible.

Acting on a hunch, I dug my flame fingers into the seam and pulled. A small door swung open midair, revealing the inside of a wooden shipping crate. It was a little bigger than a school gym locker, maybe three feet tall and two feet wide, and perhaps as many deep. Stacked inside were several plastic-wrapped bricks of white powder and compressed plant matter. The air inside was musty with a familiar sweetly weedy odor.

The patio door slid open.

"We fixed your glove," Mother Karen called, sounding more like her old cheerful self again.

"Hey, did you know someone put an extradimensional drug stash back here?" I called back.

"A *what*?" Karen strode across the yard and stared into the crate. Her expression changed from surprise to irritated recognition. "Darn that boy, I *knew* he was lying to me."

"Which boy?" I took the repaired opera glove from Mother Karen's outstretched hand and slipped it on. I hoped Jimmy wasn't in any trouble; I liked the kid.

"I fostered a teenager named Rick Wisecroft about five years ago. He had a lot of natural ability, but he seemed mostly interested in making drugs and selling them at the local high schools. I personally have nothing against adults partaking responsibly in whatever substances they choose to, but his behavior was completely unacceptable. Neither the authorities nor I could ever find anything on him, of course. He swore up and down he never brought anything illegal to the house." She sighed. "I tried to give him the benefit of the doubt, but some kids just don't want to do the right thing."

"What happened to him?" I asked.

"He stayed long enough for his eighteenth birthday party, and then ran away that night with his gifts and the cash from my purse." She paused, looking sad. "I haven't heard of or from him since. I'm surprised he left all this behind."

"Maybe he made some enemies and had to leave in a hurry. Or maybe he smoked too much of his own supply and forgot where he put it," I replied. "It was pretty well hidden."

"How did you find it?"

"Pure accident, I think. I felt the doorway in the air." I wiggled my flame fingers at Karen. "Apparently the Hand o' Doom is useful for more than wanton destruction."

"Thank goodness for that." Karen reached inside the crate and pulled out the bricks of white powder and stacked them on the grass. "These I assume are cocaine or methamphetamine; be a dear and burn them, would you? Just try not to breathe the fumes."

Karen pulled out the bricks of marijuana. "I'm going to check these to make sure they haven't been tainted with PCP or any nonsense like that. And then . . . well, no sense in wasting a perfectly useful herb."

"There's probably more of these," I said. "I mean, if I were a high-school coke dealer, I'd want to have more than one hiding place, just in case."

Mother Karen nodded. "Please check the rest of the yard, would you?"

"Sure thing."

I spent the next hour slowly going over the yard bit by bit with my flame hand. I found another extradimensional cache by the fence that contained just a couple of organic chemistry manuals, but in the trees

I made a startling discovery: doors that led into the basements or gyms of the toniest high schools in the city: Thomas Worthington, St. Charles Prep, Bexley High, Bishop Hartley, and Upper Arlington. There wasn't a door into the suburban Talent high school, Dublin Alternative, presumably because the custodians there were on the lookout for such enchantments.

"The kid was *slick*." I carefully closed the last portal.

"It does seem he was running quite the operation."

I hefted one of the kilos of anonymous white powder. "Maybe he wasn't making standard drugs. Maybe he was selling memory enhancers and love potions and stuff like that, too. I mean, seriously, kids would go *crazy* over love potions in high school."

"It's possible," Pal replied. "But I wouldn't try any of that to find out. It's so old by now it's probably unstable, assuming it was ever stable to begin with."

"I wasn't planning on it." I dropped the kilo into my flame palm and closed my fiery fingers around the package; it burned with a quick blue flame and disappeared into ash and acrid smoke that I did my best to avoid breathing.

"Know what I'm happiest about right now?" I coughed, stepping away from the smoke and fanning the air with my flesh hand.

"No, what?"

"I'm really damn happy I didn't find little Ricky's corpse stashed out here. 'Cause it's been just that kind of week."

Raising the Tent

"Hey, I found a tent for you in the attic," Cooper called from the patio. A green nylon bundle was slung over his left shoulder and he gripped a wooden mallet in his free right hand. He grinned at me, and I felt myself melt.

It was the first time he'd looked genuinely happy since I'd brought him back from his hell. The man had a great smile. Anybody can have nice, straight white teeth these days; it's what the smile *says* that matters. And Cooper's grin told me that, yeah, we'd been having an epic bad week, but everything was gonna be okay, and once we'd put things right, he had lots of delicious plans for making my toes curl.

"Aw, you're a sweetie!" I hadn't even realized I needed a shelter; it was one of those things I'd probably have thought of right around the time I was too exhausted to do anything other than crawl into the sleeping bag on the open grass and hope that Mother Karen had an antimosquito charm working.

"Well, I want you to get as good a night's sleep as you can out here." Cooper looked at Pal and chewed the corner of his mustache. "Do you want a tent, too? I think I saw a pup tent up there that I could magic up to make big enough for you."

Pal blinked his four eyes at Cooper; I wasn't sure, but I thought his expression was slightly indignant. "Please thank him for his kind offer, but I prefer the open air. And also I am quite capable of working my own spells."

"Pal says he's good, thanks," I told Cooper.

Cooper carried the tent over and we opened the big drawstring bag. We pulled out the fiberglass poles, hard plastic stakes, tie-down ropes, then the green nylon tent body, fly, and thick waterproof tarp. We spread the tarp on a nice flat spot in the middle of the lawn and got the poles threaded through the fabric to pop the tent into shape.

"It looks pretty stable," I said as we set the assembled tent in place on the tarp with the entrance facing the patio. It was basically just a one-person model, though two people could fit in it if they didn't mind close quarters. "I don't think we need to stake it to the ground. Unless there's supposed to be a rainstorm or wind tonight."

Cooper gave me a look. "With the luck we've been having?"

"Right. Better stake it down, then."

I started tying the ropes through the tent grommets as Cooper stripped off his borrowed T-shirt and began pounding stakes into the lush sod. The muscles in his shoulders and his abs seemed unusually defined; I suddenly imagined myself running my tongue through every hard groove on his belly, kissing his navel, gnawing gently on his delicious hip bones.

Pal sniffed the air. "Jessie, whatever you're thinking about, please stop thinking it."

I didn't reply; I just focused on putting the fly on the

tent. Which took a whopping two minutes, so it wasn't much distraction. Cooper was still driving hard, thick plastic into the moist, yielding lawn. A slight sheen of sweat gleamed on his smooth skin. My knees were starting to quiver.

"Jessie . . ." Pal warned.

Cooper stood up. "The grass seems pretty springy, but if you think you'll need an air mattress—hey, what's the matter? You're all flushed. And you look so *sad*."

He gazed down at me with concern. It was all I could do not to grab him by the ears and stick my tongue down his throat.

"I need a . . . hug," I replied. "Can we cuddle on my sleeping bag in the tent for a while?"

"Jessie!" Pal exclaimed.

A look of "uh-oh" realization flickered across Cooper's face. He scratched his goatee, looking conflicted. "Well, I don't think that's a good idea—"

"*Please,*" I said, as much to Pal as to Cooper. "I nearly lost you, and it feels like it's been so long since we've been able to just hold each other. For all I know I could get dragged off to prison tomorrow and never see you again. Please. I'm not going to have a flaming, gushing orgasm from cuddling, I promise."

"I suppose there's no harm in that." Cooper coolly glanced at Pal, his expression daring my familiar to disagree.

Pal pawed the ground and glared at us. "Just keep in mind that I have a bucket of very cold water out here, and I'm not the least bit afraid to use it."

Cooper stood before the tent, twisting the much-chewed corner of his mustache thoughtfully. "This thing is really kind of puny, isn't it? Not much room for more than one person. And not very comfortable for you if you're going to be in there all night."

He closed his eyes, raised his arms, and began a chant. I recognized old words for changing size and dimension. The ground and the tent simultaneously began to expand, the earth trembling, and soon the tent was as big as a small bedroom. Cooper winced and leaned forward on his knees as he finished the spell, looking pale and a bit drained. Too much, too soon.

"Are you okay?" I asked.

He straightened up and smiled at me. "I'm fine. Check it out!"

When I pushed the tent fly aside, I discovered that he'd raised the earth into a bed-size platform, the sod beneath the tarp grown thickly into a natural mattress.

Cooper helped me unzip the sleeping bag all the way and we laid it on the grass mattress. We crawled on top and lay down in the dark, sharing my pillow, Cooper spooning me. Through my skirt and his pajama pants, I could feel he had a rubbery half-erection.

"Warlock and I are planning to go to the Costco up at Polaris tomorrow to get some supplies," he said. "Five babies need a whole lot of formula. And diapers. And everything, really. Hoo boy."

"They sure do," I agreed. I wondered if he was talking about his infant brothers because they were the most pressing matter on his mind, or because he was trying to chill his libido. Probably both.

"The boys . . . wow," he continued. "I always wanted a bigger family, and now I've got it, and that's extremely cool . . . but, jeez, *babies*. I do *not* know how to take care of babies."

"Well, Mother Karen does. And there are lots of books you can read."

"I know, but . . . I don't want to screw this up. They've been through so much, and I don't want them living in those shadows. Not like the Warlock and I did. I want my brothers to grow up to be good men." Cooper rubbed his face and slipped his arms around me, his hand resting gently over my nipple. I couldn't tell if he'd done it on purpose or not. "Taking care of them properly means we'll have to wait."

"Wait for what?"

"To have our own baby."

"Oh." I laughed, perhaps too flippantly. "Trust me, I'm fine waiting."

He paused. "You . . . you *do* like the idea of us having a kid together someday, don't you?"

"Yeah, I think so." I stopped, considering his words and his concerned tone. We hadn't had this conversation before, and I didn't really know what to tell him. Babies were pretty far from my mind most of the time; if I had a biological clock, it hadn't started ticking.

On the other hand, spending time trapped in a hell was sure to put a man in touch with the grim reality of his own mortality. It wouldn't be that surprising if Cooper had started thinking about his own legacy, magic and genetic and otherwise.

"I can't honestly say I like the idea of going through labor," I finally replied. "And the thought of being pregnant freaks me out a little, protective magic or no. It makes you so . . . vulnerable. But I like everything that leads up to conception. I like that part a *whole* lot."

I should have lain there quietly and talked more about the logistics of taking care of his little brothers. Instead, I reached back and eased the itchy skirt up so that my bare ass was pressed against his flanneled groin. Immediately his erection snapped to warm attention. I began to silently grind against him.

His grip on me tightened.

"What the heck are you doing?" he whispered.

"Cuddling," I replied innocently. I almost said *And I'd like to cuddle you balls-deep in my ass,* but bit my tongue. I knew Pal wasn't kidding about the bucket.

Sweet mother of bacon, I wanted Cooper to fuck me. I didn't care if it was going to hurt or make a godawful mess or set the whole blessed planet on fire. It was like I hadn't even come earlier; my hormones were screaming for relief as if I'd spent the past decade in a convent with octogenarian nuns. Wearing a straitjacket. And a chastity belt. With the key broken off in the lock.

I have never been any damn good at keeping my pants on around a boyfriend; I have also never once cheated on a boyfriend, but honestly? Cooper was the first real boyfriend I'd ever had.

Not that I was some innocent little rosebud when I met him; far from it. I had more than my share of big dumb sex in high school, but avoided serious trouble because I was smart enough to use a condom every time and was able to work a basic silencing spell to keep the boys from bragging to their buddies (usually). In retrospect, most of the rest of the school probably thought I was a lesbian. I vocally despised the rah-rah frivolity of football pep rallies, played grumpy midfield for the field hockey and lacrosse teams, and rarely wore a dress or makeup. I liked all the boys I'd slept with, and maybe I had a little crush on a couple of them, but I'd never been in love with anyone before Cooper.

I lost my virginity when I was fourteen, thirteen if you count oral (I didn't). Yeah, I know what you're probably thinking, and at this stage in my life, I'm thinking it, too. But I can't pretend it didn't happen, because for better or worse that's part of what made me the person I am today.

I was eleven when my mom died, and her body was barely cold before my stepfather (at that point we all thought he was my biological father) started dating my soon-to-be stepmother, Deborah. I hated Deb with a sullen passion that only increased after they got married a whole two days after I turned thirteen. As the topper on my birthday cake, we moved to Plano, Texas, away from our old Lakewood neighborhood in Dallas and the friends I'd grown up with.

The new neighborhood was a dusty grid of particleboard ranch houses with miserable stick trees in the front yards. I was pretty eager to spend as little time in the new house as possible, and my stepparents didn't much seem to mind me being gone. Deb got pregnant with the twins right away, and she was definitely not in the humor to deal with a strange, moody teenage girl.

A couple of days after we moved in, I was slouched on the front porch reading one of my *Sandman* comics when a boy in his midteens pulled into the driveway next door in an old VW Beetle. I remember he was wearing clothes that were just a bit too formal and too heavy for the spring weather, and he had a fresh black eye. My interest was significantly piqued when he lifted a shiny new Alienware tower out of the passenger seat and started to carry it toward his house.

So I went over and introduced myself, probably by saying something profound like, "Whoa, that's a sweet computer." He blinked at me from behind unfashionable glasses, and we exchanged awkward geekeries until he asked if I wanted to come inside and help him set it up in the rec room.

His name was Edwin Chong, and he lived with his grandmother; she'd been his guardian ever since his parents died in a car crash near the Texas Instruments headquarters where they both worked. Even though he was sixteen, he was skinny as a skewer and not much taller than I was. He played first chair violin in the orchestra at Plano Senior High and worked as a projectionist at a movie theater on the weekends— thus his new computer purchase. Various fine young Baptist rednecks regularly kicked the shit out of him because he was half Chinese, half Jewish, and 100 percent nerd. Worse, he was fussy enough to come across as utterly gay to everyone but the actual gay kids. So, like me, he didn't really fit in anywhere.

When I started asking my stepfather if I could hang out next door at Eddie's house, he probably took one look at the boy and mentally filed him under "Completely Unthreatening." The kid's grandmother, on the other hand, dimly sensed that in his bony chest beat the same hormone-charged heart that every other teen boy possessed. And so Grandma Goldstein would haul her arthritic bulk down the half flight of stairs into the rec room every hour . . . and find us putting together a spaceship made out of Legos, or playing video games, or watching whatever new sci-fi or horror flick he'd surreptitiously recorded at his job. And she'd just sigh at the vast expanse of dorkiness on display before her, shake her head, and go back to her armchair in the living room.

After a couple of months, she stopped checking up on us. And that's when we started watching descrambled satellite porn. If I'd flipped out or acted disgusted the first time I came down there to find naked boobies on the TV, it probably would have ended there, and we would have gone back to platonic geek pursuits.

I could tell you that we started fooling around because I was achingly lonely and desperate for human touch. Or because my stepmother was conservative and ultrafeminine and I was in full-on rebellion against her and everything she stood for, be it cosmetics or Christianity or chastity. And I had all that going on in my head, sure. But the fact was, I'd been jilling off two or three times a day since I was twelve and was drowning in my own wave of hormones. So when Eddie finally got around to making his first fumbling pass, I was happy to catch.

At first it was just awkward groping, the awkwardness compounded because Eddie was more than a little squeamish about bodily fluids. It's tough getting laid if you're a teenage neat freak, but at least it means you're all for condoms. Eddie finally decided to read the fucking manual and found a copy of *The Joy of*

Sex. Consequently, he figured out how to get me off, and like good little geeks we started trying everything in the book. Sex became my favorite hobby, and he was a willing horse. If I had a crappy day at school—and, let's face it, at that age they're pretty much *all* crappy—I'd sneak out at night and hit Eddie up for a booty call.

We continued sex on the sly until my magical powers started to manifest. I got crazy-moody; it was like a whole second puberty on top of the one I was already trying to cope with. I got mad at him one night (I don't even remember why now) and his beloved PlayStation 2 blew up; it was your typical budding-Talent pyrokinetics, but I had no idea what I'd done, or how I'd done it. Afterward, he didn't want anything to do with me, and I spent a miserable angst-ridden month that climaxed in me waking from a nightmare to find my bedroom on fire.

My stepfather sent me to Columbus to live with Aunt Vicky. There wasn't room for me at the regular Talent school, so she enrolled me at Upper Arlington High, where I and a few other students got covert magic lessons (I think the classes showed up on our transcripts as Esperanto). Once I'd regained some equilibrium (and learned a silencing charm), I looked around for quiet, geeky guys with pretty eyes and graceful hands. And started deflowering them, one by one.

In the middle of my sophomore year, I experienced a nearly catastrophic charm failure. I'd done both the guys in the school orchestra's bassoon section, and each boy had jumped to the conclusion that he had been my special first time. I didn't put the ideas in their heads, but since I wasn't forthcoming about my sexual history—in my teen brain, I figured since I'd never done it without a condom, they weren't in any danger of disease so it wasn't their business—I didn't dissuade them, either. Stupid.

And at the time I didn't realize the fatal flaw in the low-grade silencing charm I was using: it stops working if the enchanted party is around someone else who knows about the taboo subject (in this case, sex with me). So, take two previously virginal guys I'd gotten busy with and put them in the same room every afternoon . . . well, bragging was inevitable.

Of course, the bragged-to boy got pretty upset, and before anyone else realized what was going on, they were throwing down right there in the practice hall, screaming, skinny fists swinging, the whole nine yards. The fight ended bloodily when one kid stabbed the other with his bassoon's curved metal reed piece. It was mostly just a flesh wound, but the kid had to go to the emergency room with the three-hundred-dollar silver-plated bocal sticking out of his chest like a faucet. Luckily the school principal made some phone calls and convinced both boys' parents to declare the fight an "accident," and it stayed out of the papers.

I tried to visit the stabbed kid in the hospital afterward, then tried to call him, but he didn't want to talk to me. Weeks later, he sent me an angsty text in which he called me a "Jezebel" and "spawn of the Devil" and claimed I'd "seduced him into perversion away from the love of Christ." I had significantly mixed feelings about his message; on the one hand, okay, I probably deserved it, but on the other hand, *what*? My "seduction" had pretty much amounted to "Hey, ya wanna . . . ?" He'd never seemed the least bit religious when we'd gotten biblical together. And, perversion? Really? I'd remembered it all being vanilla enough to flavor a vat of Dairy Queen soft-serve.

So I sent him a message back expressing my regret over the incident, and reminding him that while Christ would surely turn the other cheek, if he started spreading rumors about me, they'd be pulling another bocal out from betwixt both his. I didn't hear anything else from him.

Although I kept my own mouth shut about the whole thing, Vicky pretty quickly clued in to what had happened. But instead of grilling me or giving me any repressive lecturing, she just encouraged me to have too many extracurricular activities—convincing me to try out for lacrosse and field hockey, for instance, despite my previous disdain of sports—to have much free time on my hands. More important, she casually handed me a brand-new Hitachi Magic Wand ("I got this in a gift exchange at work, but I already have a back massager, so I thought you might want it"). And that rubbed the edge off, to say the least.

But I'd still developed a certain compulsion about sex that kicks in once I become intimate with a guy. And that leads back to me doing the Bad Idea Grind on Cooper in a flimsy tent in Mother Karen's yard.

"I'm not sure this qualifies as cuddling," Cooper whispered. "What's gotten into you today?"

"Sh," I whispered back. "Don't say anything. Don't move a muscle. And don't. Make. A. Sound."

I turned around in his arms and pushed him back onto the sleeping bag. Putting a finger to my lips, I pointed in Pal's direction; Cooper nodded silently. I eased his pants down to midthigh so his cock bobbed free.

"Great Goddess, I've seen heat-addled moose with more self-control than you people!" Pal exclaimed inside my head. "I'm getting the bucket."

My middle finger doesn't double as a clit, I thought back to him, irritated. *So back off unless something starts smoking in here. And by "back off," I mean get out of my head and step away from the tent until I'm done.*

Pal blew irritated-sounding chords, but I heard him moving across the lawn toward the patio.

I turned my attention back to Cooper. Even if I couldn't get off, *he* certainly could. Sometimes it really is just as much fun to give as to receive.

So I lay beside him, my gloved hand hot beneath us, whispering delicious filth in his ear as I worked his long, lean flesh with saliva-slick fingers. To feel him shudder beneath me, watch his face open and vulnerable beneath mine when he finally came . . . it was beautiful.

When it was over, he blinked, stunned, at the goo splashed across his chest: "Ew, I got some in my beard!"

So much for tender moments.

He snapped his fingers, extended his hand, and commanded, "Nex!" A box of facial tissues materialized on his palm, pilfered via an enchantment he'd set up one night in the Giant Eagle near our old apartment after the manager refused to refund the balance on a demagnetized gift card. It was a petty revenge, perhaps, but certainly handy at times like this. I helped him mop up and then took the spooged tissues out onto the grass to burn them.

Pal just shook his head at me.

When I came back into the tent, Cooper was curled up fast asleep.

Hellement

I lay there wide-awake beside Cooper; I'd managed to wind myself up enough that sleep seemed a distant possibility. On a whim, I pulled off my glove and held my hand above me, staring into the orange and purple flames, wondering at the mysteries that burned within.

Suddenly, the earthen bed seemed to slide sideways beneath me. I was blind, had the sensation of being smothered . . . and just as suddenly found myself standing beneath a bare yellow bulb on the concrete floor of an all-too-familiar basement. My flame hand was flesh again. I was in a small chain-link dog-pen cell in the corner of the basement; glass jars of memories I'd captured from the Goad glowed beneath the narrow single bed pushed against the gray cinder-block wall.

This was Cooper's hell, or what was left of it. The hellement was linked to the fire that burned in my hand. I'd dragged Jordan into the hellement to teach him a lesson. It had been an unthinking act in more ways than one; I wasn't exactly sure how I'd gotten in here during my confrontation with Jordan, and was even less sure how I'd come to be here from the tent.

And what would happen to my body while I was in

here? Had I physically traveled here, or was I experiencing a psychic projection? If I'd left my body behind, what if my arm dropped and set me and Cooper on fire? The thought was worrisome to say the least.

"Okay, let me back out," I said to the chain-link fence and the wall.

"Let me out, dammit."

Nothing happened.

I tried to swallow down the alarm building inside me. After all, I'd gotten out easily enough before: I'd just willed us back to Jordan's office, and there we were. It'd been easier than hopping into a pair of ruby slippers and clicking my heels. Only now . . . now that I was sinking in cold panic and not surging on the adrenaline of righteous rage, it didn't seem nearly as simple.

Taking a deep breath, I closed my eyes to concentrate. If I had made a hell for myself, how would I get in and out? Surely I'd engineer a portal, probably one just like the trans-spatial door we'd put in our old apartment that went to our practice shack in the woods.

I opened my eyes.

Before me stood a big red steel door, just like the one to the shack. I gripped the brushed stainless-steel door handle, turned it, and pulled the portal open.

And found myself lying on my back in the tent, staring at my flame hand.

Well, that wasn't so bad after all, I thought. My relief was followed by an intense curiosity. What else could I do in the hellement, and what was still in there besides the jarred memories from the Goad's victims?

I crawled out of the tent, walked to a clear spot on the lawn, and adjusted my skirt so I could comfortably sit on the grass without worrying too much about spelunking ants.

Hey, Pal!

"Yes?"

I'm going to try something. Please keep an eye out to make sure I don't set myself on fire, okay?

"I've been trying to do that all evening, if you'll recall. And what's this 'something' you refer to?"

A piece of Cooper's hell survived after I killed the Goad, and my flame is linked to it—I want to check it out a little more.

"Is it clear of devils? Is it stable?"

It seems to be, yeah . . . but I need to make sure. Thus my wanting to check it out and stuff.

"Do you think you can limit your explorations to an hour?"

Probably.

"Fair enough. I'll watch for fire and send for help if you're not back after the hour has elapsed."

I concentrated on the flames again, and quickly felt the same disorienting shift before I appeared in the basement. The hellement was much as I'd left it; the big red door was behind me now.

So the portal had persisted; I took that as a good sign that I was indeed master of this little domain. On the other hand, maybe I only thought it was little. How far did it go?

The chains on the cell door fell off at my touch and crumbled into dust. No spells were necessary here, apparently. Perhaps the hellement was partially powered by my natural Talent? Spells are just a way of tapping magical energy and redirecting it, after all. Wishing I understood more about what had happened to me when I'd stuck my hand into the Goad's heart, I opened the door and stepped out into the forbiddingly dark basement.

A flashlight would be handy, I thought, and a moment later a slim black Maglite with a bright halogen bulb rested in my left hand. The metal felt cool and comfortable, absolutely solid and real.

I shone the light around the basement, seeing the chalked ritual sacrifice symbols on the floor, the music box, random crates and old furniture . . . and then there came a flash as the beam reflected off a length of sharp, polished steel. It was the sword that had emerged from the Warlock's magic pendant, given to him by his mother as protection that hadn't come to fruition until I wore it into the hell. I went over to the sword and picked it up; the blade was still streaked with dried devil ichor, but I could see no other signs of the Goad's death in the room around me.

The basement, though apparently harmless now, was creeping me out. I had no desire to maintain a museum dedicated to the atrocities committed by Cooper's stepfather and the Goad. If I truly had control of this place, couldn't I make it look however I wanted it to? I closed my eyes, searching for a more pleasant surrounding. I'd loved the beach, but had only been there once or twice when I was a kid; I couldn't quite feel the sand beneath my toes. I knew the Panda Inn like the freckles on my arms . . . but why re-create something I could visit for real whenever I felt like taking a short drive? And anyway, the Panda Inn was only fun because of Cooper and the Warlock. I didn't know—and at that moment didn't want to know—if I could create doppelgangers of them in here.

What did I know inside and out that I couldn't visit anymore? Once I'd asked that question of myself, the answer came to me immediately as I imagined the old Craftsman bungalow that had been my home from my birth until my stepfather married Deb. I could see myself entering the front door after school, tossing my book bag down on the tweed La-Z-Boy recliner in the living room, and going past the library nook with its built-in shelves and cabinets down the hall to my haven.

I opened my eyes, and the dark basement had become my old bedroom, late afternoon sunlight streaming in through the miniblinds from beneath the wide eaves of the house. It was just as I remembered it: my stuffed animals lined up on the dresser, my Power 80 computer and a few comic books on a red wooden table in the corner, and my Buzz Lightyear comforter on the bed, complete with a pinkish stain on Buzz's white boot where I'd spilled some grape juice. The big red portal door was set in the wall beside my closet; the *My Neighbor Totoro* poster my mother had given me was taped to the front. The only other difference was that I could see the jarred memories glowing in the dark beneath the bed, barely visible past the blue dust ruffle.

I set the flashlight down on the bed, leaned the sword against my dresser, and left my bedroom to explore the house. It seemed to be perfect down to the smallest detail. I found myself constantly surprised by little things I thought I had forgotten, like the Texas-shaped Six Flags souvenir ashtray my mother kept on the mantel for company. The place even smelled right: a combination of dust, furniture polish, and potpourri. On the other hand, if I had lost a memory entirely, how would I realize it was missing from this re-creation?

And the quiet of the place was eerie. The oak trees made a soft swish as the breeze blew through their branches, but no doves or mockingbirds called from the foliage, and no cars hummed or puttered on the streets nearby. The neighbor's pugs should be barking, but weren't. I stepped out on the broad front porch to see if I could hear anything, and I found the shield that had also been part of the pendant. Its bronze surface was also splattered with ichor from the Goad larvae I'd fought off.

The bitter, metallic smell of the ichor made me shiver, and suddenly the silent porch with its view of the trees and the other beautiful old houses seemed just as creepy as Cooper's dark basement prison. I supposed that it would take more than a change of scenery to make a hell feel homey.

I took the shield back into the bedroom with me, propped it up beside the sword against my dresser, and exited through the red portal.

I found myself standing on the lawn, staring down at my flame hand. Wait, hadn't I been sitting down when I left?

"Hey, Pal, was my body here this whole time?" I asked.

"Yes; was it supposed to go someplace?"

"Well, I wasn't sure if my body would stay here, or enter the hell with me." I suddenly had a mental picture of myself disappearing headfirst into my flame hand, Girl Ouroboros. Probably for the best that wasn't the case. "I guess it's just sort of like an astral projection. Weird."

I realized that if it hadn't been for the damage I'd done to Benedict Jordan's mind, I'd have had no other proof that entering the hell was anything more than a figment of my own imagination. "When did I stand up?"

"Just a moment ago; why? Is everything all right?"

"Yeah, everything's fine. I just didn't remember standing up, that's all."

I pulled my opera glove back on, shook the grass off my skirt, and crawled back into the tent to join Cooper.

Siobhan's Boys

Cooper continued to saw serious logs, but I slept fitfully at best the rest of the night. It didn't help that Pal stuck his big shaggy head into the tent and poked me awake a couple of times on the grounds that I was dreaming, or *looked* like I might be dreaming. Shortly after dawn's first light, I hauled myself out of the tent and staggered into the house in search of hot coffee and a warm bath.

I found blond toddler Blue wandering around the kitchen, looking forlorn in his hand-me-down Superman footie pajamas.

"What's the matter?" I asked. "Why aren't you asleep?"

He stared up at me with huge cloudless-sky eyes. Because the venom from his Wutganger still tainted my blood, Blue was able to communicate with me telepathically, as if he were a kind of familiar. So far, he hadn't uttered a single sound, not a laugh or cry or even a hiccup. Mother Karen had speculated that his muteness might be traumatic. I thought the boy might simply prefer telepathy with me; he was surely able to convey much more complex information than if he were trying to wrestle unfamiliar words out through immature vocal cords.

"Tertius and Quartus woke me up," Blue replied earnestly. "I think they have dirty diapers. They are very upset."

I winced. Diaper duty before I'd had any caffeine was simply inhumane. I wished Mother Karen believed in using changeless diapers, but she didn't, at least not anymore. There was an ongoing debate among Talented parents about where the waste from the diapers actually went. It turned out there was an ambiguity in the standard baby-safe enchantment and it wasn't clear whether the waste was whisked away and destroyed or if there was a poo dimension someplace where it all just built up. The environmental/ethical concerns of dropping diaper loads on unsuspecting people aside, if the waste was simply stored someplace, there was the possibility it could be used as a pointer against the young Talents later.

"Well, let's go see if I can't get them changed." I took Blue's tiny hand and let him lead me upstairs to the nursery. He probably didn't know his brothers' real names—it was likely that their mother's murderous husband, Lake, had never bothered to name the boys at all—and Blue surely didn't know the Latin names for the fourth and fifth sons born into a family. But when he conveyed the concepts of his infant brothers to me, in my mind I'd begun hearing Tertius, Quartus, Quintus, and Sextus.

Blue sometimes referred to the Warlock as Septimus. As far as Lake had been concerned, the boys were merely components for the blood ritual intended to give his adored first son, Benedict, tremendous magical power. If the boys' mother, Siobhan, had enough mind left to give the Warlock and his numbered brothers proper names, I hadn't heard them spoken in Cooper's hell.

Names *matter* in the magical world. Knowing the true, secret name of a devil or other supernatural creature can help you gain control over it. It's one thing for a Talent to be thoughtlessly named; it's another to have never been named by your parents at all. Being a nameless Talent means you don't have full access to your own potential, your own powers. You've been cut from the grounding forces of your own family bloodline. A nameless wizard can still be a powerful wizard, but almost never a well-rounded one.

I stared down at my gloved arm, thinking of my dead mother. Whether we like to admit it or not, our parents give us everything we have to start out with, good and bad. Sometimes their mistakes hang around your neck like loops of heavy, unbreakable chain.

Blue and I reached the nursery. I couldn't hear any babies crying, but Mother Karen had probably put a sound-dampening enchantment on the room so her other kids wouldn't be disturbed. She'd surely have some kind of baby monitor working at the same time. I opened the door.

The room was in utter chaos. Mother Karen was floating in the air, surrounded by a swirling storm of stuffed animals and colorful teething toys. She was holding onto the edge of the changing table for dear life, her free hand clutching a folded dirty diaper. Her graying brown hair was blown out in a wild corona around her face. Below her, the naked baby boy on the changing pad giggled and kicked in delight.

"Karen—" I began, ducking to dodge a flying teddy bear.

"All under control! Shut the door!" she cheerfully yelled back.

"But—"

"*TakeBluebacktobedandshutthedoor!*"

I quickly did as she told me, feeling rejected and useless. And, frankly, a bit scared. Most Talented kids don't start developing their magical skills until they've reached an age of rational thought. And that's exactly as it should be. A happy baby with full-blown magical powers is far more dangerous than an angry baby with a bag full of live grenades.

And we apparently had a house full of 'em. Christ in a chum bucket.

"Okay, I'm supposed to take you back to bed," I said to Blue as I led him down the hall to his room.

"But I'm not tired," he replied.

"When adults tell you to go to bed, that mostly means they want you to stay in your room and play quietly."

"Oh."

I pulled open the door to his room. It was one of the smallest bedrooms, maybe eight by eight, with a child-size low bed in the corner, a green beanbag seat, a toy chest, and a play table and little red chair. The dissected remains of an old Batman clock radio lay in neat piles on the beige carpet. Blue had even carefully pried the transistors off the circuit board and had put them in color-coordinated piles.

"Why did you do that?" I asked, pointing at the radio dissection.

"I wanted to know how it works," he replied.

"Until you've read the manual, that's not going to

help you understand it," I said. "It's just going to leave you with a broken radio."

"Oh. Why?"

"Because you can't put it back together again the way it was, and so it won't work anymore."

Blue stared down at the radio parts, a slightly rebellious look of determination creeping across his face. "I bet I remember *exactly* how it goes together."

I picked up one of the transistors. "Remember how this was stuck on with metal blobs?"

"Yes."

"The blobs were stuff called solder. Regular glue won't work. And since solder is poisonous and soldering irons are dangerous, I'm not going to give you any to play with."

Any other kid genius would have gotten mad at this point; I was partly testing Blue to see if he had indeed shuffled all his capacity for "bad" emotions off into the demon he'd created. But Blue didn't even seem the least bit frustrated. Of course, his mind was older than mine, almost as old as Cooper's.

"Why won't glue work?" he asked.

"It doesn't conduct electricity."

Blue reached down to the carpet and picked up a twisted paper clip, which he'd apparently used as a tool in his radio dissection. "Does this conduct electricity?"

"Yes. So do you. So don't go sticking that in an electrical socket, or you'll hurt yourself."

"I don't hurt," Blue replied, turning the paper clip over in his hands. I realized for the first time that his little nails were chipped, and he had cuts and blisters on his fingers, presumably from prying the radio apart. "What if I melted this and used it to attach the transistor back on the green board thing?"

"How do you plan to melt it?"

He looked up at me. "With my mind."

Uh-oh. "It would take a lot of heat to melt that."

He shrugged. "That's okay."

"No, it's not. You'd melt the circuit board and the transistor. You also might set the house on fire. Mother Karen wouldn't be happy with you trying that."

"I can be careful." He shrugged again. "And she doesn't have to know."

"This is *her* house; she *has* to know. You couldn't hide this from her."

"I think I could. I'm good at hiding things."

And he was; he'd built a whole secret passageway in the house in hell, apparently without the Goad ever realizing. Mother Karen, for all her skill at keeping a watchful eye on her foster children, surely couldn't supervise her home as ruthlessly as a devil monitored its hell.

Hoo boy. I racked my brain, trying to figure out how best to redirect Blue onto something harmless. Or at least onto something less potentially harmful than bare-handed soldering.

"But it would be *rude* to secretly do things she doesn't like in her house," I said. "Rude and disrespectful and . . . and just plain *mean*. You don't want to be mean, do you?"

"I guess not," he replied, sounding uncertain.

Appealing to a sense of honor he couldn't have possibly developed yet wasn't going to work. I went to the closet, hoping its contents would provide inspiration, and opened the door. And there, crammed in the corner atop old boxes of Christmas and Hanukkah decorations, was an old blue-and-white, Dalmatian-spotted iMac computer, its hockey puck mouse wedged under the top handle.

"I have a better idea," I said, grabbing the iMac and hauling it out of the jumble. "This is a computer. Computers are cool. You can use them to learn lots of new things without having to destroy anything else."

I set the iMac down on the play table, then went back into the closet to disentangle the USB keyboard and power cord from some tinsel garlands.

"What kind of things?" Blue asked.

"All kinds of things." I got the keyboard free, then turned it over and tapped the back to knock out bits of stray tinsel and old crumbs. "And you can play games on them."

Blue watched intently as I attached the keyboard and mouse and blew dust off the iMac's vent holes. I plugged in the power cord, then paused, my finger over the power button.

"Okay, before I boot this up, you have to promise me something."

"What?" Blue asked.

"Promise that you won't try to take this apart. If you're super-curious, I'll show you how it's put together later. And you have to promise not to take apart anything else, either." I paused. "Especially not the cats. Or yourself."

Blue looked down at the parts on the floor. "Will you help me put this back together?"

"Yes. But later."

"Okay. I promise I won't take anything else apart."

"Good boy," I said, feeling relieved. I pressed the Mac's power button, and although the hard drive made some ominous grinding noises at first, we were soon looking at the old OS 9 desktop, littered with short-cuts to various educational games. I showed him how to use the mouse and keyboard, and then launched Reader Rabbit.

"I've got to go, but I or somebody else will check on you in a little while," I said as I put the radio parts in an old shoebox I found in the closet.

"Okay." He was already engrossed in the game.

Once I'd gotten the radio pieces out from under-foot, I left Blue at the computer and quietly shut the door behind me.

I ran into Mother Karen in the hallway; she was looking completely frazzled.

"Did you get Blue to bed?"

"Sort of . . . he wasn't tired, so I broke out an old iMac I found in the closet and showed him some games."

"Good enough!" She rubbed her eyes with the backs of her hands.

"Did you get any sleep last night?" I asked.

"Oh, one or two hours, I expect."

"Want me to make some coffee?"

"Already brewing! You're welcome to have some, of course." She pulled a wristwatch out of the pocket of her denim jumper; I figured she'd taken it off before her episode of *Iron Mom: Battle Diaper*. "We're sup-posed to mirror Riviera Jordan in about three hours; I'd like to bathe before I do anything else. Would you mind hanging around the kitchen in case any of the children go downstairs needing help with something?"

I was cheered that she finally wanted me to do something. "I don't mind at all."

I went downstairs and had just finished doctoring my coffee with a couple of teaspoons of sugar and a slug of cream when the Warlock came through the front door carrying a brown paper Kroger's bag.

"Hey, I thought you and Cooper were going to the store together." I nodded toward the bag as I took a sip from my mug. It was still a little too hot to drink, so I set it back down on the counter.

"I couldn't sleep, and I wanted to see if Opal was okay. I figured I'd stop to grab some beer on the way back while I had the chance. I'll go out again with Coop later."

"So is Opal okay?"

"She had kind of an interesting time with the Circle Jerks after we left, but now everything seems relatively calm. The critters are fine. We had to fix the front doors and one of the upstairs windows, but it could have been worse. The Jerks seem to have called off the dogs for now."

The Warlock set the bag down on the counter beside me and reached inside it. "I also picked up a little something Coop said you needed."

He tossed me a fresh six-pack of women's cotton bikini underwear. The size was right, and the colors weren't hideous. I was ridiculously thrilled.

"Yay! I don't have to go commando today! Thank you!" I impulsively hopped up on my toes and gave him a quick kiss on his bearded cheek.

Suddenly, I was lying on a concrete basement floor, my eyes covered with a cloth blindfold; "The Twelve Days of Christmas" tinkled from a music box nearby. A man intoned a command I was too young to comprehend, and the blade of a knife came down on my tender throat, a silvery pain as it sawed through my windpipe and arteries—

"Whoa, Jessie, are you okay?" the Warlock asked.

I'd fallen to my knees on the kitchen floor. My throat still ached from the relived murder, the psychic imprint of the Warlock's death during the blood ritual. It took me a moment to get any words out. "You died."

The Warlock looked supremely puzzled. "What?"

I coughed, trying to clear the phantom pain. It was gradually fading. "Your father made Cooper . . . made him sacrifice you. To steal your magic. When you were a baby. Death's all over you. You don't remember?"

He shook his head, his puzzlement changing to a look of worry. "No, I've never been able to remember what happened then."

I picked my underwear pack off the floor and slowly got to my feet. "Be glad of that."

"I am," he said faintly.

Mother Karen came down the stairs in a well-worn purple bathrobe, her wet hair wrapped up in a green towel. "Who's next for the big kids' bathroom?"

"Me," I said. "I definitely need a shower."

Riviera

Taking a shower when one of your hands is made of fire is a bit more challenging than you might expect. Almost immediately, I got water in the opera glove, and the bathroom filled with thick, sulfurous steam despite the vent fan's buzzing labor. Within a few seconds, it was pretty hard to breathe in there. I quickly soaped and rinsed all the important parts one-handed and got out to get dried and dressed.

The Warlock was waiting by the bathroom door when I emerged, toweling off my hair. He held his nose and waved his other hand dramatically when the rotten-egg steam reached him. "Sweet Zeus, woman, what have you been eating?"

"Oh, bite me."

"I'd love to, but I'm sure my dear brother would object."

I made a rude noise and whipped my damp bath towel at the back of his legs; he narrowly dodged the snap and danced into the bathroom, quickly latching the door behind him.

Downstairs, Mother Karen was busily directing her teens in the kitchen; it looked like French toast and sliced fruit were on the menu that morning. The smell of the toast made my stomach growl; I hoped it wouldn't taste of caged horror.

I went out into the backyard to take Pal's order (a bucket of peeled cantaloupes and a few dozen hard-boiled eggs) and woke Cooper, who was still snoozing away in the tent. I brought him inside and he helped me set the table.

Breakfast with eighteen kids was pretty loud, but went far better than dinner had; the French toast gave me a brief twinge from a couple of weevils that had fallen into the wheat grinder, but the ambrosia salad was quiet and sweet. Afterward, we helped clean up and then played boxing and snowboarding on the Wii in the rec room until it was time to talk to Riviera Jordan.

Mother Karen led me, Cooper, and the Warlock upstairs to her study. The room was one of many spatial surprises in the house; its door was tucked in between the master bathroom and the teen girls' room, and based on how everything else was laid out, you'd expect it to be a windowless cave at most nine feet wide and possibly ten or eleven feet deep. But when I stepped inside, I found myself in a vaulted haven bigger than many living rooms. Tall windows with gauzy curtains alternated with floor-to-ceiling oak bookshelves loaded with spellbooks, cookbooks, and various jars and enchanter's implements. The windows on the western side looked out over a rocky north Pacific beach; the eastern windows had a view of white sands and gently lapping Caribbean surf. Near the door, there was a nautical blue-striped couch and chair set around a coffee table made from glass and driftwood. Set in an alcove in the middle of the room was Mother Karen's desk, and across from it a wet bar with a coffeemaker and tea caddy. At the back of the room was a big marble fireplace with a softly burning enchanted fire that matched the sea-green wallpaper, and above it was an eight-foot-wide antique silver mirror in a gilded wooden frame.

"I've never seen anyone open a mirror," I said. It was one of a list of enchantments Cooper hadn't showed me. "Is it hard to do?"

"It's harder than opening iChat"—Karen nodded toward the Mac tower on her desk—"but I suppose having us all crowd around the webcam would lack a certain gravitas."

Mother Karen led us to the fireplace and pulled a business card out of one of her pockets; a lock of bright silver hair was stapled to the back. "Riviera's courier dropped off this pointer to her office. What happens next is I put this under the edge of the mirror's frame and recite the opening trigger."

"But what if you didn't have a pointer, or a mirror that was already enchanted? Could you still do it?" I asked.

"You ubiquemancers would have a better chance than I would, I suppose, but I'm not sure how you'd go about it," she replied.

"In theory it's doable," said the Warlock. "Any mirror will work, but you'd have to be at least somewhat familiar with the person you're trying to contact. You know, be able to keep a good solid mental picture of him and the room his mirror's in while you do your chant. And you'd have to hope that he'd either be there to respond to the mirror spell, or that his mirror has a message enchantment."

"Eh," replied Cooper. "That's a chancy lot of work, and if you don't have a pointer, you never really know who you're actually talking to. Lots of sorcerers and demons like to play mirror games. And if you know your contact well enough to have a pointer . . . shoot, you probably have their phone number, right? So just call them on your cell. No sense in blowing magical energy when there's cheap technology that does the job just fine."

"Well, wizards of the old school see resorting to technology as disrespectful and lazy," Mother Karen replied. "We should mind our p's and q's and do this the way Riviera wants us to."

She tucked the card up under the edge of the gilded mirror frame and looked back at us. "Last chance to brush hair and straighten clothes and check your teeth for strawberry seeds. Jessica, this means you."

"Oh. Yeah." A couple of the buttons on my borrowed blouse were undone; I'd gotten a little overenthusiastic playing Wii Boxing. I fixed them, and ran my fingers through my hair. "Good?"

"Good enough," Karen replied. She put her hands against the glass, closed her eyes, and spoke the trigger: "Speculus, speculus."

The mirror shimmered, brightened, and our reflections dissolved into a view of a slim, well-dressed woman in a plum business suit seated in a tall-backed antique chair. Queen Victoria could have scarcely looked more commanding. Her hair was a thick, fashionable bob of bright silver, but her face was smooth and unwrinkled. Powerful Talents have a wide array of antiaging magic at their disposal; if you don't fall into poverty or die through accident or violence, you can keep going for centuries if you're determined enough. Some people get tired of the endless and increasingly difficult rejuvenation rituals after a time and let nature take its course; one look in her sharp, intense eyes, silvery as her hair, and I doubted Riviera would ever willingly surrender her grip on life.

"Well, now." Riviera had an upper-crust Southern accent, the kind that shows its British roots. "I see you've all gathered as I requested. But we're missing one."

She turned toward me, expression still intense but not hostile. "Where's your familiar, Miss Shimmer?"

I felt a sudden urge to curtsy; instead I did an awkward little head bob. "He's too big to fit in the house. Ma'am."

"Ah." She leaned forward slightly. "I do realize that there are most certainly some trust issues on your side as well as on mine, but there are serious issues at hand that we had best discuss in person, and in private. So I have arranged for us to meet tomorrow afternoon on neutral ground: the Seelie Tavern west of Winesburg."

My heart beat a little faster; I'd always heard that there was a faery realm hidden near Amish country, but you couldn't find it unless you were invited. I'd heard all kinds of stories about the hazards mortals face when visiting Faery: those deemed graceless transformed into pigs, those found cocky turned to mice for the cats, those seen as too pretty lulled into spending the night and emerging the next morning to discover that they'd disappeared for a century and aged almost as much. Too quiet and you might become a tree, too loud and you might become a crow. What were we getting into?

"Please be there promptly at four; I will send another courier with a faery token so the guards will let y'all in. They will be able to accommodate your familiar, I'm sure," Riviera continued. "But to avoid offending our hosts—and the most serious consequences that y'all might suffer—please be on your best behavior, and dress properly. Old-world formal will do. I expect it will take you perhaps two hours to reach the tavern. So until one-thirty tomorrow, you may travel freely within Franklin County, provided it's by mundane means. After that, you'll be safe as long as you're on the highways traveling in the right direction. If you leave the county, or if you use any form of teleportation, our truce is off and I'll have to have y'all taken into custody and remanded to the Virtus Regnum.

"Do y'all have any questions about these arrangements?" she finished.

"No, ma'am," we all said.

"Good," she said. "I look forward to seeing y'all tomorrow."

And with that, the mirror shimmered and fell back to reflecting our worried faces.

"Dude." Cooper broke the silence. "Did we just have a meeting about having a meeting?"

"We sure did," the Warlock replied. "Welcome to Bureaucratica. Population: us."

Pal met me on the patio. "What did she say?"

"We're all meeting her tomorrow at four at the Seelie Tavern up near Winesburg."

"Oh dear," he replied. "That seems a somewhat perilous venue. Why Faery?"

I shrugged. "She said we should meet on neutral territory."

"But there are surely faery enclaves within this city—why not meet at one of them?"

"I'm guessing the idea is that we meet on neutral territory that's *also* out in the middle of nowhere," I replied. "And considering the mess Cooper and I accidentally created downtown, well, keeping us away from large, expensive buildings would seem prudent to her, wouldn't it? I'm trying real hard not to imagine that there's a more sinister intent here."

A sudden chill breeze ruffled my hair and a voice whispered, "Look skyward, my girl."

"What?" I looked around, looked up.

A small object was plummeting down from the clear blue sky. I stepped aside, and it hit the grass near me, bounced twice, and came to a rest. It was an old brown teddy bear; a small cream-colored card was tied to its middle with a piece of kite string. I hesitated, then picked up the bear. Something about it was familiar; I sniffed it, and immediately remembered playing with the bear in my old room in our Lakewood house. The memory strengthened; it was one of several stuffed toys I'd had since I was a baby, but my stepmother, Deb, deemed it junk and sent it off to Goodwill before our move to Plano.

Hands shaking a bit, I untied the kite string and unfolded the card. In it was a lock of copper-brown hair and on it a handwritten note:

I've missed you very much. We need to talk.

—Your dad

"What's that?" Pal asked.

I resisted my sudden, irrational instinct to hide the card and lie; if I betrayed Pal's trust, it might be a long time before I got it back.

"It's a pointer," I replied. "From my father, or so it says."

"Your father?" Pal blinked in surprise. "But the prison records indicated that he was, well . . ."

"Dead. I know." I stared down at the card and lock of hair. "He's talked to me before this, last night on the front lawn and also at the Warlock's, but I wasn't sure it was him."

"Can you be sure now?"

I held up the teddy bear. "This used to be mine, a long time ago. My mom gave it to me when I was a baby; for all I know, my dad might have gotten it for me before I was born."

"But for all you know, this could be an elaborate trick conjured up by some dark entity."

"That's true." I closed my eyes and smelled the dusty bear again; it was like an instant portal back to the happiest time I'd had as a child. A thousand questions about my family and my life crowded around the memories, questions only Ian Shimmer could answer. "But if this really is from my father, I *have* to talk to him."

Mirror, Mirror

After Cooper and the Warlock left on an errand in the Land Rover, I went looking for Mother Karen in the kids' playroom. She was arbitrating a fight over a Transformers toy; when she got the two kids settled, I pulled her to the side.

"Can I borrow the mirror in your study?" I asked.

"Sure." She dug in her jumper pocket for the key and handed it to me.

"Um." I stared down at the key. "Does your mirror have any . . . security enchantments? To protect against magical spycraft or identity spoofing, if that kind of thing happens?"

Her eyebrows rose. "It has some protections against demons and malicious spells, yes. Who or what exactly are you planning to contact?"

"My father. My real one, I mean, not my step. I think. I haven't ever met him, and it's all super-weird and hard to explain, but if it's him I really need to talk to him."

"Well." She pursed her lips. "Just don't give out any sensitive personal information, unless you're absolutely certain he's who he says he is. Saying 'oblittero' will cut off the connection if you need to; so will clapping your hands or stomping your foot twice if you can't speak."

I thanked her and went into the study, latching the door behind me. Mother Karen would surely be able to get into her own study without the key, but I didn't want any of her kids coming in there in case there was trouble. What kind of trouble could come from contacting someone (or something) that claimed to be my father, but wasn't? I didn't have a clear idea, but having spent some quality time in a hell, my imagination was supplying plenty of dire scenarios. At least two of them involved hooked chains, rusty razor blades, and a TV stuck on a *Jerry Springer* marathon.

I sat on Karen's couch and stared down at the card, mentally doing a dare-I-eat-a-peach dance with myself. In the end, it seemed better to try to get answers than to spend the rest of my life wondering what might have been. So I went to the antique mirror, stuck the card under the frame, and spoke the opening charm.

Nothing happened right away, so for a few moments I wondered if I'd done it wrong. And then the reflection changed to show an empty tall-backed wooden chair, and behind that an arcane-looking workshop that appeared to occupy an old-fashioned domed observatory. In addition to a big telescope, I saw several antique brass solar system models, an alchemical apparatus of glass tubes and distillation flasks for potions on a long table, and chalkboard walls with a mixture of spell glyphs and complicated mathematical equations written on them in the same neat, precise handwriting as on the note.

"Um . . . hello? Anyone there?" I called.

"Oh!" The reply was a deep, pleasant baritone—nothing like the somewhat sinister whisper I'd heard before—somewhere off to the side where I couldn't see. The speaker had a slight accent, maybe German? I heard a chair scoot across the wooden floor. "Is that you, Jessie?"

"Yes, it is," I replied.

I heard the sound of feet slapping across the floor in flip-flops. A tall, strongly built man with long, wavy, penny-brown hair and a full beard stepped into the mirror view and sat down in the chair. His face was deeply tan. He was wearing bright orange Thai fisherman's pants and a long madras patchwork jacket over a black T-shirt with white Courier lettering: "I Void Warranties." I began to suspect that my disinterest in fashion was probably genetic.

"It's so good to see you." He beamed at me, and I realized that if someone fattened him up a bit, gave him a pair of wire-framed glasses and a red suit, and aged him twenty years, he'd easily be able to pass himself off as Santa Claus.

"It's, um, good to see you, too." I wasn't sure what was supposed to happen next.

"I imagine you have questions." He sat back in his chair, looking perfectly relaxed. "Ask anything. Ask away!"

"Okay. Well." I paused, wondering if "ask anything" actually meant *anything*. I supposed I didn't really have that much to lose by being blunt (not that I ever have much luck trying to be delicate). "So I heard you died in prison?"

He laughed, sounding a bit embarrassed, and tugged

at his beard. I realized that his hands were spotted and gaunt, looked considerably older than his face. "Well, if you get sent to prison for life, you might as well die and get it over with, right?"

"So you, what . . . died and got better?"

"Oh, come on. By now you of all people should know that resurrection magic is entirely doable, even if the powers that be tell us otherwise. Death *never* stopped a Shimmer."

He paused. "Though mine did put me out of commission longer than I'd hoped. By the time my friends finally got to my body, it was too late for me to save your mother. Fortunately she was able to save you before the Virtii's minions took her from us."

To save you. Benedict Jordan had told me that I'd been diagnosed with untreatable cancer when I was a child, and that my mother stole the life energy of a boy awaiting a heart transplant in the hospital in her spell to cure me. He said she was forbidden from using any magic, much less grand necromancy, so she'd been quietly put to death soon after. I remembered finding my mom dead on the floor; the coroner told us it was an undiagnosed aneurysm. She couldn't really have done what Jordan claimed, could she? I had to know.

"Jordan said she murdered a kid to save me," I said.

"That boy was going to suffer a slow, painful death from his illness," Shimmer replied gently. "What your mother did for him was a mercy."

"But she could have saved him." I hadn't expected I'd be so contrary with him, hadn't expected to be suddenly feeling so much anger and sadness over what had happened so long ago. "She had that power, didn't she?"

"She had the power to save exactly one child before she would be killed for the sin of using her natural gifts. Would you expect a mother to save a stranger's dying child rather than her own? Would you rather she betrayed *you*, let you suffer and die of cancer to preserve that sick young boy? Would you rather be dead?"

"No. I wouldn't," I replied. The admission made me feel dirty, like I'd personally murdered the boy I'd never even met. "So how much more of that kind of 'mercy' has there been? Was that what landed you in prison?"

"If you ask the authorities, they will tell you I was put in prison for grand necromancy and murder. But since you're asking *me*, I will tell you I was imprisoned because I dared to study the magic of time and probability, magic that the Virtii feel is their sole domain. If I had been a good little wizard who sat at the back of the bus when I was told to, I never would have been prosecuted."

"But did you commit murder?"

"I killed a pair of cockroaches who happened to look like men. They tried to rape your mother, and I cut them down. Given the same circumstances, I would gladly do it again. It was my right as a man, and my duty as a husband. Had I used a gun or a sword instead of a killing word—well. Unfortunately my lack of a pistol gave my enemies more ammunition than I expected."

I did some quick math in my head. "So you were freed and resurrected . . . when I was eleven?"

"Yes. And I've been keeping an eye on you ever since." He beamed at me again, his slightly gap-toothed smile declaring *Aw, my widdle girl is all growed up and ain't I proud!*

I thought back on the horrible months I'd suffered through when my powers began and I didn't know what was happening to me. My cheeks flushed hot, and I suddenly wanted to smack that smile off his face.

"That was a dozen years ago," I said, my voice shaking from my sudden anger. "If you care so much about me, why did you wait so long to contact me?"

He blinked at me, apparently confused at my change of tone. "Isn't it obvious?"

"No, not really."

"I'm an outlaw," he said. "If the authorities had any inkling that I was in contact with you, they would have used you as a pawn, made your life miserable—"

"Miserable? What, you mean like being raised by people who act like you're some bad debt they're stuck paying off? You mean like having your powers come on without anyone around to tell you what they are or how to handle them, so when you inevitably set shit on fire, everyone thinks you're some kind of sociopath who belongs in the nuthouse? *That* kind of miserable?"

"You have no idea how sorry I am that you had to go through that; I contacted Victoria as soon as I could to let her know what was happening—"

"You had Vicky call my stepfather?"

Shimmer spread his hands. "She was no Talent, Jessie; she had no way of knowing what was happening to you otherwise. You thought she just miraculously decided to call your stepfather the day before you were going to be committed to a mental institution?"

I rubbed the back of my neck with my flesh hand. "Yeah, I guess I kind of did."

He shook his head, a half-smile playing on his lips. "For a girl who claims to despise Fate, you seem to accept tremendous coincidence without much question."

His gentle joke rankled like mockery, and I felt my blood rise again. "So why am I graced with your fatherly attention now, after all these years of not knowing you even existed?"

"Again, isn't it obvious? You've gotten yourself into so much trouble that my presence in your life can't possibly make things any worse."

"You're sure about that?"

"I've studied Fate and probability and chaos magic more than any human alive, so . . . yes, I'm very sure. Before you got the attention of the Virtii, it was best you didn't even know about me. But now that you've killed one of them—oh, and well done, by the way— it's quite a different story. I'd like to continue to help you, if you'll let me."

"Wait just a minute," I said, doing a little more mental math about his previous "help" and not liking the sum. I touched the scarred flesh beneath my stone eye. "This ocularis was your doing, wasn't it?"

He nodded. "I gave it a compulsion charm tuned to you and arranged for the Warlock to find it, yes."

"You arranged for him to find it . . . when I was eleven."

He blinked. "Yes, once I realized your mother was beyond my help, I did an extensive set of probability divinations to try to see where your life might take you. I picked up on Cooper Marron's thread, and the opportunity arose to get the ocularis into his brother's hands, so I took it. It seemed to be the most prudent course of action."

"The most prudent course . . ." My voice failed for a moment. My face felt like you could cook an egg on it. The only way he could have thought that the ocularis would be any help to me was if he'd been pretty sure I was going to be seriously mangled and lose at least one eye. "*You knew all that shit was going to happen from the beginning and you didn't warn me?*"

"There was only a forty percent chance—"

"How hard would it be to send me a note saying, 'Oh, hi, don't go calling the rainstorm tonight, there's a forty percent chance you'll *lose your fucking eye!*'"

"The threads were very complex, I couldn't risk—"

"*You couldn't risk? You* didn't risk *anything!* Five people died that night, you jackass!" I screamed at the mirror. I yanked the glove off and shoved my flames at the glass. "*I* nearly died. *Cooper* nearly died. *We* nearly lost everything. *You* didn't do shit!"

Hot tears were streaming down my face. "You're as bad as that rat-bastard Jordan. *Worse.*"

"Jessie, I can explain—"

"Save it. Oblittero." I yanked the pointer card out of the mirror's frame and threw it down toward the fireplace. I didn't look to see if it burned or not.

The mirror went back to reflecting my own furious, red-eyed face. The scaly scars around my left eye socket were livid, inhuman, the ocularis a cold cat's eye faintly reflecting the firelight. I leaned my forehead against the cool marble mantel and wept.

Cooper

The guys stumbled through the front door as I was coming down the stairs. Cooper was leaning heavily on the Warlock's shoulder, his eyes even more blood-shot than they'd been when he'd awoken from his potion-induced sleep the night before. I felt myself getting furious all over again.

Cooper spotted me, and at first he had an "uh-oh, busted" expression on his face, but then I guess he saw my tears and looked genuinely concerned. I was too angry to care; he *knew* I hated it when they went drinking. They could have used a pretty easy spell to get themselves sobered up after their bender, could have at least *pretended* they'd actually gone shopping, but no. That would have required a slight bit of effort and respect for my feelings.

"Jessie, whassamatter?" he slurred.

"Shitfaced and it's not even three. You guys are so fucking predictable."

"Jessie, we just—" the Warlock began.

I held up my hands as I strode away from them to the patio doors. "Save it. Just leave me alone."

Pal approached me as I stomped into the backyard. "How did it go with your father?"

"I don't really want to talk about it." I went into the tent and flopped down on the sleeping bag.

I heard Pal nudge the tent fly aside and step into the doorway. "Was it a fraud?"

"No, it was him, he just . . . he . . . gaaah!" Rage and frustration flared in me again, and I started slugging the pillow with my flesh hand. "*Why* do people have to suck so bad? Why?"

"Oh." I heard Pal shuffle his feet on the grass. "I'll be out here if you feel like talking."

I lay there, seething. A few minutes later, I heard the patio door slide open, and then a man's heavy footsteps approached the tent.

"Jessie, I—" Cooper began.

"If you're still drunk, *go away*!"

He retreated, and a moment later my anger turned to sadness and regret. I wept quietly into the battered pillow, and after a while I fell asleep.

"Jessie . . ."

I woke up, groggy. "What?"

A moment later, I smelled grilled hamburgers, and I felt intensely hungry. Stupid inconsiderate barbecuing neighbors, making delicious food I couldn't have anymore. The jerks.

"Can I come in?" Cooper asked. He sounded sober, and downright cheerful, but beneath the surface I thought I could hear a slight strain in his voice. "I thought you might be hungry, so I made us a snack."

I squinted at the fading sunlight coming through the tent flap; it was already evening. I'd been asleep for hours.

"Sure, come on in, I guess." I sat up and swung my

legs over the edge of the grassy bed, rubbing my sticky eyes. The flesh around my ocularis ached.

Cooper ducked into the tent carrying a plate of little hamburgers piled high with caramelized onions, melty cheddar, and crispy bacon. "Don't worry, these sliders are all vegan. Even the cheese. And I guarantee they won't taste like old jockey shorts."

"There's a fair distance on the tasty scale between 'good' and 'jockstrap,'" I said as he set the platter down beside me.

"Just try it."

I did. The burger patty was savory and juicy, tasted just like real beef, and the bacon was perfect and salty and crisp. The cheese was rich and tangy. I was in gustatory ecstasy.

"Dude, this is sex on a bun," I replied around my mouthful.

Cooper grinned at me. "Ye of little faith. Have another."

"Where did you learn to make this?"

"One of my exes ran into a necromantic side effect that made it a bad idea for her to eat animal flesh, too. It's more common than the pointy-hats would have you believe. Anyhow, she learned how to make a good meatless bacon cheeseburger, and she passed the recipe on to me. They're not very nutritious, so you couldn't live on 'em, but they're not as bad for you as the real thing, either."

I swallowed my mouthful, then looked around for something to wash the crumbs down. "Is there anything to drink?"

"Oh. Yeah. Left them on the picnic bench while I was grilling." He snapped his fingers, and two sturdy glass mugs of dark beer shot across the yard into his outstretched hands.

I accepted the mug he held out to me and took a sip. It was Guinness, *fresh* Guinness, not the oaky ditch-water it's usually staled to by the time we Yanks find it in a grocery store. "Yum."

After we'd cleaned the platter and drained our mugs, Cooper crawled onto the sleeping bag beside me. He cleared his throat. "Look, I'm really sorry about earlier. We really did intend to go shopping up at Polaris, but in the car I started talking to the Warlock about how bummed I was about Smoky dying and he said he wanted to cheer me up and before I knew it we were at Hooters—"

"You guys went to *Hooters*? What, were all the strip clubs closed or something?"

"They have pretty good chicken wings there."

"Breasts, too, I've heard." My tone was brittle as ice.

He held up his hands. "Look, I'm *sorry*. I wasn't thinking, and things went from dumb to stupid. I'm sorry I made you mad."

"I was already pretty mad. You just made it worse."

He gave me comically sad puppy dog eyes. "Forgive me?"

I sighed. "I suppose I have to, seeing as you made me the most kick-ass burgers I've had in over a year."

"Hug?"

I gave him a hug, and he held me close. I could feel an odd tension vibrating in his body.

"You know I love you, right?" he said.

"Yeah?" I replied slowly. He *never* asked that. First the baby talk, and now this . . . what the heck was going on with him? I knew spending time in a hell was bound to change a man, but I never expected it would make Cooper want to start talking about our Relationship, capital R. I worried about where this was going.

He took a deep breath. "You don't feel that I've been taking advantage of you, do you? Sexually, I mean?"

I sat up and stared at him. "No, why do you think I would think that?"

"It's just . . . well." He rubbed his face. "We've been together almost five years now, and . . ."

"And?" I prompted.

"I mean, your— Some people would think we should have gotten married by now. But you don't want that, right? I guess we haven't really talked about it."

True enough; we hadn't ever discussed marriage as far as I could remember. Not that I'd really cared one way or the other. I was never one of those girls who dreamed about being a bride in a fancy white dress. The only wedding I'd ever attended was my stepfather's, and that little soiree left me with a lasting impression of needless stress, unpleasantness, and expense. Until that weekend, Cooper and I hadn't had any family to stand up in front of and declare our love to, and none of our Talented friends seemed to view weddings as anything other than an excuse for a party.

As far as I was concerned, being in a committed relationship was being in a committed relationship, whether a priest and a ring and a piece of paper were involved or not. And if you needed a religious contract and the symbolic equivalent of a shackle to keep you from stepping out, well, how committed could you have really been in the first place? I'd always figured that a decent person does the right thing because it's the right thing, not because he's expecting some kind of cookie in the afterlife.

"I guess I kind of thought we more or less already *are* married," I replied. "I love you, you love me . . . how would our lives be any different after a formal wedding ceremony?"

"Things would be a lot different," Cooper replied, that odd strain coming back into his voice.

"How?" I wondered what he was getting at. Had my outburst at dinner and the fire and my not being all gung ho about having a baby with him given him second thoughts about being with me? Was he finding the scars on my face repulsive? Dammit, I'd gotten those scars rescuing *him*. My stomach began to clench. "Wait, is this your subtle way of saying you want to break up with me?"

"No!" Cooper looked alarmed. "No, no, that's not it at all."

He paused, his expression smoothing into a look of mild worry. "I just . . . I just want you to be happy."

"I *am* happy," I said. "I'm happy I got you back and that we're both in more or less one piece."

"Okay," he said, seeming to relax a little more. "I'm glad." Then he grinned. "Wanna go make brownies and play Halo?"

Faery

The next morning I got Mother Karen to try another healing poultice on my face. I sat in the rec room watching cartoons with the littler kids for close to an hour with a wet tea towel over a clammy green mudpack that stank like someone had slathered Vicks VapoRub all over a plate of anchovies. It did seem to deaden the ache around my ocularis, at least.

"Well, we've got to start getting ready, or we'll run the risk of being late," she called from the kitchen as the clock struck ten. "Come into the bathroom, please."

I followed her into the small half bath off the downstairs guest room. She had me sit on the toilet lid as she wiped the poultice off with a hot washcloth, then turned my head from side to side, frowning.

"Well, that helped a bit, but only a bit." She poked my cheek. "The scar tissue is better, but these scaly patches really just don't seem to want to go back to normal."

"Do you think it's some kind of curse?" I asked.

"It's possible." She wrung out the cloth. "Honestly, this is a bit beyond anything I've had to deal with as a healer."

She glanced down at her watch. "We better start

getting dressed. Please wash the rest of that off your face and then come up to the attic; I think I have a formal gown that will fit you."

I did as she asked, and a few minutes later found her in the gigantic cedar closet she'd installed beneath the eaves.

"Hmm," she said, shuffling through a rack of dresses and gowns. She pulled out a long strapless dress made of dark green satin with a poofy underskirt of black crinoline. "I think this would fit you. Here, try it on."

I slipped out of my jeans, T-shirt, and sports bra and wriggled into the dress. Karen zipped me up. I had to do some gyrations and tugging to get the bodice comfortably into place, but it was indeed a passable fit. I hadn't worn anything like that since Aunt Vicky talked me into going to the senior prom with some friends. The DJ mostly played a bunch of crappy love songs you couldn't really dance to, so after a while we ditched and went to someone's house. We played Texas hold 'em and got trashed on peach schnapps. I lost all my pocket money on a bad bluff and somehow ended up having to kiss a cheerleader named Brittany. She was too pretty and rich and stuck-up for me to have wanted to have anything to do with her normally, but I was drunk enough to feel like everybody in the room was made of awesome. At first I thought the two of us were just putting on a little show for the guys, but she got into it like she was trying to find the secret answers to our algebra final in my tonsils.

Over the next couple of weeks, she kept sending me text messages, asking me out. I told her as nicely as I could that I was straight, but she kept pestering me. After that, I began to suspect some kind of setup. You know the deal: she'd lure me to some seemingly private location, get me naked or close to it, and then somebody hiding in the bushes or closet would take a bunch of photos that would show up all over the Web five minutes later. Good times. So finally I just started replying to her texts with animated GIFs of volcanic porn cocks and she got the hint.

So anyhow, now I inevitably associate ball gowns with sickly sweet liquor and suspiciously enthusiastic cheerleaders. I suppose it could be worse.

"Do you think you're going to come out of that bodice?" Mother Karen asked.

"If a troll runs up to me yelling, 'Whoo boobies!' and yanks the front, yes. Otherwise, no, the puppies are safely kenneled."

Mother Karen laughed. "I doubt that would happen. Unseelies aren't usually allowed into the tavern." She paused, scrutinizing the outfit. "I can give you the other opera glove; that will look nice. I think I have some dark heels in your size—"

"Heels? Nuh-uh."

She frowned. "Heels would look very pretty with this dress."

"I am not wearing anything I can't run in. This meet could be a big ol' trap for all I know, and I want to be prepared."

She looked over her shoe rack. "All my flats are too small, unless you want Cooper to resize them, and you can't very well wear sneakers."

"I'll just wear the dragon boots. Nobody can say those aren't expensive enough," I pointed out.

She made a face, which I suppose was only natural since the last time she'd seen the boots, they'd been on the back porch tarred in dried devil ichor. "Those filthy things? They won't really match."

"So I'll get Cooper to clean them up and put some dark polish on them. The dress will mostly cover them, and anyway, who's really going to be looking at my feet?"

A couple of hours later, the emergency babysitters had arrived and we were on the road toward Winesburg in the Warlock's Land Rover. Pal cruised along overhead, hidden by an invisibility charm, although I could hear the weird calliope music of his flying spell over the engine noise. Cooper had done a great job shining up the boots, and he'd cleaned off the rest of my dragonskins, which I'd stashed in a black JanSport backpack I'd borrowed from one of the teens along with my street clothes, my Leatherman tool, a bottle of water, a couple of PowerBars, a small medical kit, hand sanitizer, and some stray spell ingredients in translucent plastic Fuji film canisters.

Mother Karen had done my makeup—doing her best to camouflage the scars—and had put my hair up in a French braid. I'd gotten wolf whistles from both Cooper and the Warlock when I came downstairs. Still, with my shoulders bare, I felt uncomfortably exposed, and also weirdly felt like I was in drag. I envied the guys being able to wear pants. The Warlock had gone back to his place and found tuxedos for both him and Cooper. Apparently the Warlock had been considerably slimmer in his early twenties, and the old tux wasn't even that far out of style. The Faeries, I supposed, cared almost nothing about current human fashion and mainly wanted to feel that we'd paid proper respect in our attire.

I also hoped that none of the seelies would take an inordinate interest in Cooper. He looked absolutely delicious in the hand-me-down tuxedo. The satiny jacket accented his broad shoulders and narrow waist, and the pants were just snug enough to nicely show off his buns and package. My inner Old Lady Mabel hated the saggy pants fashion that had reigned over American males seemingly my entire life.

A little while later, the Warlock pulled off the highway onto a dirt road running between two cornfields.

"This should be it," he said, glancing down at the magic compass he'd brought along. "Karen, you got Riviera's token?"

"Right here," she replied, patting the small beaded purse in her lap. She was wearing a long-sleeved sea-green silk gown and long strings of pearls; the outfit must have dated from the 1930s, and it looked good on her.

We got out of the Rover. The ground was soft and damp, so I was glad I wasn't in high heels. Pal's calliope was loud overhead. I slung my backpack over my shoulder and began to follow Mother Karen and the Warlock down a corn row.

Cooper nudged my backpack. "You could leave that in the car, you know."

"If something happens, it's not going to do me a lot of good if it's locked in the car a mile away."

"The seelies are probably just going to make you check it at the door."

I shrugged. "Checked at the door is still closer than locked in the car."

We came to a clearing where a battered old scarecrow hung crucified on a couple of rake handles. A cloud of dust rose as Pal touched down, and Cooper spoke an ancient word to turn off his invisibility.

A tin cup had been tied to the straw fingers of the scarecrow's left hand. When we got within ten feet of the scarecrow, my stone ocularis started to itch in my skull. I blinked through to the gemview that had shown me the invisible door to the drug stash. I saw an odd double image of the scarecrow and a set of bronze-reinforced oak doors big enough to admit an elephant.

Mother Karen dug the token—a small golden coin—out of her purse and stepped up to the scarecrow. She dropped it into the tin cup. The scarecrow shuddered, the tattered old black suit expanding as it filled with ogrish bone and muscle. The creature broke the rake handles like straws and leapt to the ground, glowering at us with coal-black eyes. It dumped the token out into a mottled, callused gray palm.

"Who seeks entry to our realm?" Its voice rolled like thunder.

Mother Karen stepped forward. "Karen Mercedes Sebastián, daughter of Magus Carlos Sebastián and Mistress Beatrice Brumecroft. And associates. We come at the invitation of Maga Riviera Jordan to dine with her at the tavern."

He turned his baleful face toward me and pointed a long black claw at my ocularis. "We don't like spies."

"What? I'm not a spy." My voice shook.

"Don't try to be clever with that sight-stone, or someone will pluck it right out of your pretty head."

I quickly blinked back to the gemview that showed the world simply as my flesh eye did. "Is this better?"

"It is acceptable."

Still scowling, the scarecrow reached into the air where I had seen the bronze handles on the great oak doors. He pulled, and suddenly the doors were visible to the naked eye, swinging wide to reveal a twilight-dimmed forest lit by a huge harvest moon. A road of ancient silver coins sunk in the damp earth glittered before us. The evergreen trees swayed gently in a brush of night wind, and tiny glowing creatures flitted through the branches.

The air from the forest smelled of midnight's denizens, deep dark earth, and night blooms headier than any liquor.

"Follow the silver path to the tavern," the ogrish guardian ordered. "Stray from it at your own peril."

"We better hold hands," Cooper said. "Things can get pretty weird in Faery."

We followed Mother Karen and the Warlock inside; Pal followed along behind us. The scarecrow shut the door after my familiar stepped onto the path, and almost instantly, the darkness seemed to solidify around us like a crush of unseen bodies just beyond arm's reach, the breeze like soft cold fingers brushing across my shoulders and the nape of my neck. Cooper's hand tightened around mine; I could tell he felt it, too.

"Girl . . ." a voice whispered.

I turned toward the sound, the will to simply not look somehow beyond me. A golden-haired young man stood in the trees, slender and pale, dressed only in a kilt of sheer material that left just enough to my imagination. I felt a dizzying, primal lust for him; he was everything I found physically sexy about Cooper amplified and intensified a dozen times over.

"Come here," Golden-Hair said with a smile that made my legs turn to water. He knelt and plucked a dandelion and blew the feathery seeds at me. "I've got something to show you."

Cooper's hand was growing slick with sweat. I glanced at his face; he was turning red as he stared at Golden-Hair, looking equally embarrassed and angry. "Don't listen to her," he whispered, pulling me along.

"Don't," echoed Golden-Hair, suddenly appearing from behind a tree in front of us, his voice like wind-chimes. "Don't just walk away . . . don't you want to see what your man sees? Don't you want to see what delightful things we could be doing, the three of us? All you have to do is take a little peek."

"Don't listen to *it*," Pal warned inside my head. "It's a trick. Stick to the path, no matter what."

What are you seeing when you look at it? I asked Pal.

"I'd rather not say," he replied.

Golden-Hair popped up in the wildflowers a few feet away from me, sitting cross-legged. "Boots? You wore nasty ol' boots!" he cackled. "Who dressed you this morning, your *father*? He should have tied a bell around your neck, because you lumber like a dimwit-ted cow. I'll bet your mother was some plow-pulling beast of burden your father turned into the shape of a woman after he couldn't stop himself from rutting on her in the barn. I bet the Virtus Regnum cut her into steaks and ate her after they killed her."

He paused, staring intently at the trails of smoke

curling from my opera glove. My pulse was pounding in my head despite my attempt to breathe slowly and stay calm.

"Ooh, everyone hide, the cowgirl's angry now! Stop chewing your cud and come over here! Show me who's boss, Bossie. Come over and try to shut me up."

For a long second, I thought about taking him up on his offer. My ocularis was itching like mad, but the scarecrow's warning stopped me from blinking for a better look, stopped me from leaving the path. We weren't here for me to get into a fight and endanger everyone else.

Golden-Hair kept after me, whispering seductions one moment and mockeries the next. I kept my gaze focused on the lost treasures embedded in the path: ancient drachms of Hermaeus and Menander, shining argentus nummus, Ottoman akçe and Indian rupees, mottled Liberty dollars, plus dozens of exotic coins stamped with the pale faces of dead kings I'd never seen in any book.

Finally, the path ended at what at first looked like vine-covered walls, but then I realized that the vines *were* the walls. The front door was a tall, thick oval mat of purple-flowered clematis lianas hinged on living tendrils; it swung open with a swish of leaves and a creak of green wood, and we filed into the tavern, everyone looking relieved to be free of Golden-Hair.

I quickly realized that the entire tavern was built from still-living plants enchanted or artfully cultivated to form a functional architecture, although certainly not one that had much use for straight lines and ninety-degree angles. The interior walls and floor were formed by smooth, densely woven strangler figs.

Ivory-barked trees rose like support columns for the leafy ceiling high above us, and luminous bracket fungi growing on the trunks cast a soft golden light throughout the rooms and passageways. Redwood-size tree stumps served as tables, and the woody figs rose from the floor to form trestle benches and stools.

The patrons seated at the nearby tables were dressed in antique finery from various eras; they scarcely gave us a second glance. Viewed straight on, they appeared perfectly human; glimpsed from the corner of my flesh eye, some became large insects, creatures of twisted bone, or strange fungal conglomerations. It was just a little unnerving.

A tall, beautiful woman in a diaphanous Aegean-blue chiton stepped toward us. Maybe she floated; I couldn't really see her feet. She was like a nymph straight out of Greek mythology: her glossy black hair was piled in ringlets atop her head, and her skin was sun-bronzed. Her eyes were the color of storm clouds rolling over the ocean. She glanced briefly at my back-pack, but didn't seem the least bit concerned about it.

"Please follow me," she said, her voice a rush of sea breeze through a mountain olive grove. "Your party awaits."

She led us through a winding passage to a room with an enormous tree-table. Riviera Jordan, dressed in a silver gown and shawl, sat on the opposite side of the table, flanked by six Governing Circle agents in crisp black tuxedos.

"Y'all have a seat," Riviera said, rising from her strangler fig bench. "We have a lot to talk about."

We took our places at the table. At each setting was a single white, highly polished plate; there were no glasses, no cutlery, no napkins. I at first assumed the plate in front of me was porcelain before I saw the fine concentric grain beneath the shine.

"Wood?" I asked Cooper.

"Probably," he replied. "Or maybe some kind of gourd or tuber."

Riviera was busy looking over some papers in her lap, so as quickly and surreptitiously as I could, I lifted my plate and licked the edge.

Instantly, I was standing on a windblown hill, rearing back to shake off the horrible jabbering prairie apes clinging to my shaggy fur, trumpeting my anger and frustration to the sky as one of them scurried between my front legs and jabbed a sharpened stick up between my ribs—

—I managed to stifle a gasp as I came out of the death-memory.

"It's wooly mammoth tusk," I told Cooper. "Very old."

"Oh. Wow." He gazed down at his plate, looking impressed. "I'll be careful with it."

And then I nearly dropped my plate when it spoke to me: "Now really, it doesn't seem very useful to lick me *before* the food's been served, does it?"

An amused elfin face was staring at me from the surface of the plate. I quickly set it back down on the table.

"I'm sorry," I stammered. "I was just trying to see what you were made of—"

"Rather nosy of you, don't you think?"

"I'm very sorry. I wasn't expecting sentient tableware."

Plateface sighed dramatically and rolled its ivory eyes. "Apology accepted, I suppose. Beverage?"

"What?"

"A drink? You know, something liquid that helps the food go down and prevents unsightly choking?"

"Oh. Uh. Water will be fine."

Another eye roll. "Boring, yet vague. Do you want it hot? Iced? Room temperature? Sparkling? Paris bottled? Detroit municipal? Dipped from a Mongolian horse trough and filtered through a wool sock?"

I frowned. "I'll take Evian natural spring water, no ice, forty degrees Fahrenheit."

There came a faint cracking noise from the table. A straight green tendril sprouted from the polished surface. It quickly formed a large bud that elongated and split open to unfurl a spiral of waxy lavender leaves that fused and rose up into a vaselike hollow flower. The remains of the bud shell thickened into a sturdy green calyx base supporting the flower, which quickly filled with a clear liquid.

"Your water, mademoiselle," said Plateface. "And for your meal you'd like . . . ?"

I blurted out the first thing that popped into my head; I suppose I was partly jonesing for more of what I'd had for breakfast and partly channeling my wish to escape: "A Monte Cristo."

Plateface sighed. "Still very, very vague. Do you want the whole sandwich dipped in batter and fried, or just the bread? And what kind of cheese?"

"Just the bread . . . and Swiss. No, wait, Gruyère."

"Since you seem indecisive, I'll give you both. And the usual assortment of condiments."

Plateface vanished, leaving me staring at the shiny blank ivory.

The table cracked again as a woody sprout erupted beside the plate. In the space of a few seconds, it grew into a small bush that produced one large red bud and three smaller purplish buds. The buds flowered into pretty blossoms that quickly shriveled, overtaken by swelling fruits covered in thick, veined skins. The big red fruit expanded like a balloon, steam rising from its green veins, until it ruptured with a *pop!* and a hot, sugar-dusted Monte Cristo sandwich toppled out onto my plate. The other, smaller fruits dropped off the bush beside the sandwich and split open, revealing what looked like strawberry jam, honey mustard, and clotted cream. A small branch I hadn't noticed fell off the bush and dropped beside the plate; it had a single long, serrated, bladelike leaf at its tip, and I realized it was meant to serve as a dinner knife. A large, velvety leaf sprouted on the plant and fell beside the twig knife: a napkin.

I'd been so focused on Plateface and my lunch plants that I hadn't been paying any attention to how the others were faring. Beside me, Cooper was pulling the purple skin off a huge berry of shrimp carbonara; he had red wine in his drinking flower. The Warlock had a T-bone and a baked potato, and Mother Karen's plant was dropping perfect little cucumber and smoked salmon tea sandwiches onto her plate. Pal was already gnawing on a large joint of some roast beast. Across the table, Riviera Jordan's plant was growing and shedding a variety of leaves and vegetables to fill her plate with salad; her bodyguards had gotten burgers and other sandwiches.

I nudged Cooper and pointed at the crispy bits of bacon scattered among the shrimp on his fettuccine noodles. "Aren't you worried about getting a death vision off those?"

"No more than you are, I guess."

"What?"

He nodded at my sandwich. "That's a Monte Cristo?"

"Yes?"

"Ham. Turkey."

I stared at it. "Oh, crap, I forgot. I only remembered it had cheese on it."

He laughed. "It's faery food . . . I wouldn't worry about it."

I cut my sandwich in half with the twig knife and blew on it to cool it a little. The bread was fluffy and moist under the crispy egg batter, and the inside was stuffed with cheese and turkey and shaved ham. I bit off a corner, expecting a kick of pain, but felt absolutely nothing. It certainly looked and tasted like meat, but I might as well have been eating a napkin for all the spiritual residue it contained.

We finished our meals in relative silence. When most of us were finished, a handsome young man in a kilt of ivy leaves shuffled into the room. Each of his eyes was covered with a bright red poppy blossom, and his face was frozen in a smile. He began to uproot the spent dinner plants onto the dirty plates and clear the table. His hands moved fluidly one moment, jerkily the next.

Mother Karen stifled a gasp when the young man took her plate; I gave her a quizzical look.

"It's Rick Wisecroft," she mouthed at me.

Her prodigal foster son? No wonder he'd left her

house so abruptly. Clearly he'd crossed the wrong people. I watched him more closely as he gathered up my plate; he moved like a marionette, and I saw thin silver chains on his wrists.

Mother Karen was staring at Rick, her face flushed, tears welling in her eyes; clearly she wanted to do *something* to rescue him from his slavery, but she couldn't do anything without risking her own freedom and probably ours as well. I felt myself getting angry again. Given our warm reception in the woods, I doubted that getting Rick as our busboy was any accident. The seelies really seemed intent on provoking us. Part of me wondered how they'd cope with a little incendiary ectoplasm, but the rest of me considered Rick's predicament and realized that was a bad, bad idea.

Riviera Jordan stood up and rapped on the table for our attention. Her eyes flickered from Mother Karen to Rick; clearly she knew something was amiss, but I could tell from her expression that she wasn't about to let it sidetrack the meeting.

"Well, now, it looks like everyone has had a chance to finish the fine lunch our hosts have provided for us," Riviera said. "And so it's time to get down to bare boards, as it were."

She paused. "As head of the Governing Circle, my primary duty is to ensure the welfare of the Talented families under my jurisdiction. A large part of that involves enforcing the laws set down for us by the Virtus Regnum; that part's usually pretty easy. But sometimes the law and our community's welfare are at odds with each other . . . and that's when things get difficult.

"I was head of the Circle for over fifty years, but after half a century of being responsible for thousands of often-ungrateful lives, I was ready to spend some quality time in my garden. My nephew Benedict seemed to want the job, seemed to be entirely qualified to do it, so we all put it to a vote, and twelve years ago, he took the reins. Everything seemed to be going fine under his watch, until last week when some well-intentioned but frankly very poor decisions blew up in all our faces."

Riviera looked at me. "When I came into the house Friday night and saw what you'd done to Benny, I was ready to kill you on sight, my dear. When I saw what you'd done to Angus and Eugene in the alleyway, I was ready to clap you in irons and drop you to the bottom of the sea. But then the butler told me what he'd overheard and I learned about the babies . . . and I realized I needed to put my judgments back on the shelf until I had my facts straight. And you're most fortunate, young lady, that you didn't destroy my nephew's mind completely, or else we'd have never been able to recover memories of his that cast your actions in a rather better light than we'd have ever guessed."

"I never meant—" I began, but she held up a hand to silence me.

"Please let me finish; you'll have your time to speak. This is a little difficult for me, and I want to get it all out here on the table."

She took a deep breath. "I told you I stepped down because I was tired. That's not the whole truth. My son Reggie . . . you know that he killed himself, Jessie. And you know why, probably better than I do. I never laid eyes on the hell my brother Lake made for himself and his family, and that's my failure, as a sister, a mother, and a governor. That's my mortal sin, one I'll carry to my grave.

"The day Reggie died . . . well, I hope none of you ever feel the way I felt. I told myself I wasn't fit to protect the city if I couldn't protect my own son. And I crumbled, I simply crumbled. Benny told me that he would take care of everything, and I took him at his word. But instead of dealing with Lake's hell, he simply kept covering it up."

"Didn't you know that my brothers were trapped in the hell?" Cooper asked, sounding deeply suspicious.

She shook her head. "Until you brought them back, I didn't even know they'd been born. When Reggie took Benedict to the farmhouse and he discovered Lake and Siobhan dead in the basement and the blood in the ritual circle . . . Reggie misjudged what had happened. He never saw the other children; the devil had probably already pulled them into its realm. Or maybe he saw the babies but couldn't bring himself to tell me about them. By then, the mundane authorities had found Cooper and his baby brother. Until last night, I thought the Warlock and Siobhan were the only sacrificial victims. Benny, it turns out, knew the truth from the beginning, but never told me.

"I should have dropped everything to investigate my brother's atrocities myself, but the Circle was in the middle of a crisis; several of the founding families were demanding we secede from the Regnum and withdraw entirely from the mundane world, and things were getting violent here," Riviera said, then looked at Mother Karen: "You lived here then, didn't you?"

"That was a bad time for the city," Mother Karen agreed. "A lot of children were orphaned. And so I hung up my wand and went into fostering full time."

"Your service to our community has been much appreciated," Riviera said to her, then faced Cooper and me. "I was convinced that if the news of Lake's madness became public, the secessionists would have turned it into a scandal to paint our whole family as closet necromancers."

Riviera paused. "So I told my son to burn the farmhouse and stay quiet."

"What would have happened if the Circle had voted to secede?" I asked.

"We would have gone to war with the Virtus Regnum," she replied. "And we would have lost. Badly. Dozens, perhaps hundreds of people would have died. I had visions of entire families being wiped out."

"What happens now?" I asked. "Is Pal or Mother Karen or the Warlock in trouble for helping me? Am I going to jail?"

"There are certainly a variety of local criminal charges that could be brought to bear," Riviera replied. "But, having reviewed my nephew's memories, it's clear he abused his power in appalling ways. He evidently commissioned some kind of third-party psychological profile on you that convinced him that you would fold under pressure, and the more you didn't do what he expected you to, the more he tried to force you . . . Well, he's as much to blame for what happened as anyone, I think.

"So, right now I'm not inclined to press any charges

against any of you, provided y'all continue to work with me and the Circle in a good-faith effort to remedy the damage that's been done. And, Jessie, seeing as you didn't respond in anger against our hosts' provocations on the silver path, I do have faith that we can work together."

I frowned. Had she set Golden-Hair on us—on *me*—as some kind of a test?

Riviera must have read the change in my expression. "I didn't ask our hosts to harass you, but I've been to Faery many times before and I know how they treat newcomers," she said. "And I had to know that you're able to rise above that kind of provocation when the situation calls for restraint rather than going in spells ablaze."

"But if I'd screwed up, we all might have been enslaved here," I protested. "And what would have become of the kids back at Mother Karen's house? You risked their safety just to see if I could ignore a Faery's 'yo mama'? *Really*?"

Riviera held up her hands. "My people have been watching the house; the children were never in any danger. We have foster parents lined up to take care of all of them in an emergency, and I was prepared to negotiate for your release if it came to that."

"But no guarantees that you'd succeed, right?" I replied.

"And who were you planning to hand my baby brothers over to?" Cooper asked sharply. "They're more than just a handful; they've got full-blown magical powers."

I leaned forward toward Riviera. "I'm pretty sure ol' Benny would have locked them up like they were all just a bunch of demons; how were you planning to do right by those kids?"

"That's the most important thing we have to talk about here today," she replied, nodding vigorously. "Obviously it's crucial that the Marron brothers be placed in loving, supportive homes where they can safely learn to control their powers. It's equally important that they get as much psychological care as they need to overcome any evil tendencies they may have picked up in the hell—"

"I don't want them dosed with magebane," Cooper said, his voice carrying a threat that made even me nervous. "They're way too young; it could hurt their brain development."

"It wouldn't be my first choice, either," Riviera replied gently, "but I can't guarantee that wouldn't happen."

"If my brothers get hurt—"

"The safety of the foster families has to come first, you know that," Riviera replied, her voice rising to match his. "I think we can both agree that blunting the boys' powers would be better than locking them away should they become violent."

"*No.*" Cooper's face was red, his hands clenched against the edge of the table. I hadn't seen that kind of sudden fury in him in a long time, not since his days of waking from bad nightmares to go drinking and looking for fights in dive bars.

"I won't let them near anyone who would even *think* of giving them that poisonous shit." He rose from his chair, scowling at Riviera. "I won't see my brothers turned into obedient little half-mundane zombies just for some country-club Talent's convenience! I can take care of them myself!"

"Cooper, please," Mother Karen said. "I'm against the magebane, too, but we don't have the resources to care for them all properly. It's been just a few days and I've barely slept, and my other kids are starting to wonder where I've gone. No offense, but I've been doing most of the heavy lifting for you so far, and I just can't keep doing it. I know you have the best intentions, but I really don't think you can do this all by yourself."

Karen turned to the Warlock. "Not unless you have other ideas?"

The Warlock shook his head, looking uncomfortable. "I want to help my brothers, honest I do, but my house just isn't a place for human babies. Opal ain't ready to be a momma."

Riviera met Cooper's furious glare with collected calmness. "You have my word that I will personally make sure that your brothers get the best care possible. As Circle head, I must also say that while your desire to protect your family and raise your brothers yourself is honorable, I am convinced the boys will be better off with more experienced parents, at least until they're a little bit older and you have a stable living situation."

Cooper sat down, reluctantly conceding her point with a noncommittal nod. "So which foster families did you have in mind?"

"My cousin Sylvia and her husband, Nikolai, have offered to take one of the boys; they have teen daughters at home who can help with child care. Rowland

Nachtcroft from the Governing Circle has offered to take another; two of his young sons have hereditary lycanthropy, so his family already has a nanny at the house who's skilled with special-needs children. Chione Gastaphar and her sisters have offered to take another, and Horatio Fox and his wife, Acacia, have also offered to serve as foster parents."

"Isn't Horatio a little old for fostering a baby?" Mother Karen asked. "He turned one hundred and fifty recently, didn't he?"

"One hundred and seventy," Riviera replied. "He still spends his weekends camping and running up and down hills at Civil War reenacts, so he seems to have the energy for it. Acacia is considerably younger, and a skilled healer; I'm willing to give them a chance if you are."

"How will you handle psychological counseling for the children?" Karen asked.

"All the prospective foster parents have agreed to bring the children in for regular therapy sessions; we're planning to use one therapist for all the boys, but we haven't decided who'll be handling that yet."

"I'd recommend Dr. Aboab Hopkinson," Karen said. "He's done well with my kids when they've been troubled."

"Dr. Hopkinson is high on our list, but he isn't sure yet if he can take on the Marron brothers without diminishing the care he gives to his other patients," Riviera replied. "The other candidates are equally qualified. No matter which families the boys go to, they'll get frequent play dates, and if they do well, we may be able to bring them back together in the same household after a while."

"I want unlimited visitation rights," Cooper said. "If I get a notion that I want to see my brothers at 3 A.M., I want to be let into the house to see them, no arguments from you or the family they're with or *anyone*."

Riviera pursed her lips. "The foster parents have a right to privacy that I won't see violated frivolously. I'll agree to your terms, if you promise not to abuse your visitation privileges."

Cooper nodded.

Riviera set a quill pen atop a set of papers and pushed them across the table to him. "The details of our foster care proposal—such as have been worked out—are all here, including the full list of potential therapists. If this looks like a workable arrangement to you, please sign, and after the meeting we can introduce the boys to their new homes."

Cooper frowned as he studied the proposal, then passed the papers over to Mother Karen so she could take a look. They exchanged glances; Karen pushed the papers back to Cooper with a hopeful nod.

"I guess I can live with this," Cooper finally said.

"I don't suppose you had people falling all over themselves offering to become foster parents, did you?" Karen asked.

"There wasn't an overabundance of volunteers, no," Riviera replied.

"There never is when there's a real need, is there?" Karen shook her head as Cooper signed his name on the dotted line.

"Well, now." Riviera looked from me to the Warlock. "Does this meet with you folks' approval as well?"

"If Coop's okay with it, then I am, too," the Warlock said.

"I don't know any of those people, but if Mother Karen thinks they're good parents, then I'm fine with them taking care of the kids, too," I replied.

"Did you have any more questions for me?" Riviera asked.

"Well, yeah," I said. "There's the little detail that your nephew burned down Cooper's shack and took all our spellbooks and guns."

"The house in Athens County is being rebuilt; the confiscated books and weapons will be put back where they were found once construction is complete. And you'll be compensated for any other damages."

She pulled another paper from her stack and pushed it across the table toward me and Cooper along with a quill pen; it appeared to be a list of everything that had been taken or destroyed by Benedict Jordan's agents. "Does that seem to be an accurate account?"

"It looks like it, yeah," I replied. The Governing Circle's accountant had totaled the damages at ten thousand dollars, partly to compensate for my lost job and garnished final paycheck, withheld by my boss because he thought I'd stolen from him.

"Will you take a direct bank transfer?" she asked.

"I'd kinda prefer cash," I replied.

"Cash, definitely," Cooper agreed.

Riviera gave us a look. "Given everything that's happened recently, are y'all absolutely certain that y'all want to be walking around with a great big wad of greenbacks in your pockets? If y'all lose physical money, I'm afraid the rules say I can't replace it, but if the electronic transaction fails or gets hijacked, we can fix it."

She reached into her purse and pulled out an iPhone. "I can show you the transaction right here."

I looked at Cooper. "What do you think?"

He shrugged. "I guess imaginary money will spend just the same in the end."

I signed the document, then passed it to Cooper. After he inked his name, Riviera logged into what I supposed was the Circle's Ohioana Bank account, and then showed us that she'd transferred the money to Cooper's checking account.

"What about my surprise criminal record, and our eviction?" I asked.

"The eviction has been remedied, and the fabricated conviction has been removed from the mundane criminal justice records," she replied.

"Any ideas about what to do about this?" I raised my left hand, still gloved. Thin tendrils of smoke wafted from the cuff.

"I myself am no expert on curse removal, so I have arranged for you to meet with Madame Robichaud next Wednesday at her parlor."

I knew Madame Robichaud by reputation; she was an accomplished Santeria priestess who'd moved north from New Orleans to help take care of her grandchildren. "Sounds good. What about Pal's overseers, and the Virtus Regnum?" I asked.

"Since Friday night, we have sent several messages to the Regnum concerning you and Palimpsest, but they have not replied to or even acknowledged our communications." Riviera looked solemn. "I will surely put in a good word for the two of you if I have the chance, but I don't know if that will happen."

That wasn't a good sign. But if they weren't talking to her, they weren't talking to her. I believed what Riviera had been telling me so far; I guessed I would just have to wait and see what the Virtii had in store for me.

A Hole in the Sky

It felt wonderful to step back out onto the damp earth of the cornfield, to feel the sun on my skin. I took a deep breath of the summer air and turned around. The scarecrow was once again just an old black suit and a straw-stuffed burlap sack head hanging on a couple of old rake handles.

"Well, thank God that's over," I said to Pal.

An unseasonably cool breeze wafted across my shoulders, and I shivered, looking upward. The sky was darkening. A late summer storm?

"I'm sorry, dude," the Warlock said to Cooper. "I . . . I just didn't know what to say in there. I don't know how to raise anything that can't live in an aquarium, you know?"

"It's okay." Cooper gave the Warlock a brotherly slap on the shoulder. "It'll work out. The kids'll be fine. You'll do better with the whole big brother thing when they're a little older."

"All the people Riviera mentioned will be very fine foster parents," Karen added. "I don't think you need to worry."

The hairs on my arms and the back of my neck prickled as the wind rose, turned downright cold, rattling through the cornfield. Sudden scudding clouds blotted out the sun, and my heart dropped when I saw four pavement-gray spirals begin to twist down from the overcast.

"Guys, look at that!" I said.

"Tornadoes?" said the Warlock. "What the hell?"

"No, I don't think they are," Cooper replied.

The tips of the descending spirals crackled with lightning, opened like the burning eyes of vast gods to reveal a blinding brightness behind them, and from them descended huge creatures that looked like crystalline orreries circling pulsing magma hearts.

"Shit, it's the Virtii!" I hollered. "Y'all get in the car and get the hell out of here!"

I slung both my arms through the backpack straps, hiked up my skirts, and pelted down a corn row, running as hard and fast as I could away from the Warlock's Land Rover.

"What are you doing?" Pal demanded inside my head.

Leading them away from you guys. I hope, I thought back, shielding my face from the lashing corn leaves.

"But you can kill these creatures!"

I killed one. *With great difficulty, if you remember. I take on four, I'm dead.*

"But we have Cooper and the Warlock to help us this time."

They'd be good if there were one or two Virtii. If we fight four, there'll be nothing left of us but scorched teeth and bad credit. Get everyone in the car and get them out of here.

"What are you planning to do out here on your own?" Pal sounded genuinely angry.

Planning to try to stay alive, first. I think I see some

trees I can hide in for a little while. I'm betting there's a back door to the Faery Tavern floating around out here someplace.

"They'll enslave you if you go back there uninvited!"

Still better than being dead, right? If that happens, tell Cooper he better come back here and break me out.

I ran out of the cornfield onto a dirt road and promptly tripped over a muddy rut. As I tumbled forward onto my hands and knees, I felt the zipper and fabric at the back of my ball gown pop and rip. Swearing, I got to my feet, held my smirched skirts up with my flesh hand, and started running toward the trees again, my bodice slipping ominously downward.

A Virtus loomed above me like a manta ray preparing to suck up a shrimp.

"Surrender or be expunged," it thundered.

Crap, I'm gonna die, I thought, still running. *I'm gonna die in a prom dress in a stupid cornfield out in the middle of BFE.*

I heard calliope music behind me, and suddenly Pal scooped me up underneath my arms and whisked me off toward open sky.

"Dammit, Coop, *move,* you're on my nuts," the Warlock complained from somewhere on Pal's back.

"Dude, there's no place for me to move *to*—" Cooper began.

"Christ, guys, why didn't you get out of here like I told you?" I hollered back at them.

"I wasn't just going to leave you out here!" Cooper sounded indignant.

"Nor was I," added my familiar.

"Warlock, what's your excuse?" I yelled.

"I didn't want to get stuck changing diapers!"

Pal's clawed fingers were digging painfully into my armpits, and my backpack was crammed up against the back of my head and neck; I couldn't turn to see if our pursuers were gaining on us or if we were making good our escape.

"Where are the Virtii?" I yelled against the wind.

"The closest one's, oh, a couple hundred yards back," the Warlock replied hoarsely, a faint tremor in his voice. "It's getting kinda glowy . . . that's bad, right?"

"Very bad, yes!" I stripped the glove off my flame hand just in case we were forced to fight. "Pal, if you can get us away from them any quicker, do it!"

"I know a teleportation incantation—" my familiar replied.

"Yes! Teleportation would be double-plus good!"

"—but I can't sing more than one spell. I'd have to land us first. They'd be on us before I could finish."

I swore. "Fly faster!"

"I'm trying!"

We rose higher in the air, and a sudden choppy crosswind caught my skirts. I felt the zipper give entirely and my bodice slid down to my hips. The way Pal was carrying me, I couldn't reach down to grab it. I tried for a charm but my adrenaline-soaked brain wouldn't come up with anything useful.

"My dress! Guys, help!" I spread my legs to try to keep it from flying away; the heavy fabric flapped between my knees like a sail, jerking my legs back against Pal's thorax. The wind whistled bracingly through my thin underwear.

"It's too much drag!" Pal exclaimed. "It's slowing us down; let it go!"

"I'm gonna be naked!" I wailed.

"And we'll be dead if they catch us!"

Pal's logic was unassailable. I closed my legs and felt the fancy green satin-and-crinoline ball gown flap away toward the fields below. Stupid fucking dress. At least I still had my boots on. "Are we losing 'em, or are they gaining on us?"

"They're gaining!" Cooper yelled. "Hey, where's your dress?"

Christ on a cracker. I took a deep breath and closed my eyes to keep from screaming in frustration. And suddenly realized that my ocularis was itching like someone had rubbed my eye socket with poison ivy.

I opened my eyes, blinked to the door-sight gemview, and began to scan the sky. And just a few hundred feet in front of us, I saw the faint outline of a wide oval, big enough to admit one of those flying Pringles cans they call regional jet planes—but maybe too small for a Virtus—hanging in the sky.

"Whoa! There's a portal! Go up, to the left!" I shouted.

Pal obeyed.

"What's a portal doing here?" the Warlock asked.

"I don't know; it's big," I replied. "Pal, stop, we're on top of it."

"They're coming fast, we can't stop long," Cooper said.

I fervently wished that I could turn my head to see behind us. "Let me try this."

I reached out to probe the edge of the portal with my flame hand. The moment I touched it, the portal sprang open with a pop, revealing a circle of bright jet-stream blue within the cloudy sky. A wind rose from the difference in pressure, dragging us toward the portal, but Pal was strong enough to resist it. I was too low to see the ground that lay beyond the portal, but it was disorienting to see the sun twinned in the second sky.

"Something's not right—" Pal began.

The Warlock and Cooper swore and shouted. A burning plasma pseudopod whipped through the air, perilously close to my head.

"Fuck it, go through, go through!" I screamed.

Pal went through.

And suddenly we were falling.

The Devil in
Miss Shimmer

A Bale of Trouble

Pal was still performing his musical spell as we plummeted toward the ground. I tried to shout an old word for "slow" but felt my magic blocked as solidly as if someone had put me in a stranglehold. Cooper was shouting an incantation, too, with no better result. More bizarrely, I realized my flame hand had been extinguished, leaving nothing but a couple of inches of coal-black stump below my elbow.

"Haystack below! Go left so I don't crush you!" Pal released me, and I twisted midair and pushed off his hairy body with my legs.

I landed on my backpack on a steep hill of scratchy hay, rolling sideways until I tumbled to a stop against some straw bales at the bottom. The pack had miraculously stayed on my back. A piece of baling wire jabbed me painfully in the side, and I gasped. Instantly, my mouth and nose were filled with a foul roadkill stench.

I rolled away from the protruding wire and came face-to-face with an eyeless, desiccated corpse, the leathery lips vermin-eaten and pulled back from the tobacco-stained teeth in a rictus.

"Augh, there's a dead guy!" I hollered, scrambling to my feet and leaping over the bales to the sandy ground beyond. "Ew, ew, nasty, ew!"

I dropped the opera gloves that were still clenched in my right hand and slapped at imagined maggots on my naked body and legs.

Pal was a dozen yards away, heaving himself over onto his stilting legs in the straw.

"Oh dear, there's a corpse over here as well." He bent to examine what I'd initially thought was just a bundle of rags. "She appears to have missed the haystack entirely when she fell."

I took deep breaths, trying to still the creepy shivers jittering up my spine. The air was as hot and thick as the blood of a man dying of fever. Every inhalation brought the bitter-sharp smell of a thousand spiny weeds and the pungent stink of rotting flesh and something I took to be gasoline or kerosene.

The pile of hay we'd fallen into was positively mountainous; the top had to be over a hundred feet high, and the base was easily the size of a football field. Cooper and the Warlock had gotten stuck in the hay much closer to the top and were struggling down the hill, sinking knee-deep in the fodder with every step; they both seemed to be uninjured. The cloudless sky was the blue of a natural gas flame, and the sun stung my bare breasts and shoulders; I'd be burned to blisters in a half hour. The makeup Mother Karen had put on me smelled as if it had some kind of sunscreen in it, so at least my face would be okay for a while. The tops of my ears and my nipples, maybe not so much.

Where were we? I turned to survey the landscape. At first glance, I thought we were in a junkyard planted randomly in the middle of a vast expanse of flat scrub, but then I realized the twisted metal frames were the wreckage of various types of smaller aircraft, from gliders to crop dusters to small commercial jets. I even saw the stripped, sun-bleached bones of a dragon. Farther in the distance I could see abandoned, intact aircraft; apparently their pilots had coasted to safe landings.

Or mostly safe: some had broken wings and fuselages, and I could see dark, muddy fuel spills beneath them. Why hadn't they exploded or even burned? And what had made them crash? Clearly we were in a magical dead zone, but planes didn't need magic to stay in the air. Or if they did, the airlines sure weren't advertising it.

Cicadas were a steady, feverish buzz in the scrubby mesquites scattered among the wrecks. The earth was a mix of exposed crumbling limestone and dry caliche dotted with tufts of brown arrowgrass, purple-blossomed nightshades, ragweeds, and horse crippler cacti.

"Hey, guys, I think we're in Texas." I shrugged off my backpack and dug out a disposable lighter.

"Texas?" The Warlock was running his purple healing crystal over a nasty scratch on his face as he limped through the straw toward me. The wound was sealing, so the crystal was still working. His gaze rested on my bared breasts for two heartbeats, then slid away to the airplane wreckage. "What makes you think this is Texas?"

"The weeds, mostly. And the general landscape." I flicked the lighter several times and didn't get so much as a spark off the steel. Huh. Planes probably didn't need charms, but they definitely needed internal combustion. Apparently someone—or something—had nixed fire as well as spoken magic. I blinked through all the gemviews; my ocularis seemed to be working properly. Whatever was squelching our spells didn't seem to affect enchanted items.

The Warlock ran his fingers through his sweaty curls and scratched his scalp. "But it's so . . . flat. Where are the mountains?"

I laughed and started digging my street clothes out of the backpack. "You've seen too many Westerns; you're thinking of Montana. Hollywood thinks it looks more like cowboy country than the Lone Star State. Or maybe it's just cheaper to film up there."

Cooper joined us. "Not that I don't love talking about movies, but maybe we should be talking about this spectacular trap we just randomly fell into?"

I wiggled into my sports bra. "Trap, yes. Random, no."

The Warlock frowned. "What do you mean?"

"Well, the trap part is obvious." I slipped on my Hello Kitty T-shirt and gestured at the hay mountain. "That or this is the shittiest theme park attraction I've ever seen."

"Did you know this was probably a trap when you had Pal go through?" Cooper asked.

"Yeah, I had an idea." I started taking my boots off so I could slip on my dragonskin pants. It was way too hot for them, but at least they'd provide a bit of protection if we got attacked. I couldn't bear the thought of putting on the dragonskin jacket, even though my arms were getting pink from the sun. For all the stuff I'd packed, I'd forgotten sunscreen.

"You *knew* this was a trap?" The Warlock looked

like he was ready to pay me back for the broken nose I'd given him. "What the hell were you thinking?"

"I was thinking we were facing certain fiery death if we didn't go through the portal." I stepped into the pants and pulled them up with my flesh hand; immediately my legs started sweating uncomfortably under the leather. "And since the portal didn't seem to lead into outer space or a live volcano or Rush Limbaugh's underwear, it seemed like the better of two lousy choices."

I was getting faint flashes of the dragon's death as the leather clung to my damp skin. If I closed my eyes, I could feel Moorish steel slashing my long neck and belly as I belched fire at the impudent raiders. But the death-imprint was old, faded, hovering just at the edge of my perception. I could get used to it, probably tune it out entirely after a while like a mild case of post-nightclub tinnitus.

"But maybe they just wanted to take us into custody," Cooper said.

"Look, guys, contrary to popular belief, I'm not an idiot." I pulled the hem of my shirt out over the top of my pants and started to put my boots back on. "I got a peek inside the mind of the Virtus I killed. They want me dead, period, end of sentence. And to be on the safe side, they want you guys dead, too. They are probably the least random beings in the universe; everything they do is carefully planned and measured against a thousand possible outcomes. The Virtus probably didn't have to miss when it took a swing at us, so they wanted us to go through this particular portal. So it was a setup from the beginning. And we just have to deal."

"But why here?" the Warlock asked. "I mean, if

they want you dead . . . well, this hay pile doesn't fit in with that, you know? Whoever is running the show here wants people to survive the fall. So are we looking at some kind of fate worse than death out here, like prolonged torture or something?"

"They're not sadists." I shook the dust off the opera gloves and stowed them in the pack. Trying to explain to the others what I'd seen and felt when I'd touched the Virtus' mind was pretty difficult. I just didn't have the words for all of it.

"I killed one of them," I continued. "That means I'm dangerous to them in a physical sense, sure. But I'm also dangerous to them on a prophecy level, and to them, that's even worse. Clearly the Virtus I took out the other day hadn't planned on dying, right? I upset their carefully-laid plans, and they just can't stand that. Their wanting me dead isn't vengeance or something—it's simply to fix a bug in their program, I guess is the best way to put it."

I tucked my pants cuffs into my boots. "And that probably means they expect I'll die here without their having to risk any more of their own people to do it. Obviously, that's not good. But there's also the possibility that they herded us out here because their calculations say I'm likely to end up fixing some other problem they don't want to deal with directly."

I stood up and faced them. "And that means we might get out of this alive."

Texas Hold 'Em

"What kind of problem could you solve for them?" the Warlock asked.

"Jeez, I don't know," I replied. "It's not like they e-mailed a memo. If certain people had bothered to share basic information with me, none of this would have happened in the first place."

I frowned, getting angry at Benedict Jordan and my father all over again.

The Warlock tugged at the crotch of his tuxedo pants, looking unhappy. "So what now?"

"Well." I picked up my backpack and shrugged into it. "We could get some shade under one of those planes, but I think we should look for civilization. I've got only one bottle of water, and out here that won't last the four of us even until sundown. It also won't last us much of a hike in this sun, so does anyone see anything nearby?"

Cooper squinted off into the horizon. "I think there's a gas station or something over that way."

I followed the direction of his gaze, and saw the sun glinting off a red-and-white sign a mile or two away, the logo and lettering unreadable at our distance. Near it was what looked like a low building, and beyond it, a gray water tower that was barely visible against the sky.

Cooper loosened his tie and slipped off his tux jacket; his dress shirt was already drenched in sweat, clinging to his tight ab muscles. The Warlock followed suit, and I stowed their jackets in my backpack.

"I think before we wander off toward the Great Unknown, we should check the planes for supplies," Cooper said, rolling up his sleeves. "Just in case the survivors left behind some water or food or something. And I don't know about you guys, but I could use a hat."

We checked out the nearest, mostly-wrecked planes first, and found more corpses that none of us felt like moving in order to search the aircraft. As we moved farther through the airplane graveyard, we spotted an American Airlines regional jet that had plowed deep furrows in the rocky earth during its touchdown, snapping off at least one of the wheels. The crew and passengers had gotten all the doors open, and from them hung the deflated remains of the emergency slides.

"I bet there's something still in that one," Cooper said. "If the crew was sticking to protocol, they wouldn't have let people take any luggage off."

"Should we try to break into the luggage hold?" the Warlock asked.

Cooper shook his head. "Probably any bottled water would be in the passenger compartment." He looked at me and then at the limp yellow slide. "That thing looks hard to climb. If we boosted you up high enough to grab the edge of the door, do you think you could pull yourself in there one-handed?"

I nodded. My stump didn't hurt and was actually feeling a bit numb for a change, so I thought I could use my elbow for leverage if necessary.

Cooper looked at Pal. "Do you mind if we stood on you to get some extra height?"

Pal blew a chord that I took as a sigh. "I suppose there's not another way for you to get up there. Please don't stand directly on my vertebral crests, because that hurts."

"He says it's okay," I told Cooper. "Stay off his spine bones if you can."

My familiar knelt and Cooper and I got on his back. Pal stood and moved directly beneath the airplane's main door. After some awkward false starts, Cooper was able to balance on Pal's thorax and I was able to climb up on Cooper's shoulders and sit on him like we were preparing for a chicken fight.

"Okay, steady," Cooper said. "Step onto my hands and I'll push you up."

Clutching his head for balance, I gathered my feet under me and stepped out onto his outstretched palms. He grunted as he pressed me upward; Cooper's wiry but he's plenty strong. I grabbed at the lip of the open hatch with my flesh hand and swung my other elbow up onto the edge and pulled myself inside.

The short blue carpet covering the aluminum floor smelled like dirt, cleaning chemicals, and stale coffee. I quickly got to my feet and surveyed the passenger compartment. No corpses here, which I was very glad to see; the overhead luggage compartments were mostly open, and I could see bags and other items still inside.

"Looks like we're in business, guys!" I called down to the others.

I rummaged through the galley compartments first. They had been ransacked pretty thoroughly already, but I found four unopened water bottles in an overlooked bottom bin along with some packets of shortbread cookies and pretzels. Someone had left a tote bag filled with beach towels on her seat; I emptied it out, keeping the SPF 45 lotion at the bottom, and loaded it with the water and snacks. Upon checking the rest of the luggage compartments, I found a bone-colored straw cowboy hat I snagged for myself, a gray felt cowboy hat I thought might fit the Warlock, and an olive-drab boonie hat for Cooper.

I went back to the hatch and dropped the bag of loot down to Cooper. "I think I can get myself down on the remains of the slide."

I sat down, swung my legs over, and awkwardly lowered myself so I could grab the slide. I nearly lost my grip, and half slid, half fell the fifteen feet or so to the sandy earth, landing on my back.

"Are you okay?" Cooper stepped toward me, looking concerned.

"Yeah, I'm fine." If I'd learned one thing in the year I'd gone to hapkido with Mother Karen, it was how to make nice with the ground during sudden encounters.

We traded the bottle of sunscreen around and slathered it on. Cooper and the Warlock briefly argued over who got to wear the gray cowboy hat but rebuffed my offer to go back into the plane to find another one.

"Well, let's get moving; maybe we can find some

help over there," Cooper said, his cheer sounding only slightly forced. He tried a couple of other old words for random simple charms, with no effect. "But I have to say, this magic block worries me. Someone went to a lot of trouble to set it up. It's taking a whole lot of power, but I can't tell where it's coming from."

"There's nothing we can do about it except try to figure out what's happened here," the Warlock replied.

We walked out across the scrubby field toward the red-and-white sign.

"We need to find a phone to let Mother Karen know what happened," I said.

"If someone's gone to the trouble to suppress magic, what are the odds that the phones are still working?" the Warlock asked.

We continued in silence. The sign soon became legible: it bore a cartoon cowboy in a red-checkered shirt tipping a red ten-gallon hat alongside the words "Howdy Y'all! Welcome to Rudy Ray's Roadstop." There were a couple of gasoline and diesel pumps out front under a corrugated steel awning tall enough to shelter a semi and what looked to be a kerosene pump and air pump off to the side. Something low and flat out back was reflecting a lot of sunlight; I wondered if it was some kind of greenhouse. The Roadstop was a single-story brick building with a flat gravel roof. It was a fairly standard convenience store construction with a few folksy flourishes like the hand-painted cartoon cowboy signs advertising ice, beer, wine, and homemade pecan pies in the windows. The parking lot was empty of cars except for a burnt-orange Toyota Prius with a Texas Longhorns bumper sticker. The lonely car was covered in a thick layer of caliche dust and looked as if it hadn't been driven all summer.

There was a "Y'all Come on In, We're Open!" sign on the glass front door. Once we got fairly close, I was able to see past the glare reflecting off the windows into the store. "Hey, check it out, the lights are on. Somebody's really here."

"It looks as though I'm rather too large to fit through the door," Pal told me. "I shall wait for you in the shade by the fuel pumps."

I went to the door first, cautiously pushed it open a crack, and stuck my head inside. The air was cool, a little stale, but clearly the place had working air-conditioning. I heard something I first thought was ice rattling around in a blender. The front part of the Roadstop was a little café area set up with a half-dozen small round white tables and chairs to the right and a glass-fronted food service counter along the wall to the left. The food service area had a refrigerated section for ice cream (all the tubs were empty and clean) closest to the door, I supposed to attract the attention of hot, tired travelers. Past that was a section that advertised various pies and pastries—nothing was left but a few dry-looking brownies—and to the right of it, what looked to have been a hot food area that once served chili dogs and tamales and such. Beyond the café tables was a small grocery store area, mainly rows of wine coolers and beer. Most of the shelves of dry goods were empty, as were the refrigerated drink coolers along the back wall. To the far left was a glass door that led into a dark room; a sign on the door read "The Liquor Locker—Over 21 Only."

Directly across from the door past the café tables was a separate counter of Texas-themed T-shirts, caps, postcards, and other souvenirs. Between the postcard display and an old-fashioned manual cash register I could see a booted pair of feet propped up on the glass countertop.

"Hello, anyone here?" I called.

The ice-chopping noise stopped abruptly, and as a chair squeaked and the boots slipped off the counter I realized the sound had been snoring. A thin man with a thick gray handlebar mustache popped up behind the cash register, running his fingers through his sparse white hair nervously.

"Sorry, folks, must have nodded off there awhile. Come on in! My name's Rudy, and mi hacienda es su hacienda!"

I shrugged at Cooper and the Warlock. They shrugged back. We cautiously stepped inside.

"I ain't had a supply run in a while, so I'm short on snacks, I'm real sorry 'bout that." The man ran his hands over the front of his red Western-style shirt, apparently trying to smooth out some of the wrinkles. "But I got Cokes and beer in the back if y'all are thirsty. Got the good Mexican and Passover Cokes, too. No corn syrup in my store if I can help it! Don't know if that junk really causes diabetus or not—the 'betus took my wife, Yolanda, God rest her—but real sugar tastes better if y'all ask me."

I was actually pretty thirsty, but didn't know if we could trust this guy or not. "Thanks, I think we're good for right now . . . but can you tell us where we are?"

"You're in Cuchillo, Texas." The man's tone was

an odd mix of pride and dread. "Really, you're about a hunnert yards past the city limits—it's a dry town, or it used to be. I don't 'spose anybody there much cares about the potential for moral turpitude from ol' debbil whiskey anymore."

"What happened here?" Cooper took his hat off and set it on a nearby café table.

The old feller scratched his scalp nervously. "I can't rightly say. We sort of had our own Hurricane Katrina blow into town and set for a spell, and things ain't been right since."

He looked at me. "You folks come through the hole in the sky, or did you take a wrong turn on the highway?"

Rudy said "highway" the way cancer patients say the word "cure."

"We dropped down onto that big pile of hay out in the field," I replied. "I don't suppose you know what that's about?"

He looked profoundly uncomfortable. "I can't say. Don't really understand it myself, but . . . well, the sky's how most folk end up here these days. I keep praying the highways will open back up so we can get some help, but I guess the good Lord's up to his old mysterious ways again."

"How are the highways closed?" the Warlock asked. "Roadblocks, or the National Guard, or what?"

Rudy shook his head. "There ain't no roadblock, none you can see, anyway. Like, for instance, say you got on the highway out here and tried to drive toward Lometa. After a mile or two you'd find yourself thinking you want to stop the car and go back where you came from, and after another mile your heart would be poundin' and your hands would be shakin' and you'd be so scairt you wouldn't be able to keep going. And if somehow you could keep your hands on the wheel and your foot on the pedal . . . you'd find yourself turned around on the road driving back this way and not know how it happened."

Rudy paused to scratch the gray stubble on his chin. "But you probably wouldn't find any of that out, not unless you had a 'lectric car, because you can't so much as light a match round here anymore. Never mind gettin' a gasoline engine or a generator started."

I looked up at the fluorescent lights. "Do you get your power from the electric company?"

"No, miss, I ain't been on the city grid for years. And the electric company went under same time as everything else round here."

"Then how are you running the lights and coolers and stuff?" I asked.

Rudy smiled, looking proud and profoundly sad all at the same time. "Come take a peek out back. I ain't got no weirdo Texas chainsaw monkeyshines going on out here, I promise."

We followed him through a door beside the cash register at the food counter. He led us down a hall past an employee restroom, the storeroom, and what looked to be his own living quarters and exited at a loading dock at the back of the building.

Before us was a solid acre of blue-gray solar panels shining in the afternoon sun.

"Ain't it a beauty?" Rudy asked. "It was my daughter Sofia's idea, going green like this. One thing we never lack out here is sunshine! The panels are real expensive if you buy 'em whole, but Sofia knew where to get the parts, and she and I spent six months building this out here with some help from some buddies of mine. My little gal's smart like my daddy was; he helped engineer the Hoover Dam back in the day. She's a physics professor at Cuchillo State. Was, anyway."

His expression fell into misery. "Well, all this is how I got lights and cool air."

I wanted to ask what happened to Sofia, but sensed that it wasn't something he wanted to talk about. He silently led us back into the café section of the building.

"You wouldn't happen to have a working phone or CB radio, would you?" Cooper asked Rudy.

The old man shook his head. "No, sir. I got a radio, but if you're looking to talk to somebody who ain't here in Cuchillo, it won't work. The landline don't work, and I haven't been able to get a signal on my cell phone since this mess got started."

"When did it happen?" I asked.

" 'Bout a year ago, give or take a month or two. The days've been kinda running together in my head."

Rudy glanced out the window toward the highway. Nervously, it seemed to me. "It's a far piece into town, but somebody usually comes by to give new folk a lift. Have a sit if y'all want to wait; drinks are on the house if you want 'em."

Cooper frowned slightly. "I thought you said cars don't work here."

Rudy's expression was unreadable. "The people in town still have some horses and mules and such. Haven't had to resort to eating 'em quite yet."

"We might take you up on those drinks in a little while," Cooper said, beckoning the Warlock and me to follow him outside to the shaded gas pumps where Pal was resting.

"I don't like this," Cooper said, his voice hushed even though we were surely out of Rudy's earshot.

"What's to like?" I replied. "There's been some kind of local apocalypse and the phones don't work and we can't escape."

"He *says*." The Warlock crossed his arms.

"Do you want to coldcock the old guy and ransack the place looking for his cell phone?" I asked. "Because I sure don't."

"The healing crystal works," Cooper said. "So, obviously some magic can still function here. I think we should try to open a mirror to call for help."

"How?" I asked. "You guys have never been good at that kind of magic in the first place. I could try it, I guess, but I don't have a pointer."

Cooper suddenly looked a bit embarrassed. "I do."

He got his wallet out of his back pocket and pulled out the folded card containing a lock of my father's hair.

I stared at the pointer. "Where did you get that?"

Cooper cleared his throat. "I found it on the floor of Mother Karen's office, near the fireplace."

I gave my boyfriend a hard look. "And why were you in her office?"

"You were really upset, and I didn't know why, and I thought I should try to find out."

"Did you mirror my father while I was asleep?"

He paused. "Yes, I did."

Cooper's admission made me unreasonably furious. "Goddamn it all to hell—"

"Jessie, he is kind of a jerk, but I think he actually means well—"

"I am *not* calling that jackass and asking him for help!"

"He seemed *very* concerned about you, and told me he wanted you to contact him again. And he might be our only option here." Cooper held the card out toward me. "I think we're in over our heads. And I think Magus Shimmer has the power to get us clear of all this."

"No way," I fumed.

Pal heaved himself to his feet on the oil-splotched concrete, looming above me. "Surely my ears deceive me. Surely you are *not* refusing to do what you can to help us all get out of this dust-blown, sweltering, fly-infested gulag because your pride has been injured?"

I bit my lip. Pal was right. And apparently also really pissed off at me. My hand still trembling, I took the card from Cooper.

"Fine. I'll give it a try. But I'm going to try contacting Mother Karen first, just so you know. What are we going to do if the mirror magic won't work because of the suppression spell?"

"We'll figure something out," Cooper said.

"Do you have the power of creation in that hell fragment of yours?" Pal asked.

Yes, I do.

"Try the spell in there. Mirror magic should be workable from within a hell dimension," Pal said.

"Okay," I said. "Let's go back inside; I'll ask to use the ladies' room and try opening the mirror in there. If that doesn't work, I'll go into my hellement."

"Hellement?" Cooper frowned. "What hellement?"

"It's sort of a long story," I said. "I'll explain later once I understand it myself."

chapter fourteen

Mirror Matter

The women's restroom was practically spotless; evidently Rudy had time on his hands and nervous energy to spare. I locked the door behind me, then turned to the mirror above the sink. Could it work? I slipped my father's pointer into a side pocket of my backpack. After rummaging through the main compartment for a few moments, I found a long strand of Mother Karen's hair. I tucked the strand up under the corner of the mirror's frame and touched the glass; it seemed impossible that I could enchant the materials. Every time I tried to focus on Mother Karen's office, tried to focus on bringing out my Talent, it felt as if a strong hand was closing around my throat, my mind.

Time to try a different tack. I went into the toilet stall, hung the pack on the door hook, and sat down on the toilet. Could I even get into my hellement in this place? I stared down at my blackened stump.

Despite having no flames to concentrate on, slipping into my hellement was even easier than it had been in Mother Karen's yard. I found myself standing in front of the red door in my childhood bedroom. Everything appeared to be exactly as I left it. I went to the mirror above my dresser and brushed the dust off the top of the frame. How would the magic work in here? Names mattered, after all, and I had Mother Karen's name and her address.

I touched the glass and concentrated on visualizing the inside of Mother Karen's office as it would appear from the vantage of the mirror. "I wish to speak to Karen Mercedes Sebastián, daughter of Magus Carlos Sebastián and Mistress Beatrice Brumecroft, of 776 Antrim Lane, Worthington, Ohio, 43085."

I spoke an ancient word for "open."

The mirror darkened, then began to clear. For just a moment I got a blurry view of Mother Karen's office. Yes! Success!

And then the mirror went entirely black. A life-size medieval knight in full silvery Spanish plate armor rose in the frame.

"Begone, hellspawn!" the knight shouted, swinging his steel longsword at me. The blade thrust out of the mirror straight at my head. I managed to duck in time, snatching up my own sword from its place against the dresser, and parried his swing with a teeth-rattling clang.

The knight leaped through the mirror, knocking everything off my dresser, swinging at me wildly. He was quick, strong, and hard to parry.

"Can't I just leave her a message?" I hollered at him as he knocked me backward onto the bed.

"Devils deserve no quarter!" He lifted his sword with both hands, preparing to skewer me to the mattress.

I saw a gap in the armor under his raised arms, and I jabbed upward. My blade sank deep into his armpit.

The knight snarled and disappeared in a puff of acrid blue mist.

I lay there on Buzz Lightyear's quilted face, clutching the sword, panting for air, my heart pounding in my ears.

That's one hell of a security spell, I thought. *Mother Karen ain't fooling around.*

Once I'd regained my composure, I sat up and checked myself for injuries. Even sixty seconds of a sword fight can slice you up good if it doesn't kill you outright. Karen's knight had nicked the knuckles of my right hand, and I had a nasty defensive gash running along my left forearm. I went down the hall to the bathroom and patched myself up with some gauze and a roll of bandages I found in the medicine cabinet, then went back into my bedroom to try again. My only remaining option was to contact my father.

I touched the glass, imagining my father's workshop as I had seen it before. "I want to speak to Magus Ian Shimmer."

I spoke another ancient opening word. Nothing happened. Not even so much as a flicker in the mirror.

My heart sank. I needed more information, or I needed a pointer of some kind, and I didn't have either one. Too bad I couldn't have brought the card into the hellement with me. I didn't even know if Ian Shimmer was his true name, and I certainly didn't have his home address.

Then I had a little duh-moment epiphany: Shimmer was my biological father. Half my DNA was also his DNA. So wasn't my own flesh and blood a kind of pointer to him?

I slipped my right index finger under the bandages covering the gash on my forearm and smeared a bit of sticky blood on the glass. Concentrated.

"I need to speak with my father. *Dvaaramud-dhaaTaya!*"

The mirror hazed, resolved. I was looking into my father's workshop.

"Um, hello?" I called. "Are you there?"

I had almost said, "Are you there, Dad?" but the D-word stuck in my throat and refused to come out.

I heard the sound of flip-flops slapping across the wooden floor, and my father appeared, still dressed in his orange pants and patchwork jacket. He sat down in the wooden chair across from his mirror, looking at me with an expression of deep relief and concern.

"Jessie, I'm so glad you've been able to contact me again," he said. "Are you in Cuchillo?"

His question surprised me. How did he know where we'd gone? And then I was surprised that I'd been surprised. After all, how had he known that I was in the backyard to receive the teddy bear message? My father kept an eye out, clearly.

"Yes, we're at a liquor store just outside the city limits."

"I see you're mirroring from a hell. Is everyone all right?"

"We're okay. Do you know what's going on out here?"

"I only know what Randall told me before he went there with Dallas Paranormal Defense. That was almost a year ago. He said that there was a report of a small town taken over by a powerful demon; he seemed to think it would be a routine operation for them, but his whole team went incommunicado that night. And then the Regnum put down a regional isolation barrier and I haven't been able to get through—"

"Wait, who's Randall?"

Shimmer blinked at me. "He's your older brother."

The word "brother" sent a shock straight down to the soles of my feet, and in the next moment I thought that surely I'd misunderstood him.

"What?" I asked.

"Randall is your older brother," Shimmer repeated.

"I . . . I have a brother?" I replied stupidly, suddenly feeling thrilled. I'd wished for a big brother to play with when I was a little kid, yearned for someone to commiserate with when I was a teenager. Like most of my childhood longings, it wasn't something I thought about much as an adult, although brotherly figures still popped up in my dreams every so often. The Warlock was too much of a hound to fill in as a surrogate, but he came pretty close sometimes.

"Yes, you have a brother." Shimmer smiled, apparently amused by my reaction, and his expression infuriated me.

"Why the hell didn't you tell me?" I scowled at him.

My father raised an eyebrow at me. "You didn't exactly give me a chance when we talked before."

"But what about Vicky?" I demanded, feeling betrayed. Having a brother was a damn big deal, and I wanted to know why nobody in my whole family had seen fit to clue me in. "She knew, didn't she? Why didn't she tell me?"

"She thought the boy was dead," my father replied quietly. "That's what the authorities told her when she went asking about him after your mother died. And so she didn't tell you about him for fear it would just upset you more during a difficult time of your life."

"And you didn't tell her anything different?"

Shimmer shook his head. "We only had a few moments to talk outside the Regnum's surveillance, and frankly I was too worried about your situation to think to mention him to her."

I paused, trying to get a grip on my roiling emotions. "Tell me about my brother."

"Randall is five years older than you," Shimmer replied. "The authorities removed him from your mother's care and put him in a foster home during our trial. She wasn't allowed to have him back afterward; they claimed we'd exposed him to necromancy and they wanted him to have some sort of fresh start. They told him we'd both died considerably sooner than we actually did."

Shimmer shook his head, looking angry and disgusted.

"How did you find him? Or did he find you?" I asked.

"I wanted to see my son graduate from high school, so I attended in disguise. Randall saw right through my careful obfuscations." Shimmer smiled, looking proud. "The lad has sharp eyes and a good memory. He tracked me back to my hotel, and we've stayed in touch in the years since. He's strong, well-trained . . . all my divinations say he's still alive, but whatever is happening there in Cuchillo is most serious and dangerous."

"I'll find him," I blurted out. "I'll get him out of there. What does he look like?"

"I think you'll see a family resemblance right away. He's a few inches taller than you, just a shade over six feet, has your and your mother's hazel eyes, but my mother's sandy blond hair. Girls find him quite handsome; boys, too, apparently, but I won't begrudge him his dalliances if he doesn't deprive me of grand-children when the time comes."

I didn't really know what to say to that; surely it was entirely Randall's business if he wanted to have kids or not. So I changed the subject: "About us being stuck in Cuchillo . . . what you're saying is nobody can get into or out of the city?"

Shimmer nodded. "That does seem to be the case. Sometime after Randall and his team disappeared and the authorities locked down the city, the demon apparently set some trans-spatial aerial traps to capture aircraft, but my sources say the authorities found and closed most if not all of them. I take it you encountered a stray open trap?"

"It was a stray closed trap; I had a choice between opening it or throwing us at the mercy of the Virtii."

"Well, those creatures haven't any mercy, so you made the wisest choice," my father said.

I pondered what he'd told me about the demon. "Putting an isolation barrier around a whole town is a pretty serious move. They must think the demon is a real threat. Do you think the Virtii stranded us here instead of just killing us because they think we're strong enough to kill the demon?"

"Apparently, yes. Or that you would weaken the demon enough to make their job of destroying it much easier."

"So we could kill it and save the townspeople who are still hanging on here?"

My father looked concerned. "Your heroic impulse is most admirable, Jessie, but I think the Virtus Regnum has wagered that you will die in Cuchillo. So I beg you to focus on getting yourselves and your brother out of there. Do you think you can get back to the trap portal you came through? It might be possible to re-open it."

I shook my head. "Magic mostly doesn't work here. The demon is casting some kind of suppression spell. And we don't have fire, either; there's no internal combustion and so no cars or helicopters. Unless I can find a tame dragon, I have no way to reach the portal, and even if I did, I'm not sure I can overcome the antimagic enough to open it again."

Shimmer tugged his beard thoughtfully. "Your brother is also quite talented when it comes to portal magic—I fear the demon may have forced him into helping it create the aerial traps. But if you can find him and free him, I'm sure the two of you together could create a new portal to escape the city, isolation barrier or no."

"Could you let Mother Karen know what's happening? I don't want her to think we're dead or blew her off or something."

He nodded. "I can get word to her."

We said our good-byes and I closed the mirror. I sat down on the bed. It was hard to process: I actually had a long-lost older brother. Who, according to his proud papa at least, was brilliant and handsome and talented . . . and possibly our main hope for getting out of this mess.

I hoped he wasn't a dick.

A Little Gift from the Welcome Wagon

I opened the red door and suddenly I was back in my flesh body . . . but I was naked, standing on hot pavement, the sun beating down on my skin, covered in something warm and wet and itchy, the taste of pennies in my mouth—

—and then the death-memories hit me all at once:

The beautiful raven-haired woman with the deep green eyes smiled and whispered, "Come join your wife" and I fell to my knees before her on the carpet of the funeral home and she touched my head and I felt the shock run through me, a tugging and tearing inside me and everything went black—

The naked auburn-haired girl came at me in the parking lot, grinning madly, swinging her black scythelike left hand at me, connecting with my neck, the spray of my blood sparkling like rubies in the sunshine—

I struggled against the dead-eyed men holding me fast as the green-eyed lady came toward me down the church aisle, my prayers dying in my throat as she reached out and touched my forehead—

The naked girl axed me down and fell on my neck, tearing at my flesh with blunt teeth.

I fell forward onto the pavement; there was something in my mouth. I spat it out: the tip of a man's finger. More twinned death-memories hammered my senses: spiritual death at the touch of the beautiful green-eyed woman followed by brutal physical death at my hand. I began to throw up blood that was surely not mine. I realized I was leaning forward on both hands, not just my good right hand, but my left was a coal-dark claw that scraped crablike against the blacktop.

"Oh God, *what happened*?" I gasped. My eyes focused on a man lying nearby in a pool of drying blood. His throat had been ripped out, his lower jaw torn away. By me, the death-memory told me. Or by something that had taken up cheerfully homicidal residence in my body while I'd been in the hellement.

"Jessie, is that really you?" Cooper asked.

I nodded, heaved again, but very little came up. The blood coating my mouth and my stomach was absolute torture. My body was trembling with exhaustion; my muscles felt completely spent, as if I'd just sprinted to the finish line of a daylong triathlon. I tried to get up, but my legs collapsed under me. Suddenly I felt incredibly cold despite the heat; I began to shiver. My eyes entirely lost focus.

"Get this—get this out of me. The blood. Get it out," I managed.

"She's going into shock," I heard the Warlock say. "What the hell happened to her hand?"

Someone brought a big towel, and Cooper wrapped me in it and carried me into the store.

"Do you have a shower?" he asked Rudy. "And any syrup of ipecac?"

"Yes sir, I got a shower back here in my apartment," Rudy said. "And I think I got some in my medicine cabinet."

The death-memories were overwhelming me. So much remembered lust for and fear of the beautiful woman, the tearing dark of souls sundered from still-living bodies, the raw agony of claws and teeth shearing skin and nerve and muscle, my own panic and horror at knowing my body had been used to commit mass murder. That the men I'd slain were soulless didn't matter, because it hadn't mattered to the entity that had possessed me. The expression of monstrous blood lust I'd seen on my own face through the dead men's eyes made me want to slit my own throat for fear of that happening again. Better to be dead than to be used for such evil. Better to be dead.

I was barely aware and mostly blind with tears as Cooper set me down into a bathtub of warm water.

"Drink this," he said, pushing a small plastic medicine cup to my lips. I opened my mouth and took the shot of sickly sweet syrup.

"Now this." A bottle of Evian was at my lips. "Drink it all if you can."

I tilted my head back and swallowed down the cool, sweet water. Mere seconds later, my stomach began to cramp and roil.

"Over the side! Bucket's right here!"

I turned my head and spent the next half hour or so being miserably sick into a galvanized steel bucket that smelled of bleach and harsh soap while Cooper sat close by on the lidded commode.

"Jessie, can you hear me? Are you all right?" Pal's voice was faint in my head.

I'm pretty fucking far from all right, I thought back.

"Oh, thank Goddess. I thought we'd lost our

connection for good. I've been trying to get through to you for quite some time."

What the hell happened?

"Do you remember anything?"

Bits and pieces. Death-memories. I . . . I can see myself killing those poor guys.

"Don't spend a second longer feeling guilty about those men." Pal's sternness was a thin veneer over an underlying tone of worry. "They were nothing more than meat puppets, and their master does not appear to have good intentions toward us."

How did you know they didn't have souls?

"That was fairly obvious: dead eyes, jerky gait, like the lad at dinner but without the pretty flowers and good complexion."

So what happened?

"Shortly after you went off to try to open the mirror, two vehicles arrived with the puppets. They demanded our surrender. Cooper and the Warlock began fighting with them, and then you came out of the store attacking whoever happened to be closest to you. Cooper is most fortunate he quickly realized you were not yourself."

I thought of the old shopkeeper. There wasn't a death-memory from him in my head, but then there wouldn't have been one if I'd simply gutted him in passing as I hurried to get to the fight outside. *Rudy . . . I didn't . . . did I?*

"No, you didn't harm him. He was tending to his solar array when the cars arrived. The Warlock has been questioning him out here since Cooper brought you back inside."

He isn't beating him up, is he?

"Oh, no. Seeing the corpses of the 'Welcome Wagon,' as Rudy calls them, has made him quite talkative. Apparently the town has been taken over by a demon or devil who simply calls herself Miko—what a Japanese entity is doing *here* of all places, nobody seems to know—and she has captured an unknown number of local Talents along with Rudy's daughter."

That fits with what my father told me.

"So you were able to open a mirror after all? Excellent. Any suggestions from him as to how to leave this lovely little hamlet?"

Not so much. There's an isolation barrier around the whole area.

"How dreadfully inconvenient."

Dreadful, yeah. Do you have any idea what just happened to me?

"Based on the fragments of diabolic babble you uttered while you turned the meat puppets to slaw, I'd hazard to guess that you were temporarily possessed by some sort of devil. A rather young one, I'd say."

I thought of the Goadlets I'd slaughtered by the dozens in Cooper's hell. It looked like at least one had escaped my blade after all. *Crap. It's coming out of the hellement whenever I go in.*

"That does appear to be a reasonable hypothesis."

My eyes were finally starting to focus again. The first thing I saw clearly was the scary appendage that had erupted from the stump of my left forearm. Two black blades had burst out from the remnants of my ulna and radius bones. The blades merged approximately where my wrist should have been in an exoskeletal joint that separated into five flattened claws: four fingerlike and the fifth a thumblike one that could oppose the others. The claws were jointed enough to curl into a cruel-looking rake, but I couldn't make a fist with them. If I straightened them out and closed the claws, they scissored cleanly together to form a flat, hard blade like a broad spearhead or narrow axe.

"Jesus. That's nasty," I slurred.

Cooper apparently thought I meant the grue in the bucket. "Sure is. Do you think you got it all out?"

The death-memories had largely subsided. I nodded. "I need to brush my teeth."

Cooper stood and rummaged through the drawers under the bathroom sink. He found a pink Oral-B, a tube of Crest, and a floss dispenser. "The brush looks clean, but I think it's been used once or twice."

I grimaced. "Considering what I've just had in my mouth, do you really think I could possibly care about that right now?"

"Right. I guess not." Cooper handed me the brush and paste, then turned away to dump the bucket in the toilet.

I brushed my teeth as best I could while I took a shower; the claw wasn't good for anything more than holding a bar of soap, so flossing was sadly not an option. As I was lathering the murder off my skin, I discovered several scratches and gouges on my body and left leg. They looked like they'd been inflicted when whatever had possessed me had pulled off all my clothes.

I had toweled myself dry and was blotting my

wounds with a paper towel moistened with hydrogen peroxide when somebody knocked on the door.

"It's just me," Cooper said. "I have your clothes and the Warlock's healing crystal."

"Come on in."

Cooper entered with my backpack and boots and my clothes in a neatly folded stack. He handed me the crystal. "I saw that you'd cut yourself up a bit."

"Thanks, honey." I started running it over my wounds to seal them.

"Your hat and your T-shirt were completely shredded, and your bra and panties were ripped, too, but Rudy had some needle and thread and I got them fixed. The pants and boots were okay."

Cooper handed me my clothes; he'd sewn up my torn underwear with thick blue thread in simple backstitches. The repairs looked like they'd hold. Instead of my borrowed Hello Kitty shirt, I now had a cream-colored souvenir tee emblazoned with the outline of the state of Texas with the words "Cuchillo, Texas" arced around it. A little red star sat off-center in the middle of the state outline, presumably to mark the location of the town.

"So do you remember what happened?" Cooper asked as I got dressed.

"Some. I got death-memories from the blood, so I know what my body was doing before I came to, and Pal told me some of what happened, but I'm still missing a lot."

I paused, staring at Cooper's face. His eye was blackened and his lip swollen under a freshly sealed split. "I didn't hurt you, did I?"

Cooper shook his head. "The meat puppets you killed rolled up on us in some big hybrid SUVs and came at us with baseball bats and stun guns when we told them we weren't going anywhere with them."

"Stun guns?"

"Enchanted, by the vibe of them. The meats seemed intent on bringing us in alive, but clearly their master wasn't going to mind us having broken arms and busted jaws if it came to that."

"I'm guessing their master is this Miko creature? Does Rudy know anything about her?" I sat down on the toilet lid to put on my socks and boots.

"Not much," Cooper replied. "Just that she's pretty much drop-dead everything. And if she actually *is* some kind of kuro miko, I'm curious to know what she's doing so far from her native land."

Japanese witches weren't exactly my forte, so I couldn't begin to guess what she might be doing in Cuchillo. I took a deep breath. "So. Pal thinks I'm possessed by a devil. I think maybe it's one of the larval Goads from your hell."

He blinked at me as though I'd just told him the sky was blue. "Well, obviously."

"So what are we going to do?"

"I've done plenty of exorcisms. No biggie."

His breezy tone annoyed me. "It's a biggie if you can't work magic!"

"Miko needs magic to do whatever she's doing, yeah? So this dampening field can't be everywhere. We find a weak spot in the field, exorcise you, take Miko to school, save what's left of the town, and we're out of here."

He unzipped my backpack and withdrew a well-used, elbow-length brown suede barbecue mitt. "Try this on your claw. Rudy found it in his shed."

I pulled the mitt on; I had to keep my finger-claws together but that was probably just as well. That hand wasn't really useful for anything but mayhem and destruction. At least the worn pigskin would keep me from forgetfully scratching an itch and mangling myself.

"But what if only diabolic magic works out here?" I asked. "The devil possessing me sprouted the claw right off the bat. What if Miko's not using standard magic?"

Cooper reached into my pack and pulled out a Gatorade, cracked the lid open, and handed it to me. "We'll be fine. Drink up, get your strength back. We might have a lot of walking ahead of us if we can't get those SUVs started again."

I followed Cooper out to the parking lot, sipping the Gatorade slowly. My stomach was threatening another return-to-sender and I knew I had to keep the drink down if I could. But the scene in the parking lot before me was making that especially hard. The carnage was even worse than the death-memories had suggested, and flies were buzzing around the human wreckage. At least none of it had been reanimated by my touch.

Rudy and Pal were at work with shovels in the field across the highway, digging what I guessed would become a shallow mass grave in the rocky caliche. The old man had apparently seen so many grotesque oddities since Miko took over the town that he was able to take a giant spider monster pretty much in stride.

The Warlock was kneeling beside a severed head,

frowning down at it. "These dudes don't look so good."

"Decapitation does that to a guy," Cooper replied drily.

"No, I mean they look like they were sick. Look at their skin. This one's got jaundice and a rash." The Warlock stood up and started digging in his tuxedo pants pocket. He produced a small carving of a phallus; it was maybe three inches long and looked like it was made from a quartz crystal. "Jessie, come here and hold out your hand. Your good one, I mean."

I did as he asked. He touched the crystal phallus to my palm and it glowed brightly, flashing several different colors. He cleared his throat, looking pained.

"So, do you want the good news, or the bad news?"

"Uh . . ." I was afraid to choose.

"Well, the good news is you don't have crab lice, scabies, chlamydia, gonorrhea, syphilis, HIV, or donovanosis. Nor do you have viral lycanthropy." He pushed his gray cowboy hat back to sit higher on his head.

"Viral lycanthropy?"

The Warlock looked grim. "Some lyes change to beast-form when they come. That's a surprise you don't want on your birthday, believe me. So I check for everything. And it's nice to know when you don't need the condom."

"Doesn't that thing check for vampirism?" I cocked an eyebrow at him.

"No need. The icy hands and body glitter and neck-staring always gives 'em away."

"So what's the other news?"

"You're fertile—guess that means the ol' contraceptive charm isn't holding up out here—and also you've got viral hepatitis."

"What? Goddamn it. Is it B or C?"

"Uh . . ." He touched the phallus to my palm again. "Both."

"Shit on a stick! Goddamn it!" I kicked the severed head across the pavement.

"Well, the viruses are just in your bloodstream; it could be your immune system clears them before they get settled in," the Warlock replied.

"What if my immune system doesn't clear them?"

He paused. "Then we might have a problem, if we're stuck here for a long time. Curing hepatitis can be kind of tricky; we'd need a really good healer for that."

"Better than Mother Karen?" I asked.

"Maybe, yeah," the Warlock said.

"As bad news goes, that kinda sucks."

"It could be weeks before you get any hepatitis symptoms," Cooper replied. "Maybe even months. I wasn't planning on spending months here, were you?"

"No," I replied.

He smiled at me. "So let's stick with the plan. And step one is to see if we can get either of those SUVs started . . ."

Highway

The SUVs were a pair of white Cadillac Escalades; the tires were so new that they were still prickled with rubbery sprue. Cooper cautiously approached the nearest vehicle and tried the driver's door; it opened easily. He stepped up onto the running board.

"Nobody in here," he said, craning his neck to see into the back. "I guess let's see if this will start again."

Wincing as if he expected the car to explode, Cooper cranked the key in the ignition. The engine chugged to life without a stutter.

"Hoo-rah," the Warlock said.

Cooper squinted at the hood and dashboard. "I can't really tell through the antimagic, but I'm guessing somebody enchanted the starter and spark plugs."

"Is it safe?" I asked.

"Seems to be." Cooper shrugged and turned the engine off. "Let's go help Rudy and Pal get the mess cleaned up."

Rudy directed us to his stock of cleaning supplies inside the store, and we all gloved up and started hauling bodies and parts out to the grave in the field. I got shaky and sick after just a couple of minutes in the relentless sun. The guys sent me inside to sit in the cool of the café area and drink more Gatorade.

"You feeling any better?" Cooper asked, shaking water droplets off his hands as he came into the store; Rudy had set up a makeshift hand-washing station with some buckets of fresh and sudsy water on the concrete bench outside the store. The old man was at the side of the building hosing off Pal's forelimbs.

"A little," I replied. "That syrup of ipecac is some harsh stuff."

"It gets the job done. But yeah, you'll probably be feeling kinda sick for a while. Do you think you're up for the drive into town?"

I nodded. "So what's our plan once we get there?"

"Well, Rudy thinks that some survivors have set up a camp at the local university. He says someone came out here to try to rescue him a few weeks ago, but he was worried that if he disobeyed Miko's orders, she would kill his daughter."

"So she's got him staying here to keep fresh victims from wandering off too far so she can send her guys out to capture them?"

"Yeah, pretty much."

"Okay, so do you think you can trust what he's saying about people being at the university?" I asked.

Cooper spread his hands. "I think he's a nice guy stuck in a really bad situation. I don't think he's lying to us. Admittedly he's been a lot more forthcoming since you slaughtered Miko's welcoming party, which I guess nobody had done before, but I can't blame him too much. He probably figured at first that we were doomed no matter what, so there was no reason to risk his daughter's life by giving us a heads-up."

"Well, we're all probably better off if we get out of here." I stood up, my legs still rubbery, and stared out the window at the Escalades. "But I don't guess Pal can fit into the SUV, so that's a problem."

"Perhaps he can sit on top and hang onto the luggage rack?" Cooper suggested.

"Maybe. Let's see what he wants to do."

Pal agreed to the idea of trying to ride on the roof, but when he climbed atop the Caddy, it became obvious that the vehicle would tip over the moment we had to take a turn at any speed, even if he flattened himself down.

"I think I can stride alongside the vehicle at a reasonable pace," he told me. "Just drive slowly so I can comfortably keep up."

"Pal thinks he can run beside the car," I told the others. "Just go easy at first, and he'll let me know if we can speed up."

"Sounds like a plan." Cooper got into the driver's seat, I hopped onto the cushy leather seat beside him with my backpack in my lap, and the Warlock got into the back behind Cooper with the tote bag.

"Well, y'all be careful," Rudy told us, standing near my open passenger door. He handed the Warlock a couple of six-packs of Gatorade and bottled water for the road. "Miko's a dangerous character, and again, I'm real sorry I didn't tell y'all about her from the get-go . . ."

"Don't worry about it," Cooper said. "You stay safe yourself."

Rudy looked at me, tears welling in his eyes. "If you see my daughter Sofia . . . please tell her that I love her?"

The old man looked heartbreakingly sad and lonely, and I felt all my misgivings about him vanish.

I reached out and touched his face with my good right hand. "You'll have the chance to tell her that yourself soon enough. I promise."

Rudy held my hand to his face for just a moment, his callused hand warm and trembling. "Thank you, miss. Godspeed."

He released my hand, wiped his eyes on his shirt-sleeve, and headed back to his empty store.

We put on seat belts and shut the doors, and Cooper started the engine. The automatic locks clicked down and the Caddy lurched forward, the tires slewing gravel as we pulled out onto the highway.

"This isn't my idea of a slow start," Pal complained inside my head.

"Whoa, easy on the gas," I told Cooper.

He'd gone pale, and I realized he was stomping on the brake, not the accelerator. The car was continuing to speed up.

"Shit." Cooper was yanking at the key in the ignition. "I can't kill the engine."

"Drive us off the road, we can hit that fence over there and maybe bust the axle," the Warlock said.

Cooper pulled hard on the wheel, but it wouldn't budge.

I whipped off my barbecue mitt and jammed my claw into the ignition, pulling a handful of plastic and sparking wires free. Nothing happened.

"What's your man trying to do, give me a coronary?" Pal complained. He was galloping alongside the car, apparently just barely keeping up.

We're in trouble. The car's enchanted and won't stop, I thought back.

"Everyone belted in?" Pal asked.

Yes. The rush of adrenaline had banished my exhaustion and sickness.

"Brace yourselves!"

I barely had time to say, "Hang on, guys," before Pal broadsided the SUV. The Caddy tipped onto its left two wheels, then tipped back as if it was going to right itself and speed away when Pal rammed it again, sending it rolling sideways. I saw stars when one of the six-packs whacked into the back of my head. The car came to a rest upside down in the drainage ditch, the engine screaming in outrage as it revved high. The smell of gasoline filled the passenger compartment.

"Get out of there!" Pal sounded frightened.

Shielding my face with my flesh arm, I smashed my window open with my claw and slashed my seat belt, falling awkwardly onto my backpack and the car's upholstered ceiling. Pal had bashed in the back window and was pulling the Warlock outside. I reached over and cut Cooper's seat belt, then slung my backpack over my claw arm, grabbed his hand, and pulled him out with me.

We had just staggered clear of the ditch when the gas tank ignited, turning the inside of the car into a flaming crematorium.

I dropped my backpack on the ground and leaned forward on my knees, trying to catch my breath and steady my nerves. That had been a little too close. The guys were banged up but didn't look like they'd lost anything more than their hats and the tote bag.

I looked over at Pal, who was rubbing his left shoulder, or what passed for his shoulder. "Thank you. We owe you big time for that. And also if we ever play football, I want to be on your team."

"It's quite all right," he replied. "I'm just pleased I was able to stop the vehicle without any of you being seriously injured."

"Are you hurt?" I asked him.

"I don't think so. I'll probably be a bit sore tomorrow, but I haven't broken shell or bone."

The Warlock was holding his healing crystal to his bloodied lip. He gave Cooper a look. "Safe, huh?"

"Hey, you didn't see this coming, either, now did you?" Cooper shot back.

"Speaking of seeing things coming, there's another car approaching," Pal told me.

I followed his gaze down the highway. A battered blue van was speeding toward us, dust rising from behind its wheels. The sides and front bumper of the van were armored with old tires beneath rusty iron plates, and a .50-caliber machine gun had been mounted to the top, just in front of the sunroof opening. There wasn't anything to hide behind aside from the burning SUV, which was too hot and noxious to approach.

The blue van screeched to a stop in front of us, and almost at the same moment my claw burst into purple flames.

"Dammit!" I jerked the claw away from my side and slapped out my burning T-shirt with my flesh hand. Fortunately only the hem over my dragonskin pants had ignited, so my skin hadn't burned.

"Whoa." A brown-haired, freckled, bespectacled girl of about eighteen or nineteen had jumped out of the van. She had a blue baby sling across her chest and an AK-47 in her right hand. At her hip was an army-green flask canteen. A yellow Post-it note was in her left hand. Her left forearm bore nasty-looking jagged scars, white on her tanned skin. I wondered if a dog had mauled her.

The girl goggled at my flaming hand, then at Pal, and looked down at her note. "Are you Jessie Shimmer?"

"Yeah . . . ?" I replied slowly.

"Um. I'm Charlie, and I'm supposed to pick you up." She had a square-shouldered, stocky look about her that made her seem overweight at first glance even though she was probably mostly sinew and bones under her loose jeans and oversize blue "CSU Tae Kwon Do Club" tee.

"Are you working for Miko?" Cooper asked sternly. "We're not going anywhere with you."

The girl looked horrified. "No, I ain't working for Miko! I'd sooner *die*. Sara sent me."

"And how did this Sara person know we were out here?" Cooper asked.

Charlie bit her lip. "The cats told her."

We all stared at her.

"Uh. Yeah. That sounds kinda crazy, huh?" She pulled down the edge of the baby sling to reveal that she was carrying not an infant but a large orange tabby. "Miko made it so that we couldn't shoot guns or start fires, but the cats fixed that. And they know stuff, but they only talk to Sara. We all thought it was nuts, too, at first, but then she kept being right all the time. Like now. She told me you'd be here and here you are."

I looked at Cooper, who looked down at my burning arm. He held out his palm and whispered an old word for "fire flower." A rose of purple flame appeared in his palm. He quickly blew it out, and stared sidelong at the cat. The cat just blinked green eyes at him and purred.

"Oh, cool, you guys can do magic stuff." Charlie seemed impressed. "So *that's* why Sara was all in a hurry for me to get y'all. Miko always grabs people like you real fast."

"Where does she take them?" I asked, thinking of my brother Randall and Rudy's daughter. I blinked through several gemviews. The cat in Charlie's sling looked pretty strange through some of them, but I didn't know how to interpret what I was seeing. Clearly the creature was not what it seemed.

Charlie shrugged. "Someplace downtown. But I mean, you don't want to go there. There's zombies all over. We mostly stay at the university where it's safer."

"Does Sara have a plan for fighting Miko?" Cooper asked.

"Well, she did, but people keep surrendering to Miko, so we only have enough guys left to guard the dorms and the greenhouse and physical plant." Charlie's face fell. "At first we were doing okay, because the zombies aren't any tougher than we are and we can move faster, but Da— I mean, the guy who makes the zombies, he started infecting them with all kinds of diseases so we'd be afraid to fight them. A bunch of people got really sick before Sara and Doc Ottaway figured out what he'd done. Some of them caught AIDS and stuff and they figured that Miko was better than wasting away."

I thought on Miko's words to her victims in the death-memories. "She's promising people some kind of afterlife paradise?"

Charlie nodded, briefly looking wistful, then added

quickly, "But I don't believe her. You'd have to be dumb to believe her, right?"

The girl's expression turned uneasy as she looked down the highway. "Hey, um, we should go now. She'll send more cars for sure."

I dug through my backpack one-handed to find the opera glove to contain my fire. And then quickly realized there was no way it would fit on the claw.

"Can you guys reenchant this to make it a bit bigger? And cut resistant?" I asked Cooper and the Warlock.

They looked at each other, and Cooper shook his head. "No, sorry—Mother Karen actually did most of the fabric magic on that. I doubt we'd be able to do a new enchantment over her work without wrecking it entirely."

"Well, crap." I stuck the glove back into my pack.

"We could probably enchant that grilling mitt Rudy gave you," Cooper said.

"Unfortunately, it's barbecue." I nodded toward the burning SUV.

"Well, any leather glove that was the right size for you from the start would work, too," the Warlock said. "The fire resistance we can do easily enough, it's just hard to get multiple enchantments to stick without a lot of time on the spellwork."

"What do you need a glove for?" Charlie asked.

"This." I waved my flame hand at her. "So I don't set fire to everything I touch."

"Lee's Western Wear & Rodeo Supply is a few miles away." The girl pointed her AK-47 in the direction she'd come from. "They have all kinds of gloves there. We'll pass the store on the way to CSU."

"Well, that sounds like a plan." I looked at Pal. "Do you think you can fly?"

Pal began blowing his weird calliope music and rose a few inches off the ground. He stopped and fell back to earth. "Yes, I believe so, provided we stay in range of that cat-creature."

After some logistical debate, Charlie agreed to give me a walkie-talkie and a Glock 17 semiautomatic, just in case. She opened the back doors of the van to retrieve the pistol. The rear of the vehicle held a mini-arsenal of rifles and shotguns racked into a battery of modified Rubbermaid yard tool towers. Cooper took a black Beretta AL391 Urika 12-gauge shotgun for himself and checked the magazine and firing mechanism on the Glock for me to make sure it was loaded and operational. I'd have preferred one of the pistol-grip Mossberg 500s I saw on the leftmost rack, but there wasn't any good way for me to fire one single-handed. And I wanted to be able to take out the van's back tires if Charlie tried to go speeding away. Not that I told Charlie that, of course.

"Okay, then," I said as Cooper strapped the pistol's holster around my hips. "Let's get this show on the road."

chapter seventeen

Meat Puppetry

I rode Pal a few yards above and behind the van. Charlie was good to her word, and kept her speed at a steady fifty-five on the highway. As soon as the first wayward grasshopper smacked me right in the forehead, though, I wished I had a helmet and a pair of goggles.

Fields gradually gave way to modern ruins: a boarded-up gas station, a gun shop with smashed-out windows and the bars behind crumpled as if they'd been rammed with a large truck, the blackened wreck of a Dairy Queen that had burned sometime before Miko squelched fire.

The walkie-talkie crackled on, Charlie's voice tinny and faint against the wind: "The store's coming up on the left. I'm going to pull into the lot."

"Okay," I replied.

The strip mall came into view; the Kmart-size Western store was wedged between a Michaels craft store and a Mexican grocery. All the front plate-glass windows had been smashed, but at least from the outside only the grocery seemed to have been looted heavily. Not surprising, since the city had been cut off from fresh supplies for a year. The parking lot was littered with abandoned cars and overturned grocery carts rusting in the sun. By the cart corral I saw the bleached, rodent-gnawed bones of a large dog and near it, scattered human remains, and shreds of clothing. Weeds had cracked through the worn blacktop all across the lot. The place smelled of caliche dust and old rot.

Pal touched down as Charlie parked the van in a clear spot a few dozen yards away from the entrance to the Western store.

"We don't want to stay too long." The girl opened the driver's-side door and stepped onto the pavement, looking nervous. "There aren't so many dog packs now, but you never know when you'll run into Miko's creeps. Or worse."

"I'm guessing lycanthropes." The Warlock got out of the passenger seat, hefting an M249 machine gun onto his shoulders. "When an isolated town like this starts to go into the darkness, it attracts bad characters from miles around. Like rats to garbage."

"Didn't the local Governing Circle have a defense plan?" I slid off Pal onto the pavement, holding my left hand high to keep from scorching his fur.

Charlie looked perplexed. "A Governing Circle? I never heard of anything like that, sorry."

"The Talents out in these Western towns like to think of themselves as lords of their private domains." Cooper heaved the sliding door shut behind him and checked the feed tube of his shotgun. "No rules, no tedious Circle meetings, nobody poking their nose into your craft. Works great until shit like this happens."

"Whoa." I stared at him, unable to keep a half smirk off my face. "Did I just hear you defend the *government*?"

"Governing Circles are a necessary evil." Cooper shrugged. "I don't have to like them any more than I have to like the taste of dragon eyeballs."

"We should really get that glove." Charlie adjusted the cat sling, shouldered her AK-47, and started across the lot, beckoning us to follow her.

"I'll wait out here and keep watch for more SUVs," Pal told me.

The front glass door to Lee's Western Wear & Rodeo Supply was hanging brokenly on its steel hinges. Charlie pulled it aside and we followed her into the store. There were five checkout lanes and a customer service desk; all the cash registers had been forced open, the dumped-out money trays lying atop discarded checks and small change on the conveyor belts. The floor was covered with stray pennies and dust and grit that had blown in. Someone had smashed a glass case of knives, taking everything but the tiniest pocket folders. There was an impressive collection of rodent droppings and shredded cardboard and plastic beneath what used to be display racks of beef jerky and cactus candies. Most of the rest of the store looked relatively undisturbed, however.

I spotted an aisle sign for "Bull Riders' Bazaar" toward the back of the store. It occurred to me that a bull-riding glove would be long enough to cover my burning bits and surely sturdy enough to resist being pierced by my claws.

"Hey, guys, I'm going down this way to look." I started toward the aisle.

"I'll come with you." Cooper hurried to catch up to me.

The Warlock glanced up from inspecting the Damascus blade on one of the looter-spurned pocketknives. "I'm gonna stay up here looking for stuff we can use for the enchantment."

"Watch out for rats," Charlie said. "If they're starving they'll jump out at your face and try to blind you."

"Been there, done that," I muttered.

Cooper and I stuck to the middle of the aisles, nervously watching for sudden movement on the shelves. My fire abruptly went out when I was about fifty yards away from Charlie and her mysterious orange tabby. We passed rows of dusty leather chaps, helmets, gear bags, ropes, and vests until we came to the gloves.

"Well, at least you can actually try one of these on now." Cooper started sorting through the boxes of left-hand bull riding gloves. "What kind do you want?"

"That Heritage Pro model up on the top shelf looks good," I replied, looking at a black deerskin glove with a wide built-in Velcro wrist wrap.

Cooper plucked the box off the shelf and slid the glove out. As my sweaty hand touched the leather I got a faint echo of the deer's death. I carefully slipped it onto my claw; the death-memory was gone. The glove was several times bigger than anything that would have fit on my flesh hand, but I wanted it to have some give to accommodate the claws; the built-in wrist strap would tighten it down enough to keep it from slipping off. It seemed as though the leather and padding would resist being sliced fairly well, and the neoprene cuff came up high enough to cover everything that would be on fire.

"So do you think you and the Warlock could strengthen this up a little bit?" I handed the glove back to Cooper. "I'm pretty sure it will work as is, but my claw tips are kinda sharp."

"Yes, I noticed that." He stretched the cuff and peered inside at the foam padding. "Why don't we go to the craft store next door and get some thimbles to stick down in the fingers? That would make things a whole lot easier."

"Oh. Yeah, good idea."

But Cooper didn't move. He chewed the corner of his mustache thoughtfully, glanced down the aisle toward the front of the store, and pulled me closer to him.

"I'm trying to decide what to do here," he whispered. "On the one hand, I do want to help the townsfolk. I feel bad for Rudy, and Charlie seems like a nice girl. I'm curious to meet this Sara person. But on the other hand, I'm worried about my baby brothers. I'm worried that someone in the Circle might've sold us out, and that Riviera might go back on her word and drug the kids or lock them up. But on the *other* other hand, Mother Karen is not to be trifled with. I pity any idiot who tries to hurt a kid in her care."

Now that he had brought it up, I was a little worried about the babies, too. I felt that Riviera had been straight with us at the meeting, but considering we'd been ambushed right after it, I couldn't be sure about her true motivations. "I couldn't get through to Mother Karen, so I don't know what's happening there."

"We could take Charlie easily enough," Cooper continued. "Not, you know, hurt her or anything, but put a short-term sleeping charm on her, grab that cat of hers, and have Pal fly us back to the haystack and see if we can get the portal open."

"Um. I'd be all for that . . . except I talked to my father, and he said my brother Randall's here."

"Whoa, you've got a brother? I didn't know that."

"Me neither, until today."

"Wow, looks like we're drawing every king in the deck, huh?" Cooper lifted his fist for a bump.

"Yeah, go Boy Power, huh?" I dapped him gently on the knuckles. "My father says Miko captured Randall, and wants us to go rescue him."

"Hm." Cooper scratched his goatee. "That definitely tips the balance for staying here to see what good we can do, at least for a while."

We went back up to the front and passed the glove off to the Warlock, who was busy chipping the red phosphorous tips off a bunch of matches and crushing them into powder on the glass customer service countertop. Charlie was taking slow drags off a Virginia Slims cigarette and staring out the window at Pal, who in turn was gazing solemnly at the empty highway. The girl held the cigarette carefully, almost reverently, and when she brought it to her lips, she had the expression of a penitent taking communion.

"Hey, we're going next door to get some thimbles," I told her, holding my now-flaming hand high.

She gave a start. "Oh. Okay. Watch out for—"

"Rats. Right." I gave her a wave and followed Cooper outside.

The craft store had been looted more lightly than the Western store, and most of the damage aside from the smashed cash registers seemed to have been from a fit of vandalism: somebody had overturned most of the shelves of silk plants and flowers so the faux flora was in piles on the floor. My fire went out as we headed into the sewing section, but I wasn't concerned because we almost immediately saw a display of steel thimbles on white cards. Cooper grabbed a handful and stuck them into his pants pockets.

And then came a raspy wheeze to our left. I turned. A gaunt, bent old lady of seventy or so was standing there, swaying on weak legs, her knobby, spotted hands gripping a battered aluminum walker. Her bare feet were dirty and rat bitten. She smelled sourly of old sweat and fermenting urine. A stained pink "World's Best Grandma" sweatshirt hung practically to her knees. Her permed gray hair was stiff with weeks of grime, and her mouth hung open, her lips and tongue flaky and dry, her eyes clouded.

I felt as if I were looking at somebody who had died about five minutes ago, but her body hadn't quite gotten the message yet.

Cooper glanced down at my cooling claw and swung his shotgun around, gripping it by the barrel to use it as a club. "Meat puppet. Be careful."

"What the heck is she going to do? Doesn't look like she could so much as spit." Despite my words, I felt nervous that I couldn't fire my pistol. I wasn't sure I had the stomach to slice her up if she somehow managed to attack us. "We should just leave."

I took a step back. The old lady took a torturous breath and groaned, her lips and tongue working to form words. She released her walker and took a wobbly step toward us.

And in the space between heartbeats, she wasn't an old woman anymore. Short gray hair had become a thick, dark, silken cascade. She'd shot up about a foot, lost fifty years, lost her *clothes*. Her breasts were astonishing. I'd heard guys wax rhapsodic about breasts my entire life, and I'd never seen what the big deal was. The world was filled with boobies, and I grew even more jaded to them once I had a pair of my own.

But this woman's rack was *perfect*. It was a piece of art that Michelangelo himself could never replicate. Drunken fumblings with cheerleaders aside, I'd never had a single seriously sapphic thought in my entire life, and now I wanted to kiss those breasts, bury my face in them, rub expensive lotions on them, and name them after muses.

The woman laughed, a husky, throaty sound that made every single gland in my body pop to Pavlovian attention. "My eyes are up here, Jessie."

I blinked, swallowed, my heart pounding in my sweating chest, and took in the rest of her. She was built everywhere else, too. No weak-limbed supermodel body here; she was the very definition of fit, looked like she could take on Zeus himself. Of course, all she'd probably have to do was to show up and he'd pass out from the sudden rush of blood out of his brain to his nether regions.

When I saw her face, I had no doubt that I was looking at no mere demon. She was some kind of goddess, and when I saw her deep green eyes I knew who she was.

"What do you want with us, Miko?" I stammered.

She smiled down at me. "Why, I want *you*, little girl. And your boyfriend, too. But mostly, I want you."

I followed her gaze to Cooper, figuring he'd be standing there dazed with an epic erection . . . and was surprised to see him red-faced and flaccid, his features twisted in rage, his whole body trembling with a paralytic fury.

"What's wrong? What did you do to him?" My voice broke like a teenage boy's.

Miko smiled again. "Oh, he's just thinking about all the things I can do to you, all the pleasure I can bring you, and he knows that all the sex you've ever had or ever will have with him won't even come close. He knows that once I've had you, whenever you close your eyes beneath him, you'll be wishing I were making love to you instead. He'll never, ever have you all to himself again, because part of you will be thinking about me."

"That's not true." It was hard to speak.

"Oh, but it is."

She reached out and ever so gently took hold of my right wrist, and her touch was an electric arc that went straight to my pinks, and I was coming, coming *hard,* and I fell to my knees with a wail and a gasp and she didn't let me go and I was at her complete mercy in the throes of the orgasm—

—and then I was inside her head, inside her memories, reliving them in nonlinear flashes as if I were inside her body. Miko was death, through and through, and her memories were more vivid than anything I'd tasted in any flesh:

I lay in the slagged wreckage, small and weak, my infant voice wailing in pain for the mother who'd expelled me from her rotting womb and abandoned me. The metal and brick and charred bones around me were hot with radiation, my flesh burning and healing over and over, the hunger in me far brighter than the sun trying to force its rays through the smoke-dark skies—

I walked into the bookstore, sizing up the shopkeeper and his fat old wife through the corner of my eye as I pretended to look at comics. I could take them both right there, tear them apart and devour them hot and nobody would ever know. Mother, I had gone so long without even a broken-down derelict to fill me, and the hunger made my ribs and teeth ache. But I had to wait a little longer. He could be the one. After all these years, this painfully mundane old man could be the one—

I straddled the muscular GI on the brothel cot and slipped his eager flesh inside mine. "Oh, you so big, I fuck you long time." I knew good English, but the GIs on leave didn't want to hear good English. They wanted their girls skinny and underage and stupid, so I moaned nonsense like any other Tokyo whore while he whined drunkenly about wanting to be on top, but I put my hips into it, making it feel good for him while I got myself off on his tight ripe body, and as the sweet orgasm shuddered through me I grabbed the sides of his head and gave a hard, practiced twist that instantly snapped his neck, and his life was flowing into me, filling my hunger, the taste of his soul an electric ecstasy that eclipsed any moment I'd spent pinioned on a man's cock and it was all I could do not to throw my head back and howl—

"You fucking bitch, let her go!" I distantly heard Cooper shout above me.

He'd snapped out of his paralysis and swung the butt of his shotgun at her head, connected with a sharp crack of fracturing bone.

Miko fell, but it wasn't Miko anymore, it was the old woman, but Cooper didn't seem to notice as he bashed her again and again, her skull splitting horribly. Blood splashed onto my pants and shirt.

"Cooper, Cooper, stop!" I grabbed his arm, but he shook me off. "Dammit, stop, she's gone!"

He finally stopped, still holding his weapon high, breathing hard through gritted teeth. I'd never seen him so angry in my entire life, and it scared me.

"Fuck." He turned on his heel and stomped over to a nearby fabric display where he began to furiously scrub the blood and hair and bits of tissue off his shotgun. "Fuck."

I went up to him and touched his shoulder. My hand was shaking. "Are you okay?"

"I'm just *dandy*." He gave the gun a final wipe and turned on me, scowling. "Let's get out of here."

He grabbed me by the wrist and practically dragged me along behind him, looking neither to the left nor to the right as he marched us back into the Western store.

"I got thimbles." Cooper reached into his pocket and slammed the cards down on the counter in front of the Warlock.

"Whoa." The Warlock looked at Cooper's red face and the blood spatters on our clothes. "What happened?"

"Don't want to talk about it." Cooper stripped off his ruined dress shirt and tossed it angrily on the floor. He turned away from us and went over to Charlie, who was still smoking Virginia Slims by the window. "Can I have one of those?"

"Yeah, sure, they're kinda girly—"

"Don't care, I just need a smoke."

As Charlie tapped out a cigarette for my boyfriend, I whispered to the Warlock, "Since when is he a smoker?"

"Since *never,*" he whispered back. "I mean, Coop sometimes bums a clove off Opal when we're out drinking, but I've never seen him smoke outside a bar. What the hell happened to you two over there?"

I suddenly felt acutely ashamed about what Miko had done to me, and even more disturbed at what I'd felt inside her memories. "We ran into a meat puppet, and things got weird."

He raised an eyebrow. "Weird how?"

"Weird like I don't want to talk about it, either."

Cooper took a long drag off his cigarette and turned toward us, bitter smoke jetting from his nostrils. "I am going to kill that cunt. *Kill* her. How *dare* she touch you like that. She . . . she fucking *molested* you. I am going to kill her, then raise her from the dead so I can kill her again!"

Cooper slung his shotgun over his bare shoulder and headed for the door.

"Honey, wait, where are you going? We don't even know where she is!"

He glared at me; he had the expression I always thought he might wear if he caught me kissing a boy at a bar. "I need a walk."

Charlie looked worried. "You shouldn't go out by yourself, there could be zomb—"

"Oh, I hope so. I'd *love* to find something else that needs a skull cracking!" He snatched the pack of Virginia Slims out of the startled girl's hand and stormed outside.

Hey, Pal, I thought to my familiar, who was still standing guard in the parking lot watching the highway.

"What's going on?" he replied inside my head.

Cooper's pissed off, and he's not thinking straight. I'm worried he's going to get himself hurt. Could you keep an eye on him for me?

"I certainly will."

The Warlock was staring at me, both eyebrows high. "The meat puppet molested you? Do tell."

"It wasn't the meat puppet. It was Miko. She took over the puppet's body." Embarrassed, I started pulling the thimbles off their white cards.

"What did she do to you?"

"Just, um, grabbed my wrist." I pried at a difficult thimble with my thumbnail.

"And then?"

"I came." I barely whispered the words.

"You what?"

I cleared my throat and stared up at him, suddenly feeling intensely annoyed. "I came."

The Warlock rocked back on his heels and crossed his arms, giving me a look. "Oh really?"

I felt myself blush, and I looked away. "Yeah, really."

"And then Coop had an alpha-dude shit fit."

"Yeah."

The Warlock began to chuckle.

"It's not the least little bit funny," I protested. "The

meat puppet was an old lady, somebody's grand-mother, and Cooper bashed her skull in. It was really ugly. I've never seen him like that before."

The Warlock scratched his chin through his beard. "Coop always acts real cool, but underneath that cucumber façade he's got a temper worse than Opal. Takes a while to get him there, but once he's good and mad he stews for a while. Give him time, he'll get over it."

"You're sure?"

"Positive." The Warlock winked at me. "Wanna help me enchant your glove? Not that the fire doesn't look good on you, and I love hanging out with hot women as much as the next guy, but even I have my limits."

I stretched, trying to work some of the tension out of my back. My spine popped. "Sure, let's do the glove. Maybe Cooper will be back by the time we're done."

Once I worked the thimbles down into the finger-tips of the glove—the death-memories from the deer-skin were pretty minimal as long as I kept my hands dry—we started on the enchantment. It was mostly me handing the Warlock supplies when he asked for them and otherwise following his lead, since I didn't have a clue about this type of enchantment. As we worked, I started noticing that he smelled good, and I mean *really* good. Lickably good. I found my eyes drifting down toward his crotch in my idle moments while the Warlock recited incantations. I'd never given his gear much thought before—and had man-aged to avoid seeing it in action despite his and Opal's tendency to get busy pretty much whenever and wher-ever the mood struck them—but now I was hard-pressed to keep speculations about his dimensions out of my head.

It would be okay, I told myself, shutting my eyes. We could get to wherever we were going for the night, Cooper would calm down, we'd find some way of keeping my arm from spewing burning ectoplasm everywhere. He'd exorcise me. And then we'd find a condom. Several condoms. And a dental dam. And then Cooper would make love to me, and I'd have a really satisfying, mind-blowing orgasm, and I would not infect him with hepatitis or anything else. I would not hurt him. My brain would be wiped clean of thoughts about Miko and the Warlock and anybody who wasn't Cooper. Period. I would get properly laid sometime very soon and it would all be okay.

It would all be okay, it would all be okay.

"Jessie? Hey, Jessie?" The Warlock snapped his fingers near my ears.

I opened my eyes. "Sorry. What?"

"Are you all right? You're looking all red and sorta sweaty."

"It's just the fire. My arm. Makes me feel weird," I half lied.

"Well, the glove's done." He held it out to me. "Want to try it on to see if it works?"

"Sure." I took the leather glove from him and gingerly pulled it on over my flaming hand, my claws clacking into the thimbles. The neoprene extension on the cuff covered everything that needed covering, and the Velcro wrap made the fit just about perfect. Thin trails of smoke rose from the cuff, but there was no sign that the material itself was burning.

"Looks good," I said.

Charlie came back into the store; she'd gone to the grocery to hunt for cigarettes, and was now carrying a couple of packs of Benson & Hedges. "We should leave soon."

I shook my head. "Not until Cooper comes back."

"We can't stay here tonight; this place really isn't defendable." The girl looked worried.

"Another half hour won't kill us, will it?" I asked her sharply, then turned away and closed my eyes to concentrate on contacting my familiar.

Pal, are you out there? What's going on? We need to leave soon.

No response. I tried again: *Pal, are you there?*

Nothing.

He was just out of range, I told myself, trying to quell the anxiety building inside me. I chewed on my thumbnail.

"You okay?" the Warlock asked.

"I'm fine." I smiled at him, probably completely unconvincingly considering the look he gave me right afterward. And despite my anxiety, looking at him filled my head with a hundred wet unwanted thoughts, a swarm of vermin fleeing the flooded tunnels of my id.

"I'm gonna do a little more shopping back here," I told him and Charlie, hoping that out of sight would mean out of mind. "And yes, I'll watch out for rats."

I went into the T-shirt aisle first; I was wearing way too much of the World's Best Grandma and wanted something cleaner. A black shirt bearing a cartoon of a stick man being thrown from a stick horse above the caption "I Do My Own Stunts" caught my eye. I pulled off my old shirt, used it to scrub the blood spatters off my dragonskin pants, and put on the new tee.

Finished with changing, I went down the horse-riding equipment aisle. Pal was much better able to fight at his current size, so there was no point in asking him to shrink himself down to a size that would fit in the van. I'd probably be riding him the rest of the way to the university; having my butt wedged between his vertebrae was surely not that comfortable for him. Clearly he found my libido horrifying—hell, *I* was finding it fairly horrifying—and if I was going to get all juiced up the moment a stiff wind blew across my nipples, well, some extra padding between my muff and his fur would help us both maintain what was left of our dignity.

None of the saddles would accommodate his alien physiology, so I took a look at the saddle pads. I found a moss-colored SMx Heavy-Duty Air Ride pad that seemed flexible enough to conform to Pal's back and that promised breathability and shock absorption. Farther down, I found their stock of saddlebags; I picked out a glossy leather model with spacious panniers deep enough to temporarily hold a rifle stuck in catty-corner. They had several types of leather gun scabbards, but since I couldn't use an actual saddle there wouldn't be any good way to secure one to Pal short of probably disastrous experiments with braiding his fur. Remembering the sting of the airborne grasshopper collision, I went to their riding helmet section and picked out a visored Troxel Cheyenne covered with embroidered chocolate leather. With a little luck, the padded fabric lining would keep most of the unpleasant memories from the leather at bay.

I slung the saddlebag over my shoulder and tucked the pad under my arm and headed for the front door.

"I'm going out to the van for a little bit," I told Charlie and the Warlock in passing.

"Why?" she asked.

"I'm going to drop all this in there for safekeeping until Pal gets back, and I'm going see if you have anything with a little more oomph than this Glock. And then I'm going to shut my eyes for a little while, because I'm tired."

Charlie looked impatient. "We really need to—"

"Leave. I *know*. Gimme fifteen minutes of quiet time, okay? And then I'll start looking for Cooper and Pal."

I carried the tack out to the van. My fire went out halfway there. I got in the passenger side, shut the door, and climbed into the backseat. It was like an oven in there, even with the vent windows cracked. I tossed my backpack into the seat beside me, piled the tack on the floor between the seats, pulled one of the Mossberg shotguns I'd coveted out of its rack, and laid it on top of the saddle pad.

And then I sat there in the sweltering dimness, eyes closed, and focused on contacting Pal, hoping that the extra fifty yards would somehow make a difference.

Are you there? I thought. *Hey, Pal, are you there?*

Still nothing.

Keeping my eyes shut, I started trying to clear my head of the building panic and carnal thoughts that threatened to wreck my strained nerves. Breathed in, breathed out, slowly, rhythmically, just like my hapkido instructor taught us in concentration exercises. I pictured my mind as a smooth ocean wave rolling out to sea . . . and promptly imagined myself going down on the Warlock in the warm sand and foamy surf. Dammit.

There was nothing to do for it but take matters into my own hands. Hand, anyway. I unbuckled my gun belt and loosened the drawstring on my dragonskin pants so I could slip my fingers into my underwear. It was a hot mess down there, and I regretted bringing only a single change of underwear in my backpack. Buddha in a biscuit. At the rate I was going, someone might as well tattoo NO SELF-CONTROL right across my face and be done with it.

Everything was so slippery it was hard to get much satisfying friction going at first, but I leaned into it and bore down and pretty soon I was coming hard enough that I was pounding my head against the back of the seat in front of me to keep from crying out. I fell back, sweating, forehead hurting, stomach roiling again, legs sprawled. And suddenly aware that I stank of tang, and the moment I went back into the store the Warlock would know that I'd been pathetically jilling off in the van. Charlie would probably know, too. And so would everybody else I'd meet that day. Yay for good first impressions.

I found an old bandanna on the floorboards that had been recently employed as a dipstick rag and used it to wipe my hand off. Hopefully the motor oil and diesel would mask my funk. And also kill off any hepatitis I just managed to get on the rag. Crap.

There wasn't a trash receptacle in sight. I pulled up

my pants and buckled on my pistol, then stood on the seat so I could lean out of the sunroof and wedge the rag under the .50 gun; I figured in lieu of fire the heat of the sun would be the best I could do to sanitize the thing. And at least it wouldn't be floating around on the floor of the van looking like something someone could use for emergency nose blowing.

"Jessie!" It was Pal's voice inside my head.

Thank God, I thought back. *What happened to you and Cooper?*

"We've run into a spot of trouble, I'm afraid . . . we're coming your way. Please have a machine gun ready. All of them if possible. I don't think we can have too many guns right now."

What? Crap.

I stuck my shotgun up on the van's roof and boosted myself up to sit behind the .50 gun mount. And promptly realized that although I thought I could figure out the firing mechanism, I had no way to shoot the weapon without Charlie's cat nearby.

"Charlie! Warlock!" I hopped up and down, waving my arms at the Western store. The van rocked ominously beneath me. "Get out here; I need the kitty!"

I stood on the roof of the van and scanned the highway as the Warlock and Charlie came running up.

"What's going on?" he asked.

"I'm not sure yet. Pal contacted me. He and Cooper are coming and it sounds like they might have some company."

"Some company" turned out to be one of the biggest understatements I'd made all year, followed closely by "I think the habañero diablo might be a little spicy."

Pal came galloping down the highway with Cooper clinging to his neck for dear life. Six heavy-duty pick-ups were speeding close behind; the truck beds were packed with meat puppets armed with bats and axes. Some were wearing what used to be nice suits and dresses, and others were wearing sweats and pajamas. There were close to forty puppets in all as best as I could tell.

Pal ran straight toward us, playing his flying spell, unable to get airborne because he wasn't close enough to Charlie's cat. We didn't have much time. I went to a crouch on the roof of the van, trying to decide whether to go with option A, start blasting with the shotgun, or option B, try to figure out how to operate the .50 machine gun. Smoke rose from the cuff of my glove as my anxiety built, and I suddenly decided to go with option C, yanking off the deerskin and holding my flaming claw high.

Pal's spell finally took hold, and he rose fast in the air. The lead truck sped up, apparently intent on ramming the van and dashing me to the pavement.

"Get clear!" I hollered.

As soon as Pal and Cooper had flown over my head, I let loose on the trucks. The burning purple ectoplasm came out of me in a firehose jet, and for a moment all I could see was the stuff flaring into an unnatural fire-ball in the air before me. I hit the lead truck, and the vehicle went up in a hot burst of flames, swerving and rolling clear of us as the melting tires blew out. It was absolutely horrible what happened to the meat puppets in the bed. They were eerily silent as they burned.

But I didn't have too much time to think about

what I'd just done; the other trucks were still coming. I lit them up, too, with equally gruesome but effective results. The air was filled with the stink of brimstone, molten metal, burning tires, and charred flesh.

As I torched the third truck, I realized that my ecto-plasmic jet was thinning, growing weaker. Was I running out of energy? Dammit. A few trucks of puppets would be a hell of a thing to blow my remaining power on considering we hadn't dealt with Miko yet. And surely there would be a few Virtii waiting in the wings for the final act.

I used my fire more carefully after that. Soon it was all over but for a few puppets that had been tossed out of their trucks before they had a chance to be na-palmed. They lay twitching in pools of blood, still trying to reach their weapons and get up even though their limbs and bodies were mangled. I felt intensely sick and looked away, looked down.

Charlie was standing there beside the van, staring at the carnage, muttering a prayer over and over under her breath, clutching her AK-47 in shaking hands.

I pulled on my glove, picked up my shotgun, and cleared my throat. "Charlie, do you think you could . . . you know. Help me put those last few down? Please?"

"Um. Yeah." She flicked the safety off her weapon and stumbled out into the parking lot.

"You take that bunch on the right, I'll take the ones on the left." I slid down onto one of the tires armoring the side of the van, then hopped onto the pavement.

I figured her orange cat would leap out of the sling and run away the moment she pulled the trigger, but it continued to lounge against her chest, purring loudly. Charlie stepped through the bodies, firing single rounds into the skulls of anyone who still appeared to be moving. Her shaking aside, there was almost no hesitation in the girl's movements; I got the feeling that she'd had to do this before.

I lifted my shotgun and set about the unpleasant task of blowing the heads off any puppets that were still moving. It was one of the most depressing, disgusting things I'd ever had to do. But at least it didn't take very long, and afterward I walked back to join the guys.

The Warlock was tending to Cooper with his healing crystal. Based on the huge purpling knots on my boyfriend's face and body, he had taken another club to the eye and a couple to the shoulders and forearms before Pal spirited him away to safety. Pal stood close by, giving me a look I couldn't quite read.

"Nice job," Cooper said, apparently without irony or sarcasm.

My cheeks flushed. " 'Nice job'? No. There was nothing 'nice' about what I just did. That was really fucking horrible. I am going to see those bodies burning in nightmares the rest of my life, and no, I don't care that they didn't have souls and I was doing them a favor or whatever. I do *not* want to have to do that again, okay? So if you go off looking for a fight, don't bring it back to me to deal with, dammit!"

Cooper stared back at me. "Okay. I'm *sorry*."

He still had a look and tone of anger I didn't like, but I bit my tongue on another heated reply. Now was not a good time to get into an argument with him.

I turned away to retrieve my backpack and the shotgun and Pal's tack from the van. "We're leaving."

chapter eighteen

Crazed State Unhinged

The sun was sinking low on the horizon as Pal and I followed Charlie's van down the highway to the Cuchillo State University campus. The survivors had set up a tall chain-link fence topped with razor wire around a cluster of tan brick buildings in the middle of campus, walling off the Student Union, the health center, and two high-rise dormitories. The inside of the fence was buttressed with four-foot-tall sandbag walls with a rifleman keeping watch behind them every fifty yards or so.

A squad of skinny college-age boys dressed in a mix of coffee-stain desert combat fatigues, tiger-stripe airman battle uniforms, Air Force ROTC T-shirts, and grubby jeans were stationed at the sliding gate. They raised their rifles toward me and Pal, but Charlie waved at them from the driver's window and told them to stand down. The young militiamen opened the gate for the van, and Pal flew us over the fence and landed us in the courtyard. People stared at Pal, but as with Rudy, they seemed only moderately surprised to find a giant ferrety spider monster landing in their compound. The crowd was mostly more young college- and military-age men and a few girls my age and a little younger.

And the courtyard was filled with cats: they rode in backpacks and slings and lounged on the concrete picnic tables. More cats napped on the sandbag wall or in the branches of the oak trees shading the courtyard. Something seemed oddly familiar about the cats, but I couldn't quite put my finger on it. I supposed that there are only so many different kinds of cats, and sooner or later one was bound to remind me of another. But all of them? It made me uneasy.

A swarthy thirty-something man in a short-sleeved Air Force uniform approached us. I saw gold oak leaves on his epaulets.

"Air support at last . . . fantastic." He stuck his hand out to me as he looked Pal up and down. "I'm Major Woodrow Rodriguez, USAF, out of Fineman AFB, acting commander of military defense operations here. Got any more of these?"

He looked me square in the eye as I shook his hand, and in his gaze I saw a certain profound lack of interest in me as a woman. Guys usually either check you out a bit at first or dodge serious eye contact entirely to avoid seeming like they're attracted to you. But as far as the major was concerned, I got the feeling I could have been a piece of talking furniture. When he saw the Warlock and my shirtless boyfriend get out of the van, though, there was a faint spark of interest in his face. Faint, but definitely there.

"More like Pal?" I replied. "No, sorry, he's unique . . . but if you're with the Air Force, why don't you have planes and helicopters? And why is everybody here and not at the air base?"

I looked around at the whip-lean cadets and young militiamen standing guard and repairing weapons and attending to other duties in the courtyard, and I realized that if I were single, I'd be hard-pressed to find a date around here. Well, it made sense: I of all people knew the fierce tweak Miko could put on your hormones, and these boys had all survived at least a year of her tampering with their minds and bodies. Any gay kid growing up in a military-minded family in a small West Texas town would learn a monk's restraint, or he'd probably end up broken, bloody, and crucified on a barbed wire fence before he turned twenty-one. Don't ask, don't tell, and most important, don't die.

The major gave a harsh, barking laugh. "Fineman AFB is little more than a smoking crater now. Miko infiltrated the minds of some of our key personnel and brainwashed them into committing coordinated acts of domestic terrorism and treason against the base and their fellow airmen. Only a few dozen of us survived the assault on the base; we scavenged some small and medium arms, but most of the vehicles and all the aircraft were destroyed. Once Miko revealed herself and her intentions, we chose to activate the ROTC cadets here at CSU and reestablish our base of operations in these core campus buildings."

Despite his scowling demeanor, the major had truckloads of square-jawed, take-charge charisma. A man's man, through and through. My body was reacting to the smell of his testosterone-laden sweat; it didn't care that he was gay. It didn't care that I was in a committed relationship. It wanted what it wanted. And what it apparently wanted was to drive me to hang myself in frustration.

Oblivious to what was happening in my pants, the major gestured toward the high-rise dorms. "This isn't your everyday college campus. In addition to generating its own power at the physical plant, it has its own sewage treatment and water reclamation facilities. Part of Miko's attack on Fineman involved dumping psychoactive drugs in our water tower, so from the outset we knew we needed to keep tight security on our food and drink supplies. However, since her initial attack, she seems content to wage a war of attrition through demoralization."

"So what did she say she wants?" I unbuckled the chin strap on my riding helmet and took the stifling headgear off.

The major gave me another coldly direct gaze. "She says she wants our souls. I was never religious before all this happened—and I certainly never believed in magic and flying spiders—but whatever she takes from a man, it's the very essence of what makes him human. Nobody's the same after she touches them. We've lost a lot of good men to her."

"And women, too, I expect."

The major looked away toward Cooper and the Warlock, who were unloading some boxes of ammunition from the back of the van into the waiting arms of the cadets. Gave a slight shrug. "Women, too. We did manage to evacuate as many mothers with children as possible before the city got locked down. It was only the right thing to do."

Charlie came over to us, adjusting the cat's sling nervously as she looked at the major. "Um, I need to take her to see Sara."

"Of course." The major straightened up and glanced down at his wristwatch. "And I need to attend evening security inspections."

He gave me a curt, formal head bob, turned on his boot heel, and strode away.

"I think she's in the North Tower," Charlie told me. "But, um, your spider won't fit so good in the lobby."

I turned to Pal and pulled off the riding pad and saddlebags. "Do you think that just this once you could shrink yourself down? I'd hate for us to get separated given that things are mind-bogglingly screwed up around here."

He blew a chord that sounded like a sigh. "Fair enough." He began playing a different tune, and his body shrank until he stood about as tall as a mastiff. "Better?"

"Yeah, that should get you through a regular door," I told him.

We collected Cooper and the Warlock and headed into the dormitory lobby. The building was only weakly air-conditioned, but it did provide some respite from the oppressive heat outside. A couple of young men were playing Team Fortress on an Xbox hooked up to the TV in the corner, and some others were reading books and playing cards at the tables. Sleeping boys were stretched out on all the sofas. It could have passed for a men's dorm in most any college if not for the uniforms, general dinginess, and looming feeling of despair.

And the cats. There were cats *everywhere*: lounging on the TV, lurking in the bookshelves, curled up on the sleeping students. I felt a shiver when, as a group, they opened their yellow and green eyes and stared at me.

Charlie passed her AK-47 to the tired-looking blond girl stationed behind the front desk. "No guns allowed past the lobby unless you're a resident advisor or an officer."

We dutifully handed in our weapons. The blonde tagged the guns and gave us pink paper claim stubs. "Now, don't lose these," she admonished.

"We won't," the Warlock replied.

"I think Sara's probably going over the scout reports in the RA lounge—" Charlie began.

She was interrupted by a scream in the hallway to our left. A large black cat came rocketing out of the corridor with a balding, middle-aged man in a Catholic priest's black cassock close behind. The priest was carrying a large sledgehammer and mumbling something in Latin between panting breaths.

The cat slid to a stop in front of Pal and fluffed up its fur, hissing at my familiar. The priest stormed up on the stymied feline and brought the sledgehammer down on the cat with enough force to break its body wetly in two.

Shouting his Latin prayer now—I was starting to recognize it as one of the old demon banishments that really didn't work too well—the priest brought the sledgehammer down on the cat's skull.

A woman in her midthirties came rushing out of a back office. She was wearing a light blue T-shirt on which someone had Sharpie-markered "Mayor Pro Tem," baggy mom jeans, and a child's red plastic cowboy hat over her prematurely white hair. She was also wearing a big-ass .480 Ruger Super Redhawk revolver strapped to her hip.

As the priest raised his sledgehammer for another blow to the cat's corpse, the woman drew the Redhawk with both hands, put the nine-inch barrel to the back of his head, and pulled the trigger. His skull came apart like a watermelon, and suddenly all of us within ten feet were wearing him.

The woman wiped a bit of skull and blood off her cheek with her thumb and frowned at the priest's headless corpse. "Now, Padre, I've warned you three times, you *don't hurt the kitties*. I can't have you acting like this. I just can't. I think I've been more than reasonable about this."

The woman finally seemed to notice all of us standing there gaping at her and smiled at me. "Oh, hello, you must be Jessie! I'm Sara Bailey-Jones, acting mayor of Cuchillo. The kitties told me you'd be coming. I'm *so* sorry about your clothes—ask Brittney at the front desk for a fresh tee. I think they have some leftovers from World Peace Day. You'd take a large or an extra-large?"

As I looked into Sara's Adderall-blue eyes, it occurred to me that she was utterly, completely, break-out-the-straitjacket batshit crazy. And also she appeared to be in charge. And based on the general lack of reaction to her blowing the priest out of his socks, this wasn't the first time this had happened in the dorm.

"Extra-large, please." My voice was a hoarse squeak.

"Ooh, look, kittens!" Sara squealed like a teenage girl.

I looked down at the floor. The pieces of the smashed cat were healing themselves, sprouting legs and heads and tails and turning into fluffy little black balls of cuteness.

"Okay, I'm officially freaked out now," the Warlock whispered.

Sara didn't seem to hear him. She reached down

and scooped up the kitten that had formed from the cat's back legs and held it out to me. "It's dangerous to go alone. Take this."

"But—but I'm not alone." I wished I could keep my voice steady. "I have Pal here, and Cooper. And the Warlock."

"You need a kitten. They're *crucial*."

"But . . . what do I feed it? And where are the litter boxes?" It finally occurred to me that one of the things that was disturbing me on a subconscious level was that, despite there being twenty-odd cats in the immediate vicinity, it didn't smell the least bit litter-boxy. All I could smell was blood and gunpowder. And sweaty guy funk. But no cat poop.

Sara waved her free hand dismissively, as if I'd asked her how often the city plowed the streets during snowstorms. "Oh, we don't worry about that here! Please, take the kitten."

Her voice hardened a little on the word "please," and there was a gleam in her eye that worried me, so I reached out and took the little creature from her. The kitten settled into the crook of my arm, purring. It smelled like hot electrical wiring.

"That's better." Sara beamed at me. "You can keep him in that saddlebag of yours; they like riding around in sacks and slings. I think they're sort of like cockroaches that way; they like darkness and a little pressure on their bodies. Only they're cute, of course. And cockroaches don't like ear scratchies and belly rubbies."

"Yeah, um, I'm pretty sure Jessie and her friends are tired." Charlie looked a bit embarrassed and worried, as if she didn't know what Super Nutty Nutbar thing Sara was going to say or do next. "So could we maybe get Britt to give them the key to their room?"

"Certainly," Sara replied. "Be a dear and get that for them, would you? We're giving them the corner quad on the eighth floor."

I held the kitten out in front of my stone eye and blinked through a couple of gemviews, trying to figure out what I was looking at. "So . . . where did these cats come from?"

"My television set." Sara picked up another kitten and handed it to the Warlock. He took it from her gingerly, squinting at the purring fluff ball as if it were a ticking bomb.

"Your television set." Cooper stared at her.

"Oh, yes!" Sara scooped up the last kitten and cuddled it under her chin. "So soft! I heard the president say on TV that we Americans make our own reality, and I thought, you know, he was right about something for a change! That man screwed up *everything* . . . I wanted to give him a real piece of my mind, and then one night my mom and I were watching a Ronald Reagan Western, and a kitty came out of the screen! I named him Ringu. He brought more of his friends from commercials and old sitcoms and cable movies."

Sara stopped cuddling her kitten and squinted at it. "I think this one came out of *The Matrix*. But it doesn't matter where they came from, what matters is that they want to help me put things right. And they gave me the idea that we should go visit the president during one of his live speeches."

Sara stared at me earnestly, and I felt supremely creeped out by the look on her face.

"Did you know," she asked, "that pound for pound, cats are the deadliest predators on the planet? Yes. It's true! And so we got ready to go see the president, and his speech was about to start . . . and the power went out! Miko did it. I *hate* her. She screwed up *everything*."

What the heck is going on here? I thought to Pal.

"My educated guess," he replied, "is that this woman is a latent, untrained Talent whose powers were triggered by an emotional trauma that also set her on the road to madness. Very dangerous. I would avoid upsetting her if possible."

What about these cats?

"I'm not sure what they are quite yet." Pal's claws scratched on the floor as he shifted his weight nervously. "Electrical spirits, perhaps? Figments of her mind that her powers have made tangible? Some type of devils? We'll have to watch how they behave. But clearly they're able to counteract Miko's antimagic field, so it would seem prudent to keep one nearby."

"Mein Gott, what a mess you've made!" An old woman in a short-sleeved purple dress tottered out from the hallway to our right. At first glance I thought she was a meat puppet—her body was positively cadaverous, and she certainly smelled like she was close to death—but there was a sharp intelligence behind her yellowed eyes.

"Must you do this?" The old woman waved her cane at the dead priest. I saw an old, faded concentration camp tattoo on her nearly fleshless left forearm.

"Would you do this to a rabbi, too? You're acting like you belong in the SS-Totenkopfverbände!"

"Mom!" Sara turned on the old woman, her face flushing red. "Don't say that. That's mean. I have to keep order here!"

At that, the young men in the lobby started quietly closing their books, setting down their cards, pausing their video game, and slipping out of the room. Behind the counter, Britt looked as if she wished she could do the same.

"This is not order, this is fascism!" The old woman pounded her cane on the floor, punctuating every word.

The kitten in my arms was starting to vibrate, and I could see tiny electrical sparks arcing between the hairs of its fur. It felt like the static when you put your hand on an old cathode-ray TV screen.

"Mom, do you want to go back to the graveyard? Do you want that? Because I'll take you back there!"

"Is that anything like sending someone to the cornfield?" the Warlock whispered. I silenced him with a backward kick that connected solidly with his ankle.

Charlie tugged on my sleeve. She was carrying a stack of tie-dyed T-shirts, sheets, towels, and some boxes of white soap. "I have y'all's keys. We really should go upstairs now."

We quickly followed Charlie down the right-side hall to the elevators. Once we got in, Charlie and the kittens seemed much calmer.

"They get into fights like that sometimes. It's really better not to be near them when that happens," Charlie said.

"So does Sara murder a lot of people around here?" Cooper asked.

Charlie looked pained. "Only when Major Rodriguez ain't around. And only when they do stuff that makes her really mad. Hurting the cats is right at the top of her list. I feel bad for the padre, but he knew what she was gonna do. He must have lost his shit completely. Or, I dunno, maybe he *wanted* Sara to kill him, just so he wouldn't give his soul over to Miko."

We got out on the eighth floor and Charlie led us down to a corner suite of two bedrooms joined by a large shared bath. Each of the bedrooms were furnished mostly with built-ins: two couches that pulled out into single beds, two blond wood desks, and a set of shelves. The only freestanding furniture was a pair of wooden dressers, a couple of wooden chairs, a torchière-style floor lamp, and an old steel trash can. Narrow sliding doors led to cramped closets, empty except for dust and some wire coat hangers.

"Most of the rooms on this floor don't have their own bathrooms," Charlie said, "but Sara wanted you to be as comfortable as possible. I'm not sure what she's wanting you to do, but she's got something in mind."

"Oh, goody," I heard the Warlock whisper to Cooper.

Charlie set her armload of T-shirts and towels down on the closest couch-bed. "Y'all can get cleaned up and rest up here for a while. They'll be serving food in the cafeteria until midnight, but it's just canned beef stew and butterscotch pudding today. There might be some salad left. We're running pretty low on everything, but the ag students are still able to harvest veggies from the greenhouses every so often. Let Britt at the desk know if you need anything else."

Charlie left us staring at the stack of tees. The shirts themselves had been tie-dyed in gaudy spirals of orange, yellow, green, and purple, and the fronts of the shirts had been silk-screened with the image of a cheese-dripping slice of pepperoni pizza and the slogan "I Got Me a Piece at World Peace Day!"

"Wow. Those are . . . bright," Cooper said. "I think I'd rather just wear the tux jacket."

The Warlock shook his head. "The lady at JCPenney said I'm a winter. I can't possibly wear lime green and shrimp orange in public."

"Laundry charm?" I asked them.

"Laundry charm," the guys agreed.

I called dibs on the shower, grabbed my remaining change of underwear from my backpack, and pulled Cooper into the bathroom with me. He completely undressed while I stripped most of the way down. I didn't really want the Warlock handling my dirty underwear on general principle and certainly not after the day I'd had. It wouldn't take a genius to look at the state of my panties and know what had been going on in my head the past few hours. Besides, it would be easy enough to hand-wash those on my own, even if I couldn't find anything better than the tacky white institutional soap Charlie had given us with the towels.

Cooper passed our clothes out to the Warlock to charm-clean while I folded my unmentionables, set them aside under the sink, and readied the shower. It had one of those annoying, clunky single-knob controls set in the tile wall, and it provided seemingly a single-millimeter zone between freezing cold and scalding hot.

After a couple of tries, I got the water tolerably warm. "Hey, honey, come on in."

Cooper got into the shower stall with me and stood under the spray, head bowed and eyes closed, the water running down through his dark curly hair in rivulets over his delicious smooth back and chest. I had the sudden fantasy of Cooper holding me against the damp wall, my legs wrapped around his waist, his hands all over me.

I took the soap out of the tile-bolted dish and lathered it up, rubbing suds into his shoulders. His muscles were knotted with tension, and I could feel a vibration in his body that wasn't just regular stress. Miko's fury still had him deep in his guts.

"Are you okay?" I asked.

"Fine." The word was a clipped grunt.

I lathered my hands again and ran them in gentle circles over his back, down his sides to his groin.

His spine stiffened and he pushed my hands away from his genitals. "Sorry. Too much on my mind right now. Maybe later."

Not looking at me, he took a quick rinse and stepped out of the shower, leaving me frustrated and horny. And also feeling too contaminated and rejected to do anything to relieve my own tensions. Yep, if this kept up I was going to be looking for a rope and a ceiling beam that could take my weight.

The rational part of me realized there was no point in making a big deal about it. If Cooper didn't feel like fooling around, he didn't feel like fooling around.

It wasn't necessarily because he was repulsed by my infection—his coldness was probably just the result of Miko's tampering.

And once we took care of her and got the heck out of this godforsaken town, our relationship would go back to normal, wouldn't it? And if not . . . well, surely we could find a healer to cure me, at least.

But before we could go after Miko, there was a small, dark matter we had to take care of first.

Exorcism

"So, yeah," I said, stepping out of the bathroom, dressed in charm-clean clothes, toweling off my hair. "About me being possessed by a baby Goad . . ."

Cooper chewed on his mustache, still not meeting my gaze. He'd put his pants back on, but hadn't put on his tux jacket. "Well, devils don't much like being exorcised, so the first order of business is to find some way of keeping you strapped down so you don't hurt us or yourself. Would you rather be lying down or sitting up?"

At least he was speaking to me in full sentences.

"Um." I tried to imagine what the devil might try to do to my body if it was intent on hurting me out of spite. "I guess sitting up might keep it from wrenching my spine around quite as much? And it would leave you guys more room in here. But what about my flame hand?"

"That shouldn't be a problem," the Warlock replied. "I'm pretty sure I can build enchanted fire shielding out of this trash can over here. And I can make a good strong bondage chair pretty quick using the furniture we have in here—I've made lots of 'em for play parties and such. Just have to find some material for straps and spend a little extra time reinforcing it with some steel."

The Warlock and Cooper brainstormed a list of items to look for, mainly steel folding chairs, nuts and bolts, leather belts, plus a few spell ingredients for the exorcism, and we went on a quick scavenger hunt. Once the Warlock and I had collected some items from the residents down the hall, we went back to the room and I helped him build a restraint chair using the wooden pair as a base. The twin black kittens crouched side by side on top of one of the dressers, watching our labor with rapt interest.

After an hour of magic and elbow grease, the chair was complete, and Cooper had returned with a couple of vials of holy water and some other items that he had apparently gotten from the dead priest's room.

"You ready for this?" he asked.

"Sure." I sat down in the Warlock's creation. The apparatus held my arms out at my sides at chest level, my left arm fitting into a steel overgauntlet that the Warlock had forged from the trash can and part of a folding chair. He'd fashioned an upper back and head support from the second wooden chair. When they got me strapped in, I couldn't move more than to breathe, but the position I was in was actually fairly comfortable.

Cooper held up the football mouthpiece he'd sanitized and adjusted. "Open wide."

He slipped the mouthpiece in, popping it into place around my upper teeth and gums. It tasted unpleasantly of plastic and felt like I'd just bitten into a huge piece of stale taffy. "You shouldn't be able to seriously damage yourself with this in, but just to be safe, we'll strap your jaw closed so the devil can't make you bite off your own tongue."

"Or cast any diabolic spells to counter the exorcism," the Warlock added.

The first prickles of claustrophobic anxiety danced up my spine as Cooper tightened a leather belt around my head to close my lower jaw around the mouthpiece. I wondered if this was what it felt like to get strapped into an electric chair.

Please stay close, I thought to Pal.

"Of course," my familiar replied. "I wouldn't think of leaving you at a time like this."

Cooper sat cross-legged on the floor in front of me, head bowed, staring down at the vial of holy water in his hand. We weren't Catholics, of course, and I didn't expect Cooper to invoke Jehovah's help, but the blessed water holds spiritual purification powers most Talents can tap if they know how.

Cooper looked at his brother. "The doors locked?"

The Warlock nodded, nervously flipping one of the holy water vials through his fingers.

"Okay, then." Cooper knelt before me, closed his eyes, and began chanting old, old words.

My heart jumped in my chest, and I felt a sudden pain in my head, my guts. I could feel the incendiary ectoplasm jetting from my hand, spilling over the edge of the glove, turning the enchanted steel gauntlet red, smoking like an overheated skillet, but the metal was holding.

Cooper chanted louder, rose to his feet, and poured holy water onto my face. It burned so badly I thought my skin was peeling off. I screamed against the mouthpiece, my muscles jerking spasmodically against the restraints. My vision started to fade, going black at the edges, and I felt myself falling backward—

—I was standing in my old bedroom in the hellement, the floorboards rattling beneath me as if there was an earthquake—

—I was back in the chair, screaming louder, throat aching, but it didn't even sound like my own voice, it sounded like a couple of *cats*. My vision cleared. Cooper was standing over me, and past him I could see that the kittens were clawing at the hallway door, howling loud as twin klaxons, fluffed-out black Tesla fur showering blue sparks onto the carpet.

"Keep going, Coop, you've almost got it by the balls!" The Warlock tried to pick up the kittens but jerked his hands away as if he'd been burned or shocked or both.

The door boomed as if somebody in the hall had slammed it with a battering ram. The kittens dashed away under the closest bed, and the Warlock stepped back. Another boom, and the cheap steel lock gave, the door slamming inward, the doorknob denting against the cinder-block wall.

Sara stood there in the doorway, Redhawk pistol raised and pointed at the Warlock's head. "Stop. Right. *Now.*"

Cooper didn't stop.

"We can't—" the Warlock began.

Without another word, Sara stepped forward into the room and fired her pistol at Cooper. I jumped in my restraints. The bullet ripped through his calf muscle. He swore and collapsed backward onto the hard carpeted floor, clutching his profusely bleeding leg.

Oh my God, get me free, get me free! I thought to Pal. I was torn between wanting to help Cooper and wanting to burn Sara right down to her bones.

As Pal moved toward me, the kittens raced from beneath the bed past Sara into the hallway, and my fire went out. *Shit. Wait.*

"Jesus fuck!" the Warlock bellowed, raising his hand, whether to strike her or to try to cast a spell, I couldn't tell.

Sara pointed the pistol at his forehead. *"Don't."*

"We could kill you with a *word,* lady, don't you get that?" The Warlock looked angrier than I had ever seen him. "One word, and your crazy ass is nothing but red mist!"

"Go ahead." Her voice shook, but she looked strangely elated. "Kill me. If you can. But do you think that any of my kitties will have anything to do with you after that? You . . . you people think you're hot stuff, but you are *nothing* special if you can't work your magic. You'll *die* here."

The Warlock knelt, grabbed one of the unused belts lying on the floor, and cinched it below Cooper's knee to stanch the bleeding. "And my brother could die, thanks to you."

"He won't die." Sara holstered her pistol. "Dr. Ottaway can take care of him."

"I'm not letting any goddamn mundane doctor touch me," Cooper growled through gritted teeth. "Why the fuck did you shoot me?"

"I can't have you hurting the kitties."

"We weren't hurting them, we were trying to ex—" the Warlock began.

"I don't care what you were *trying* to do; what you

were doing was hurting my kitties, and I will *not* have that. Period, end of discussion. And if this happens again, I *will* shoot to kill. I'm not in the mood to give third chances today."

Sara turned and left.

"Goddamn it." Cooper slapped the floor, pain and anger distorting his face.

Pal moved behind my chair and began to undo my straps.

The Warlock got out my Leatherman tool and began to cut away Cooper's pants leg. "The bullet went clean through; looks like it's stuck down in the carpet pad over here. We're lucky it didn't ricochet and hit anybody else. But I think it pulled some fabric into the wound. Gonna be a bitch to get that out with the pliers on this thing."

There was a knock at the doorway. Standing there was a young ginger-haired guy in an airman's battle uniform with a medic's Red Cross armband. He carried an olive-drab medical kit.

"Y'all need some help?" the medic asked, staring uncertainly at Pal, then at me strapped into the chair, then down at Cooper bleeding on the carpet. "I . . . I got a radio from Sara saying there had been an, uh, incident."

"Got a pair of surgical tweezers?" Cooper took the Leatherman tool away from his brother and finished sawing through the seam on his pants leg.

The young man nodded.

"Then come help me get this thing cleaned out." Cooper picked a fragment off his wound.

"I don't have no lidocaine or nothin'—"

"Kid, I don't *care,* I just want the wound clear so I

can get this healed up! Warlock, go find us a damn cat so I can cast a spell."

Pal freed me from the last of the straps as the Warlock went into the hallway. I stood up, and immediately my head swam and my knees buckled and I collapsed back in the chair.

"You should rest for now," Pal told me. "Even an interrupted exorcism is quite hard on the system."

By now, the medic was crouching over Cooper's gunshot leg, holding a penlight in his mouth like a cigar as he pulled slick bits of dark cloth from the wound. Cooper winced and growled obscenities under his breath.

"I think that's all of it," the medic finally said.

The Warlock popped back into the room carrying one of the black kittens in the crook of his arm. "Found this one hiding under the sofa in the common room by the elevators."

"Groo. Vee." Cooper gripped his injured calf, closed his eyes, and began a healing chant. The angry red bullet wound shrank, fresh pink tissue growing in concentric rings from the outside in.

He stopped his chant and frowned mightily at his healed leg. "I guess that's good enough. Thanks for your help, kid."

The medic stood up, looking awed and a bit nervous. "I have to take y'all to see Doc Ottaway."

Cooper scowled at the young man. "What the hell for? I'm fine now."

"It's a standing order from Major Rodriguez. Anybody who gets any kind of serious wound has to be examined by the camp doc. We had some people who got attacked by dogs . . . well, they *said* they was dogs. And they said they was okay and didn't need medical treatment. But then they . . . they turned into these *things* . . ." The medic trailed off, looking like he was remembering something horrible. "Anyways, it's a standing order. I gotta take you to see the doc, or the major will kick my ass."

Cooper blew out his breath and got to his feet, favoring his newly-healed leg. "Fine. Whatever."

He looked at me, and then at the Warlock. "You guys coming with me, or you staying here?"

"I'm not really feeling up to a walk in the heat right now," I replied, "but Warlock, please go with him if you want to. I'll be fine here with Pal. We need to track down the other kitten anyhow."

"Sounds good." Cooper stepped toward me and gave me a quick, perfunctory kiss on the forehead. "Don't get into any trouble while we're gone."

He limped out the door with the medic and the Warlock close behind.

Pal blinked his eyes at me. "What's going on between you and Cooper? His pheromones smell all wrong."

"I don't really know. Miko messed with his head. Made him really angry, and he's staying that way."

I chewed my thumbnail, pondering our situation. Made my decision. "Strap me back into the chair. I need to talk to my father."

Magus Shimmer

I slipped easily into my hellement, went to my vanity, and used a pair of cuticle scissors to cut my thumb so I'd have some blood for the mirror magic.

"Are you there?" I called as the mirror cleared, showing the inside of Shimmer's workshop. "It's Jessie, are you there?"

"Oh! Hang on a moment, if you please." I heard him flip-flop across the floor and soon he came into the frame.

He sat down in the wooden chair before his mirror, gazing at me with an intent look of concern. "How are you? Is everything all right?"

"Well . . . no, not really. We haven't found my brother yet, but . . . well, it's worse than that." I licked my lips, trying to figure out a quick way of telling him everything that happened. And then did my very best, leaving out the parts where Miko turned me into her sex puppet and I'd been miserably horned up ever since.

"Well, that is quite a press of problems," he said when I finished.

My father leaned back in his chair and rubbed his chin thoughtfully through his beard. "Not being able to exorcise the Goad in you, well, that's most serious.

But it sounds as if you are taking all the proper precautions. The blood disease, it is serious, also, but I believe you can be cured. The sisters of the local convent are quite skilled in healing spells, although of course they believe them to be miracles granted by the saints after prayerful rituals. We humor them. It does not matter where they source their powers as long as they freely share them with our family."

He gave a shrug and leaned forward. "The soul harvester is a far greater threat than the devil or your disease. You must not lose yourself to her. Remember that above all else, she wants your souls, and she finds them most delicious when they're given in despair rather than taken by force."

"What about Cooper?" I asked. And almost said, *Do you think Miko's made him hate me?*

Based on what he said to me next, the unspoken question had been clear on my face: "Miko can sense a person's weaknesses. And your man is weakened by anger. It distracts him, clouds his intellect, makes him forget the people he loves. But he *does* love you, loves you very much in fact, make no mistake. And he will remember when his mind is clear again. Until then, you must be watchful and patient with him. You're all in danger, and the baser impulses that Miko inflames make your risks all the greater. So please, try to be careful. Find your brother and do whatever you must to get out of there."

"I'll do my best," I replied.

"I shall do another set of divinations to try to get you some helpful information; it's difficult to see past the Virtus Regnum's magical barriers, but I think I can manage something." He paused. "But *promise* me you

will focus on getting out of there. I know that you
have a charitable, good nature and you want to help
the surviving townsfolk . . . but those people are not
your blood. Family must always come first. Please do
not gamble your or your brother's safety for the welfare of mundane strangers. Please promise me this."

He looked so sad and worried I found myself saying, "I promise."

And then immediately wondered if it had been the
right thing to do.

Doppelganger

Once I said good-bye to my father and closed the mirror, I sat down on my bed to think. He was right; clearly Miko meant to drive us all to so much angst and misery that we'd surrender ourselves to her. The meat puppets hadn't been serious adversaries because they weren't *supposed* to be. Their attacks were intended to exhaust our bodies, fill our minds with horrible memories of carnage, and burden our souls with the guilt of having had to slaughter people's grandmothers. Attrition through demoralization, as the major had put it.

If I could just keep my head on straight, I knew I could blaze through everything and get us home, somehow. But my lust made that damned difficult, and Cooper's anger wedging us apart made it thornier still. It wasn't just that I felt as if I would go insane if I couldn't get laid; I *missed* him. I missed hugging him, missed the comfort of his touch, missed laughing with him. Our stolen moments together in the tent in Mother Karen's backyard seemed like a lifetime ago.

I looked at the bedroom around me. This was my dimension now. I created all this, purely from memory and will. What else could I create in here?

I held my hands out in front of me and closed my

eyes. Thought of Cooper, his powerful legs, his lean body, his muscular arms, his runic tattoos, his curly black hair, the sound of his voice, the warmth of his touch . . .

Strong, familiar hands took mine.

I opened my eyes.

Cooper was standing before me, smiling down at me. He was naked, his long handsome cock half hard. Glad to see me, clearly.

"I missed you," he said. A moment later, I realized it was what I'd wanted him to say. And decided that right then, I didn't really care.

"I missed you, too." I stood up; with a thought, my clothes were gone. We kissed; his mouth tasted like Nutella, as if we'd just come in from making a mid-morning snack in the kitchen. His skin smelled like fresh gingerbread and clean healthy man.

When we broke from our embrace, Cooper cupped my breasts in his warm hands, leaned down, and began to suck on my right nipple, sending an electric thrill through my chest and belly down to my vulva. The sudden spark blossomed into a sharp, insistent ache in my loins that made me moan. Smiling, Cooper straightened up and gently pushed me down so I was sitting on the edge of the bed. I lay back, my legs hanging over.

He knelt on the carpet between my legs and spread my lips with his thumbs. My flesh ignited at his touch; the anticipation was killing me. He began to run the tip of his tongue around the opening of my vagina in light, teasing circles. And then slowly up, up my juice-slick groove to my clit, which he circled, tapping gently just beyond my pleasure's reach, tormenting me.

"Fuck me," I whispered. "Please fuck me."

He wet his fingers against my pussy and began to rub my flesh in gentle circles, still just barely touching my clit. I sucked in my breath. He slowly stood up, gently brushing his hard cock along the length of my inner thigh to my vagina. He pressed the tip against my waiting flesh and began to slowly push into me as he rubbed my clit directly—

—I moaned again as the dam of my pleasure swelled, ready to burst—

He drove his cock in deeply and I came, my flesh shuddering around his shaft. I threw my head back against the mattress and wrapped my legs around his waist, trying to pull him in as deep as possible.

When the surge of my orgasm had passed, he worked his flesh in mine more slowly, gently, giving my tension time to build, and then he thrust faster and faster, pinning me to the bed, my body at his mercy. I felt his cock shudder inside me as he came, and the feel of his seed spurting inside me sent me over the edge and I was coming again, gasping for air, my nerves singing with so much carnal joy I nearly passed out.

We collapsed, spent, after that. I fell asleep in the slow afternoon light filtering through the silent windows.

chapter twenty-two

Fever

I awoke with a start in the hellement; Cooper's doppelganger was gone. How long had I been in there? There was no way to tell. I rolled out of bed and opened the red portal door.

When I came to in the restraint chair, I immediately knew something was wrong. My vision was blurry. My head was throbbing. Fever chills were washing through me. I tasted bile in the back of my throat, and my guts were in an uproar.

Pal? I thought. *Pal, are you here?*

"Oh, thank goodness you're back. You had me worried sick," he replied. "You were gone all night."

I feel like crap. Can you untie me, please? I blinked my eyes to try to clear my vision; Pal came into focus, hovering beside me.

"Certainly." Pal undid the straps binding my head and jaws, then released my arms and freed my legs.

I pulled out my mouthpiece and got up slowly, my stiff joints and strained muscles bitching at me with every inch. My stomach was cramping, acidic. The floor felt like it was tilted at a weird angle. The furniture seemed to be undulating, and suddenly I realized I was seeing small, indistinct creatures scuttling in the periphery of my vision.

"I'm seeing the fey," I slurred.

"Oh dear." Pal put a clawed paw to my forehead. "You're burning up."

I sat back down on the chair. "I thought the hepatitis wouldn't set in for weeks."

"This doesn't look like hepatitis to me. Admittedly I am not especially familiar with the disease, but you don't seem to be jaundiced. A different blood-borne infection that the Warlock's fetish couldn't detect is the likely culprit."

"Where are the guys?"

"The Warlock and Cooper came back about an hour after you went into your hellement—Cooper was apparently given a clean bill of health by the doctor—but an airman came to get them soon after. Evidently they were needed to help repel an attack by the meat puppets. Unfortunately I have no idea when they are likely to return."

"Well, damn." I licked my lips; my tongue felt like it was covered in paste. I could see the fey more clearly now: the weird little creatures were all over the place. A vermilion-feathered starfish was napping on my knee. "Could you grab me a bottle of water?"

"Certainly." Pal turned away to get into my backpack.

One of the kittens mewed, attracting my attention. In my fevered vision, it no longer looked much like a kitten: it was a rangy creature of utter blackness with huge mirrorlike eyes and a gaping mouth of long, curving teeth. Its head reminded me more of a deep-sea anglerfish than anything truly feline.

I watched, horrified, as it pounced on a fey that

looked like a fleshy daisy with tentacle legs. The "kitten" devoured the fey in two savage bites.

"Hey, Pal?" My voice shook.

"Yes?" He handed me the water bottle.

"I just found out what Sara's kitties eat—they're fey predators."

"Oh dear. Well, given their reaction to the exorcism magic, we can be certain that they're some type of devil."

I looked around the room. "Also we're apparently surrounded by paradimensional cat poop."

"I must say I'm pleased that I do not share your enhanced vision." He put his paw against my forehead again as I took a long drink from the bottle. "I think you should go see the doctor."

"No argument here."

Pal helped me up out of the restraint chair, and I leaned on him as we made our way down the hall to the elevators. It was probably five in the morning, and the dorm lobby was utterly quiet. A new girl was napping in the chair behind the counter. Once we got outside, the heat made me queasier and dizzy and I tripped on the curb in the early morning darkness. Pal caught me, sang himself a bit bigger, and carried me the rest of the way to the clinic.

The broad entry hall of the Student Health Center was completely lined with military cots on which meat puppets lay blindfolded and earplugged, their arms and legs tied down. IV drips carrying nutrition and drugs were taped into every arm, and catheter bags hung beneath the cots. At the end of the hall, I saw Sara sitting in a folding chair beside one puppet, holding his hand, her eyes wet with tears.

A petite young woman in green scrubs goggled at Pal and came hurrying over. Her name tag read Arleen Barnes, RN. "Can I help you?"

Pal, put me down.

"I'm sick, got some kind of fever," I told the nurse as Pal gently set me on the floor. I nodded toward Sara. "What's that about?"

She followed my gaze, and her face fell. "Oh. Yes. That's Sara's husband, Bob. He was taken from us about six months ago, and she hasn't been right since."

"So you're just keeping all these bodies alive in the hopes you can get their souls back somehow?"

Nurse Barnes nodded. "Yes. That's our job, and we're doing it the very best we can." She pulled a digital ear thermometer out of her breast pocket.

"Why the blindfolds and earplugs?" I asked. "Are they sensitive to light and sound?"

"No. We found out the hard way that Miko can use them to spy on us." The nurse looked uncomfortable at the thought. "Lean down a little so I can get your temperature."

I did as she asked. The tip of the thermometer was cold and uncomfortable in my ear canal.

"Goodness, you do have a fever," she said. "It's 103.5. Come with me, we need to get your temperature down."

Pal sang himself mastiff-size, and he supported me as I followed the nurse back to a cramped beige examining room that was absolutely filled with mushroomlike fey with tiny butterfly wings. At the nurse's request, I sat down on the vinyl-upholstered exam table. There wasn't a sheet of paper covering it; I supposed they'd run out some time ago.

The nurse took hold of my hands, frowning at the angry red marks the straps had left on my wrists. "What's this all about?"

"I . . . had a seizure. My friends tied me down to keep me from hurting myself." I got the feeling that the nurse was already plenty freaked out by Pal, and she didn't need to know that I was possessed by a devil.

"Do you have seizures often?" She held open my eyelids one by one and shined a penlight in my eyes. "And what's this thing?" She frowned at my ocularis.

"It's a makeshift artificial eye," I replied.

"Did you start getting the seizures after you lost your eye?"

"Yes." It wasn't a lie.

She turned away to furiously write notes on a clipboard, looking up only to ask for my name and Social Security number, both of which I gave her.

"What about your rash?" she asked, pen poised above the clipboard.

"Rash?" I looked down at my arms, and sure enough, my skin was covered in itchy-looking red bumps. "Wow. I didn't even see that. This is new."

"Have you been exposed to the blood of one of the Taken?" she asked.

I guessed that the medical personnel had been discouraged from using terms like "zombie" to describe Miko's puppets. "Yes, a couple of them bled all over me yesterday. And . . . I've been recently exposed to hepatitis, but I don't know if I've actually got the disease yet or not."

The nurse hmmed and wrote more notes. "Well, a lot of people around here have that as well. Dr.

Ottaway should be up by now . . . let me go see if she can take a look at you." She set the clipboard down, went to a nearby cupboard, and pulled down a big bottle of ibuprofen 800s.

"Do you have any bleeding problems? Are you allergic to Advil or aspirin or tetracycline antibiotics? And are you pregnant?" she asked.

"Nope, nope, and nope."

"Good." She filled a paper cup with water from the tiny sink, and handed me one of the ibuprofen horse pills and the cup. "Take this . . . it should help bring your fever down. We'll give you more to take back to the dorm with you."

"Thanks." I swallowed the medicine.

The nurse left, and a few minutes later she returned with a tired but pleasant-looking woman in a long white doctor's coat. Her thick graying brown hair was parted in the middle and pulled back from her face; the style reminded me of Frida Kahlo, but wasn't as severe. I guessed the doctor was just a few years older than Cooper.

She gave a start when she saw Pal crouched attentively on the floor beside me. "Holy smokes, what's that thing?"

"This is Pal," I replied. "He's cool."

"But what is he?"

I racked my fever-addled brain for a believable response. "He's a . . . spider weasel . . . bear . . . from . . . Japan. They're the hot new pets there these days."

It had finally occurred to me that although he was a spider in general form and a ferret in coloration, there was something distinctly bearish about his teeth, broad skull, and the texture of his fur.

"I'll have to take your word for that." She straightened up, seemed to recover her professional demeanor, and stuck out her hand. "I'm Christine Ottaway, M.D. And you are"—she glanced at the clipboard—"Jessie Shimmer?"

I took her hand and shook it. Her grip was strong, and she had a guitar player's calluses on her fingertips. "Yes. Thanks for seeing me on such short notice."

"Honey, it's *all* short notice around here." She laughed. "I'm lucky if I get a solid five hours of shuteye. But let's not make this about me. So. You've got a pretty bad fever, and a rash, and you've had some blood contamination. Any new headaches and body pains? Upset stomach?"

I nodded. "All that, yeah."

She stepped up beside the table and started feeling the lymph nodes in my neck and under my jaw. "You've definitely got some swelling in here."

She pulled a wooden tongue depressor and a penlight out of her breast pocket. "Open your mouth, stick your tongue out, and say 'Aaah.'"

I did as she asked.

"Okay, you can close now." She turned away and tossed the depressor into the trash. "I think, my dear, that you've got the local superbug: *Ehrlichia mutans*."

I suddenly felt a bit queasier. "What's that?"

"It's a bacterium in the family *Anaplasmataceae*." She went to the sanitizer dispenser on the wall, pumped some clear alcohol gel into her palm, and vigorously rubbed her hands together. "Normally it's transmitted by tick bites, and normally symptoms don't develop until a few weeks after exposure, but things aren't exactly normal around here, are they? Our local mutation is a speedy little bugger. It mostly causes the flulike, rashy ick you're feeling now, but I've been seeing it destroy some people's kidneys. To my regret we haven't had much luck at keeping people alive on dialysis around here, so aggressive treatment from the start is our best option. Knock it out before it knocks you out."

I nodded. "Sounds good to me."

Dr. Ottaway turned to the nurse. "Please bring me a bottle of doxycycline, the usual strength, and a bottle of ibuprofen 200s."

The nurse left to fetch the antibiotic, and the doctor pulled a small notepad out of one of her front coat pockets and started writing down some directions. "I'm going to give you a bottle of hundred-milligram doxycycline tablets. I want you to go straight to the cafeteria, have some food, and take *three* of the doxy pills. You've already had eight hundred milligrams of ibuprofen, and you're likely to make yourself sick if you take all this on an empty stomach. And then tonight when you get ready for bed, I want you to take two more doxy pills, and then one in the morning and one at night until the bottle's empty. I'm also going to give you a bottle of ibuprofen, but do *not* take more for at least eight hours . . . after that, take two every four to six hours as you need them for fever."

She paused. "Also, try to stay out of the sun as much as possible—both these drugs can make your skin burn very easily. Do you understand everything I've told you?"

I nodded. "I think so."

"Good." She tore the instructions off her notepad

and handed them to me. "If you see any blood in your urine, come back in here *immediately*."

"I will. Thank you."

Nurse Barnes returned with my medication in a small brown paper bag, and the good doctor bade me good-bye and sent me on my way.

chapter
twenty-three

Monsters

After a breakfast of antibiotics, rubbery powdered eggs, and watery oatmeal in the student center's cafeteria, Pal helped me back to the dorm and strapped me back into the restraint chair so I could take a nap.

"That egg ration wasn't terribly filling," Pal said. "I'm still feeling rather peckish. I think I smelled rats when we were in the lobby . . . do you mind if I go down to the basement to see if I can do a little hunting?"

I don't think that's a good idea, I thought back, unable to speak with my head immobilized. *I mean, I don't mind for myself, as long as you locked the doors so nobody could come wandering in here while I'm asleep. But you look like a monster and practically everybody here has a big gun. I wouldn't want you to get shot.*

Pal looked offended. "I was aware of that, thank you. I planned to turn myself invisible. And I am otherwise perfectly capable of defending myself against firearms."

Still. I just don't think it's a good idea . . . how about I go down there with you once I've rested for a little while?

Pal blinked at me and scratched the carpeted floor

impatiently with one of his middle legs. "I am really *quite* hungry, but I suppose that would be an acceptable compromise, provided you don't sleep too long."

Cool. My eyelids were already growing heavy, and soon I was fast asleep in the chair.

I woke with a start when I heard a key scrabbling in the lock. Based on the angle of the sunlight streaming through the miniblinds, I'd been asleep for at least two or three hours. It was hard to look around, but I was no longer seeing the fey, and my headache and chills were gone, so apparently the medicine was working. Unfortunately, I also couldn't see my familiar.

Pal, where are you? Someone's coming into the room, I thought, suddenly aware of how vulnerable I was. And I didn't know how many people might have access to the dorm's master keys. *Pal, are you here?*

No response came. The door swung open and I was relieved to see the Warlock come in. But when I saw that he was alone I felt anxious all over again. He was dressed in a pair of tiger-stripe camouflage pants and a tan T-shirt; based on the soot, smudges, scratches, and bruises on his face and arms, I guessed his tuxedo pants and shirt had been ruined during his overnight mission.

He had an olive-drab canvas map bag slung across his shoulder; he set it down on the nearby bed. His black kitten crawled out and climbed up to the shelf above, blinking its yellow eyes at us. Its twin crept out from under the bed and clawed up the bed up to join it.

"Where's Spiderboy?" The Warlock's eyes were glassy, bloodshot. He had the thousand-yard stare of somebody who'd been up far too long but was too wound up on adrenaline to sleep. He looked at the strap holding my jaw shut. "Right. You can't possibly talk with that on, can you?"

He locked the door behind him and came over to my chair to take off the restraints binding my head. His hands were dark with dirt, grease, and speckles of what was probably blood.

"Wash first, please," I slurred around the mouthpiece as he reached for it.

He gave me a slightly annoyed look, but went into the bathroom to quickly scrub himself off at the sink.

"Thanks," I said after he pulled the mouthpiece out with clean, damp hands. "I guess Pal got hungry and went off hunting rats. Where's Cooper?"

"He's off killing meat puppets, still. He's enjoying it far too much if you ask me." The Warlock set the mouthpiece aside on one of the dressers and pulled a folding chair over to sit in front of me. "But who am I to deny my own brother his pleasures?"

Something about the way he said "pleasures" set the Gothic bells tolling in my head. I gave him a harder look. "Get me out of this chair, please."

He was staring at my breasts. "You know, you look really hot all strapped in like that. Really, really hot."

My heart beat faster in mixed alarm and—goddamn it—arousal. No, no, this was *not* happening. I met his gaze, and knew that part of his mind was just *gone*. His superego had fled the building, leaving his id in charge of the party.

"Did you see Miko out there?" I stammered. Obviously, he had, and she'd triggered a lust in him that was at least as bad as mine. Worse, maybe. "Please just unstrap me. This can't go anywhere good."

"I saw . . ." He trailed off for a moment, then leaned in and breathed deeply near my neck. My skin prickled under his hot exhalation. "I saw you naked in the desert. I'd wanted to see that for a long, long time. I think I want to see it again."

I tried to squirm away from him, but the chair held me fast. I started trying to summon the words for a spell to free myself, but all I could think of was letting the Warlock take me to the bed and fuck me blind. Panic rose along with my abject lust, chasing the ancient words from my mind.

"Please don't," I begged. "You're not thinking straight. *I'm* not thinking straight. Miko's messing with us."

He didn't seem to hear me. "You've got a gorgeous pair, Jessie. Did you know I can make a woman come just by sucking on her nipples? Oh yeah. That's one trick I *know* I can do better than Coop. He doesn't half deserve a fine woman like you."

"Christ, Warlock. He's your *brother*."

"I don't see a ring on your finger. If he wanted you all to himself, he should've made the vow by now."

"I've. Got. Hepatitis!"

"And I've got condoms." He started to pull my shirt up. "And I can tell when a woman's getting all juicy. You look like you're getting a whole bunch of honey on those tight leather pants of mine."

"No, dammit, *no*. I don't want you to do this. *Stop*." I was starting to get angry now. *Really* angry. So what if I was obviously aroused by him? That didn't give him the right to jump on me like a dog that had found a bitch in heat. He owed me more respect than this, damn him.

The Warlock stood up and unzipped the fly of his camouflage pants. Levered his cock out. His organ was about as long as Cooper's but much thicker and gnarled with hard veins, the purpling mushroom head boastfully flared, and I couldn't help but wonder how it would feel inside me. Damn Miko to oblivion.

"This is another thing I know I've got on Coop," he said, stroking his cock slowly with his left hand. "All the ladies who've done a taste test with both of us have always come back to *me* for seconds. And usually thirds and fourths."

"If you touch me," I warned him through gritted teeth, "I will kick your ass like it's never been kicked before."

"Oh yeah?" He cocked an eyebrow and smiled at me as if he'd taken my threat as a challenge. "Well, we'll just have to see about that, won't we?"

He pulled up my sports bra, leaned down, and took my left nipple between his lips. His death-memory hit me, and the sensation of the phantom blade sawing through my throat fired my anger into a profound rage that overwhelmed my lust and panic. He *had* to know kissing me would hurt me, and he did it anyway, goddamn him!

Screaming in pain and fury, I pulled us both into my hellement.

The Warlock was standing in my bedroom, dressed in his tuxedo again, looking exactly as he had when we drove out to the Faery Tavern. He looked around, startled. "What the—where are we? What is this place?"

I slugged him right in the mouth, and he tumbled backward into the closet and slid to the floor, his lip bleeding. He was no physical match for me in here.

"You're supposed to be my friend!" I screamed down at him. "You're supposed to show me common decency and respect, not *rape* me, you jackass!"

He tried to get up. "I—I wasn't—"

His protestation put my rage right into orbit. Screaming obscenities, I fell on him, straddling him, and punched him over and over and over as hard as I could, feeling his nose and cheekbones and jaws and teeth shattering under my fists. After a dozen blows, his face looked like fresh roadkill, and he was gurgling for air through the blood filling his wrecked mouth. He didn't even look human anymore.

Something hard was poking my inner thigh. I rocked back on my heels, grabbed the waistbands of his tuxedo pants and boxers, and ripped them open. His cock bobbed up, huge and hard and insolent.

"You're still horny?" I snarled at him. "After all that, you're *still* horny?"

His lacerated tongue twitched and he moaned, his mouth too destroyed to form any words. I could feel my sanity slipping away from me, but was too angry to care. The Warlock hadn't learned his lesson yet, and by God I was going to give it to him.

I started to strangle him with both hands. Miko's memory of killing the GI echoed darkly in the back of my mind. The Warlock gagged and tried to pry my fingers off his throat, but he couldn't budge them even a millimeter.

"You wanna fuck?" My clothes had disappeared,

and I could feel his dick hard against the mound of my loins. "Well, you're gonna get fucked, bitch!"

I lifted my hips and drove my cunt down on his cock, imagining my gash not as an organ of love and life giving but as the callous, toothless maw of a savage forest hag, the kind that consorts with ancient horned gods, devouring haughty princes and fattening bratty children in cages of bone deep in the blackest heart of the wilderness.

I pounded down on him, choking him, waiting to feel his pelvis ground to wet rubble beneath me, and was surprised to find myself coming, coming hard.

Crying out, I fell backward against the side of the bed, my flesh still shuddering. The Warlock looked dead; surely I had suffocated him. Jesus, what had I done?

Maybe there was still time to save him. I got up on shaky legs, grabbed his wrist, and started to drag him toward the portal door.

He suddenly came awake with an animal growl and lurched to his feet, glaring at me, blue eyes bright in the ruin of his face, his tool hard again. I could have muscled him over to the door, could have stopped what happened next, but his sudden show of force had ignited my damnable lust again and I just stood there staring back at him.

The Warlock threw me facedown on the bed, and in a heartbeat his rough hands were jerking my hips up in the air, pulling me onto my hands and knees. The jarred traumas rattled in the darkness beneath us. He wedged my legs apart, pressed the blunt tip of his cock against my tightness, and there was a sun-bright pain as he forced himself inside me, and oh God it hurt, but to my hellish need agony was just as good as ecstasy. He thrust again, and an orgasm unwound inside me, fast and relentless as a striking rattlesnake. I howled into the mattress, my muscles rhythmically clamping down on his cock and he was coming, too, shooting stinging heat deep inside me.

A little sanity returned, and I realized that if we stayed in the hellement, we'd tear each other to pieces, and Miko would laugh all the way to the graveyard. *Christ, we've got to get out of here.*

Suddenly the room tilted and we were on our feet; the Warlock was rutting me against the portal door. I reached down and turned the handle, and we both tumbled through.

We came back to our bodies in the dorm room in the same positions we'd left. My jaw ached as if the Goad had been grinding my teeth. The Warlock spat out my nipple and straightened up, his unbloodied face pale and frightened. His semiflaccid cock lolled from his open fly, a bit of semen still beaded on the tip; it felt as if he'd ejaculated copiously all over my chest and belly.

"What was that?" His voice shook. "What the hell just happened? Oh God, what did we just *do*?"

"Get me out of this chair," I begged.

The Warlock nodded, tight-lipped, quickly got himself zipped up, and moved to undo the straps on my arm, but there was the sound of a key in the lock and suddenly Cooper was standing there in the doorway dressed in tiger-stripe fatigues.

We all three froze. Cooper's shocked gaze moved from the Warlock's guilt-plastered face to my bared breasts and the drying ropes of spunk that adorned them. His face contorted, turning a deep heart-attack red.

Without a word, he launched himself at his brother and rammed his knee into the Warlock's groin. The Warlock gave a strangled gasp and fell to the floor in a fetal heap. Cooper was right on top of him, brutally punching him, trying to do to him in the real world what I'd done to him in the hell. The Warlock tucked his head under his hands and elbows, rolling into a tight ball. The blank fury in Cooper's eyes scared me to death. He'd kill his brother.

The twin kittens were still crouched on the shelf above the bed, eyes bright, both purring loudly.

"Help!" I screamed as loud as I could. "Somebody get help!"

Pal! I thought. *Pal, I need you! Get up here!*

Still no response. Where could he possibly be? I started hollering for help again.

After what seemed like an eternity—probably it was actually only a minute or so—a quartet of cadets came rushing in, Sara close behind.

"Break it up!" Sara barked. "No fighting in the dorm! Y'all take this outside!"

The cadets wrestled the brothers apart, hauled the Warlock to his feet—I could tell his nose was broken, and he had a nasty gash above his left eye—and frogmarched them both out into the hallway, dragging them toward the elevators.

Which left me alone in the room, still strapped in the chair. Well, not entirely alone: the kittens blinked at me from above the bed, clearly pleased with the proceedings.

Dammit, Pal, where are you? I thought again.

Still nothing. Panic started creeping up my spine. Would Sara bother to keep Cooper from killing the Warlock? My gut told me she wouldn't. And what had happened to Pal?

So I started hollering again, my voice getting hoarse: "Somebody! Get me out of this thing!"

Charlie stuck her head in the doorway and goggled at the chair, the straps, my bared breasts. "Whoa. What happened in here?"

"*Please* get me out of this. I gotta get downstairs— I think Cooper's gonna kill the Warlock!"

Charlie came in and started undoing the straps. "Were you and the Warlock . . . uh. Fooling around on this thing here?"

I squeezed my eyes shut and took a deep breath. "It's complicated. But Cooper thinks we were."

"Oh." Her cheeks reddening, Charlie finished freeing me.

When she opened the last strap, I muttered, "Thanks," and jumped up, ignoring the pain in my joints, ignoring my dizziness and sudden headache. I yanked my bra and shirt back into place and ran down the hall to the elevator to try to stop Cooper.

chapter twenty-four

Sprung Traps

I got downstairs as fast as I could and ran out into the courtyard, breathing hard. If I'd been thinking straight I would have stopped for my shotgun and to grab a cat, but between my fever and my panic I was lucky to be able to speak in complete sentences. All I could think about was getting to Cooper. Dark spots were blooming in my vision, but at least I wasn't seeing the fey again. I scanned the courtyard, but couldn't see a ring of curious cadets surrounding a fight; I listened, but couldn't hear grunts of men laboring to murder one another, nor the thud of fists hitting flesh.

So I hurried over to an airman who was reading a gun repair manual at one of the shaded picnic tables. "Did you see those two guys who were fighting? Did you see where they went?"

He looked up, blinking at me from behind glasses that were held together with duct tape and electrical wire. "Uh. Yeah. One of the dudes swore at Sara and then started yelling these crazy-sounding words at her, and she got really mad and had 'em both thrown out of the compound."

Panic crested in me like a tsunami. "Thrown out? Where?"

"Just over there." Looking puzzled, he pointed at the main entrance we'd come through the day before.

I swore and ran to the gate; thinking back, I still don't know what the hell I was planning to do. "Let me out!"

The guards shrugged at each other and pulled the chain-link panel aside. I sprinted into the empty streets, hollering the men's names until my voice was nearly gone.

After a few minutes of running, sweat and tears were streaming down my face, my blood was pounding in my ears, and the edges of my vision were starting to darken. I stopped, leaned forward, hands on my knees, trying to catch my wind.

"Jessie . . ."

I looked up. Miko was standing right in front of me.

She smiled down at me. "I've got your men. Give yourself to me, and they'll go free. If you don't . . . well. I'm sure I can find lots of delightful uses for their bodies once I've taken their souls."

I swore and yanked open the Velcro cuff of my bull-riding glove, intending to strip the deerskin off and slash the bitch in the face. But in a blink she had me by my flesh wrist and just as suddenly I was at her mercy as she flooded my nerves with ecstasy one moment and agony the next and I fell to my knees on the pavement.

"I think that deep down, you like the taste of murder just as much as I do, little girl . . . I think you and I could make a great team, if you would just learn to *cooperate* a little."

The pleasure turned to pain again, and one of her memories rose in my mind:

I flipped on the light in the motel bathroom and examined my body in the full-length mirror. The pain had worsened as my body had made more blood and my nerves reawakened. I looked ghastly, even by my standards. There was a baseball-size entry wound in my back above my left kidney and a saucer-size exit wound above my belly button. Buckshot ground between my vertebrae. The ragged ends of a few broken ribs had pierced my skin. My T-shirt was almost a vest. I was pincushioned with cactus spines from my thighs to my chin. Dirt and dead grass matted my wounds. I pulled my switchblade and pliers out of my rucksack and took a deep breath, steeling myself for another fun Friday night of do-it-yourself surgery—

With effort, I pulled myself out of Miko's memory and gave my free hand a hard shake to shuck off the glove. No cat meant no fire, but I still had my claw. I rose up against her with as much strength as I could muster and drove my blades deep into her body.

Miko left, and the meat puppet she'd possessed collapsed. It was Major Rodriguez, his eyes staring wide at me, unseeing. I'd slashed his chest open, and my claw shone with his blood.

The sight of his corpse turned my exhaustion to lead bricks on my bones, made my fever and sickness feel a thousand times worse. I sank back to my knees on the hot pavement and wept. I had failed, utterly failed. I'd lost the love of my life and one of my best friends and slaughtered the only person who could seemingly keep Sara's madness in check. I'd failed, I'd failed, we were all lost . . .

After a few minutes, I heard the sound of someone running up the street behind me. I didn't care.

"Jessie?" It was Charlie's voice. "Jessie, what hap— Oh no. Oh God, no."

I heard her step toward me more slowly.

"Miko tricked me," I whispered. "He was her puppet. I didn't know until I killed him."

"I believe you. But some of the others won't. They . . . they'll want to blame you for his death, because you're killable, and Miko ain't." She tugged at my sleeve. "We gotta get back to the compound; it ain't safe out here."

I numbly stared down at the major's body. "We can't just leave him out here. It doesn't seem right."

"We have to. If we bring him back with us . . . you're covered in blood. You'll be dead in an hour. There ain't no helping him now; Miko's got his soul. It doesn't matter to him if the animals take his body, and if they do, well, his men won't figure you did it, will they?"

Charlie helped me to my feet and poured her canteen over my claw to wash away as much of the incriminating blood as she could. She pulled a tan bandanna out of her cat sling and let me use it to dry off my claw.

"Have you seen Pal? My spider?" I pulled my bull-riding glove back on, and in the movement imagined pulling myself together. Maybe everything wasn't lost. And even if it was, well, I couldn't give Miko the satisfaction of my surrender.

She shook her head. "Did you see your guys?"

I felt tears well in my eyes, and I savagely wiped them away with the back of my flesh hand. "Miko's holding them hostage. She says she'll let them go if I give myself up."

Charlie looked worried. "You're not gonna, are you?"

I didn't answer, and we walked on in silence. Halfway back to the compound, my heart soared with happiness and relief when I heard Pal's calliope music overhead, but almost immediately I found myself getting mad all over again.

"Where the hell were you?" I hollered at him as he touched down on the street in front of us.

He was holding one of the black kittens curled in his left front paw. His legs were crisscrossed with nasty-looking scratches. Patches of his fur had been torn out all over his body.

"I'm quite sorry," he replied. "You seemed to be resting so comfortably, and I was getting so very hungry, and I thought it would only take a half hour at most to find a few rats to snack on . . ."

"Whoa," Charlie said. "He looks like he's been down in the steam tunnels."

Pal's alien face was still hard for me to read, but it seemed to me that he looked embarrassed. "The girl is quite perceptive. While I was in the basement, I found a sealed door to the tunnels, and to my great regret, my hunger drove me to pick the lock and go inside."

"What's in the steam tunnels?" I asked both of them.

"Rats," Charlie said, hugging her orange kitty. "Really huge, nasty rats."

"More specifically, a pack of murothropes prowls the tunnels," Pal told me. "They used genuine Norway rats to lure me out of range of the cats' magic field, and they attacked me in great numbers. I count myself lucky to have escaped with my shell intact."

"Wow." Wererats are worse than werewolves; what

they lack in brute strength they more than make up for in pack size, cunning, and sheer viciousness. My anger toward Pal vanished, and I kicked myself for believing he'd thoughtlessly abandoned me.

Promise me you won't go off by yourself again? I thought to him as the three of us started walking back to the compound. *Things got really screwed up today because we got separated. And I promise I won't go to sleep if you're hungry.*

"I gladly promise you that. This does not seem to be a good place for any of us to get separated." Pal held up the kitten. "And on that same subject, I found this in the room, but I haven't seen Cooper or the Warlock. Do you know where they are?"

I felt the tears coming again, and I shut my eyes against them. *Miko's got them. She laid a trap for us and we fell right into it.*

I telepathically gave Pal the short version of everything that had happened after he left to go hunting.

"Oh dear. That's . . . dreadful."

We passed "dreadful" several miles ago. And I have no idea what to do now.

"Well, might I suggest that we can best do our decision-making on a full stomach? Breakfast was surely a long time ago for you, and I never did get to eat a rat."

Sounds good. "Hey, Charlie, any idea what they're serving for lunch?"

The three of us sat at an isolated table in the corner of the cafeteria. Our keeping to ourselves wasn't entirely intentional, but none of the people who came in seemed eager to be near Pal. Charlie and Pal had bowls of the leftover beef stew and some rice. The server took pity on me when I said I couldn't have the stew and she gave me a double portion of rice and a handful of peanut packets. It wasn't much, but it was food and it wouldn't make me feel worse than I already did.

"I really am trying to look on the bright side here." I popped two Advil in my mouth and washed them down with a swig of Gatorade. It hadn't been quite eight hours since my visit to the clinic, but the fever was kicking me hard. "But every way I look at it, Miko has completely boned us."

"Sara sent me to find you for a reason; she doesn't send us after just *anybody* who falls out of the sky, you know." Charlie took a drink of her Coke. "The cats told her you were here to do something important."

"Then why the hell did she throw Cooper and the Warlock to Miko?" I asked. "How are Pal and I supposed to do anything but die horribly without the guys to help us fight?"

"She didn't send me to get *all* y'all," Charlie pointed out. "Jessie Shimmer was the only name she gave me. It's *you* the cats were interested in, not anybody else."

"And clearly the Virtii lured you here for a reason," Pal added. "Perhaps these cat-devils know what the Virtii know: that you—and, dare I say it, perhaps I—have the ability to defeat the town nemesis."

"Well, I wish someone would fill me in on exactly how I'm supposed to take on Miko," I fumed, replaying her bathroom surgery memory in my head. Once we found her real body, my shotgun clearly wasn't going to do much to stop her. Provided, of course, that the memories I was getting from her were authentic and not designed to trick me. "It would be real nice if one of the cats could leave me a little note: 'O hai, she haz bad left knee' or 'LOL, peanut allergy!' A little help, somebody, *please*!"

I was ranting louder than I realized, and the people at the other tables had turned to stare at me and whisper to each other.

"Inside voice, Jessie." Pal downed his bowl of beef stew in one gulp and looked longingly at the food line.

"Right." I passed him a packet of peanuts and stuck my tongue out at the staring airmen.

"I know some stuff." Charlie absently rubbed the jagged white scars on her forearm. "Not about Miko, but about the zombies. She can possess them, but she can't make them. Someone else does that."

I sat up and leaned toward her. "Do tell."

She bit her lip and pulled a pack of Marlboros out of her pocket. Nobody paid the least bit of attention to the "No Smoking" signs on the cafeteria walls.

"I've never told anyone about what happened to me." Charlie's voice was low. "It's kind of a long story. I don't know what to leave out."

"I think we have time," I said.

"Okay, then . . ."

Charlie lit up a cigarette, took a deep drag, and began to tell us about her shadow.

chapter twenty-five

Charlie's Story

Charlie's real name was Charlotte, and she met her shadow when she was eleven. Her parents had unwittingly let the monster into her life. Her mother was a wedding and party planner, the kind of self-centered yuppie whose friends all got pregnant so of course *she* had to have a baby, too. And while the baby was little and cute and everybody oohed and aahed it was all good. But once Charlie started getting bigger, her mother started losing interest. And her father? He was a Paris-trained chef who owned a very successful pair of restaurants in Miami, but he never should have been allowed anywhere near other people's children, much less been given one of his own, and I'll leave it at that.

Her parents trotted Charlie out at social functions so they could show off what solid family types they were to prospective business clients. And one Saturday Charlie found herself on the deck of a boat off the shore of St. Augustine, Florida.

She was off by herself when she heard something whisper her name: *Charlie* . . .

She gave a start and stared over the railing into the sparkling green water. Nobody was there. But as she looked harder, she thought she saw a dark shape moving beneath the waves lapping against the hull.

I can give you what you want, Charlie, the voice said coyly, a little louder. It was a little girl's voice, and it was almost as if she heard it inside her head.

Tell me what you want, Charlie.

"I don't want anything." It was wrong to want things, she knew, because wanting things made her parents mad. Wanting just made her chest ache and her eyes burn. Wanting never helped her get anything.

"What did you say?" her mother asked behind her.

Charlie jumped; she hadn't heard her mother walk up.

"Uh, nothing, Mama . . ."

Her mother bent down to whisper in Charlie's ear. Though she still wore the smile she used with her clients, her voice and eyes were cold.

"What did I tell you last night?" Her voice took on a nasty edge.

"You told me to act happy, and smile, and play with Mr. Bannister's kids, 'cause you want him to hire you," Charlie stammered.

"So what the hell are you doing over here sulking by yourself, *honey*? Put a *smile* on your face. I swear, you'd better not mess this up for me . . ."

Letting the threat hang unfinished in the air, her mother turned away and gave the rest of the boat party a bright smile.

"Is she okay?" called Mr. Bannister. He was a huge, hairy man, but he had a nice smile, and he told silly jokes. ("What's brown and sticky? A stick!") Charlie decided she liked him.

"Oh, she's just a little seasick," her mother replied. "She's never been on a boat before."

"Well, how 'bout a swim? That'll help us work up an appetite. Not that some of us need any help," he added, laughing as he patted his belly.

His two little boys shrieked in delight and scampered to the ladder. Mr. Bannister stripped off his bright Hawaiian shirt, and her father slipped off his polo shirt and Bermuda shorts. The sight of him wearing nothing but his Speedos made her feel sick to her stomach, and she had to look away.

Tell me what you want. She peeked over the railing and saw the dark thing spreading like black ink beneath the waves.

"Are you coming?" her mother asked.

The thing in the water scared her worse than anything her parents might do to her later. But she knew her mother wouldn't believe her if she said she saw something down there. "Can I please just stay up here?"

"Fine." Her mother smiled tightly, then peeled off her T-shirt and went down the ladder.

Charlie moved around the railing to watch the others swim. The Bannister boys giggled as they splashed water on each other. They probably got to go to the beach all the time. She'd lived in Florida all her life, but her parents never took her to see the ocean. *They'd* gone to the beach, but always left her behind with a babysitter. Until today. Today she was finally *convenient*.

A knot of rage tightened in Charlie's chest as she watched her mother laughing and smiling that fake, fake smile of hers as she treaded water and chatted with Mr. Bannister. And there was her father, floating on his back and looking so very unconcerned and happy with himself, but Charlie knew that men who did what he did deserved to go to hell . . .

"I want them gone," she whispered through clenched teeth.

Suddenly, the dark shape surged up under her father. He had just enough time to let out a shriek before it dragged him under and tore him apart, staining the water with his blood.

Her mother screamed.

"Oh Jesus, get in the boat, get in the boat!" Mr. Bannister yelled frantically to his kids.

Her mother, who'd always been a strong, graceful swimmer, had already reached the ladder and was almost clear of the water when the thing grabbed her leg. It yanked her down so hard that Charlie heard her bones snap. Then came another furious churning under the waves. The water bloomed red.

Then silence.

Mr. Bannister, who'd stopped when he saw her mother snatched from the ladder, was treading water with his boys a few yards away. The children were crying, and Mr. Bannister's face was gray.

Finally, when it was clear the thing had gone, Mr. Bannister towed his kids to the boat and boosted them onto the ladder. After they'd scrambled up to the deck, he hauled himself up with shaking arms.

Charlie was still staring at the fading bloom of blood, numb with shock. What had she done?

Mr. Bannister put his arm around her and gently pulled her away from the railing.

"Oh, please don't look, you shouldn't see that," he said. "Jesus. It musta been a shark. I had no idea they'd be out this time of year. God, I'm so sorry . . .

you poor kid, nobody should have to see something like that."

She wasn't sorry, but she was terribly afraid.

The Coast Guard never found any trace of her parents' bodies, nor did they manage to catch any sharks. After the memorial service, Charlie left Florida and went to live with her aunt's family in Cuchillo, Texas. It was hot and dry and far, far away from the ocean.

Her mother's sister, Lois Wilson, was a real estate agent, a tall blond woman in her early forties who'd married the local tennis pro right out of college. They had two teenage girls, Misty and Jennifer, who were just as tall and pretty as their mother, and like their father they had dazzling smiles, good tans, and killer overhead volleys.

Charlie, like her father, had bark-brown hair, freckles, and a pug nose. And, as her mother had often told her, she was fat. She'd taken a lot of teasing back in elementary school, so she *knew* deep down that she was worthless and ugly, but moving into the Wilsons' big limestone house just drove it home.

Summer came and school let out, and Misty and Jennifer went off to sports camps. Mrs. Wilson deemed Charlie too young to be left at home alone. So she was sent along with Mr. Wilson every morning as he went to work at the Swim & Racquet Club at the edge of the city.

They'd arrive early, before the club opened. Mr. Wilson would go off to check the courts and open the pro shop. Charlie would be able to swim by herself for an hour or so, when the whole pool was her private blue ocean. She'd pretend she was crossing the

English Channel, or she'd throw pebbles in the deep end and pretend she was diving for pearls. Sometimes she wondered about what had really happened at St. Augustine. The voice *couldn't* have been real. Could it?

But when the club opened and people started trickling in, her paradise rapidly turned into purgatory. By noon the pool was clogged with screaming kids; the poolside became a maze of greased adult bodies basking in the sun. Even worse, her breasts were growing, perpetually sore little lumps that made her feel even more self-conscious. At school, she was covered, camouflaged. Here her every flaw lay blazing in the sun.

One boy, a big red-haired thirteen-year-old named Jason, delighted in harassing her. At first, it was just the usual taunts about her weight. Then his tactics changed alarmingly.

It started when she was near the four-foot mark in the pool, mutely watching a group of seven-year-olds play Marco Polo, when Jason grabbed her butt. She whirled around, a protest on her lips that died when she saw he'd pulled down the front of his trunks, just enough to expose his genitals.

"Touch my monkey," he drawled.

The sight made her remember her father. Charlie splashed away from Jason, numb with shock and nausea, and got out of the pool to sit in the cold shade of the snack bar.

Jason was still in the pool, smirking at her. She watched as he called over two of his buddies and whispered something to them. Then all three of them started pointing at her and laughing.

Charlie felt herself blush a deep red. She wished the

ground would open up and swallow her. She couldn't tell the lifeguard what had happened, not *now*, because even if Jason got in trouble, he'd just tell all the other kids what a pussy she was.

She prayed that Jason would get bored and find someone else to bother, but he didn't. The very next day, he rubbed up against her in the deep end.

"My big brother said you fat chicks are good fucks," he giggled. "He said it's 'cause you're so ugly, you're grateful to get any dickin' you can."

Charlie fled from the pool and went to the ladies' locker room. She changed back into her shorts, sandals, and a dry T-shirt. There was no way she was going back into the pool. She'd just go watch her uncle give tennis lessons.

But when she stepped outside, she saw that Jason and his two friends were standing around on the sidewalk that led to the tennis courts. Charlie bit her lip. There was no way she could avoid the boys.

Then she noticed that the back gate was open. There wasn't much to the land beyond, just patchy grass and a winding arroyo obscured by short mesquites and thick brush. The arroyo snaked around the whole west side of the city, a shallow, muddy gash in the arid landscape. Mr. Wilson said that the club owners wanted to turn the land into a golf course, but some local environmentalists had gotten it protected as a wetland. He'd told her not to go back there because people had seen coyotes skulking in the brush.

After St. Augustine, coyotes just didn't seem all that scary. And there would be butterflies and rocks and plants and stuff, much more interesting than tennis.

Charlie went through the gate and padded across the dry grass toward the arroyo. The sun seemed hotter out here, and now that she was away from the pool and its smells of chlorine and suntan lotion, her head practically buzzed with the scent of a thousand weedy wildflowers. She waded into the brush and stopped beside a patch of sunflowers that towered over her. She stared up at the bumblebees fumbling in the heavy, nodding blooms. A beautiful black-and-yellow butterfly flitted past her face and lighted on a small thorny bush a few feet away. Charlie stepped over and bent down to get a better look at the butterfly. Her shadow crossed it, and it flittered away. The stench of rotten meat slid up her nostrils.

She looked down and saw the fresh carcass of a headless jackrabbit just a few inches from her toes. Shiny black ants covered the ragged stump of its neck and crawled through the blood-matted fur. She could do nothing but stare at it, morbidly mesmerized.

"Hey, fatso!"

Charlie jumped away from the dead rabbit. Jason and his two friends had put on their sneakers and come through the back gate. They were sauntering toward her, grinning. Her heart pounded hard in her ears as she realized the horrible mistake she'd made coming out here where none of the adults could see. The boys would be able to do whatever they wanted if they caught her.

She plunged into the brush, tripping over rocks and fallen branches. Thorns tore at the bare flesh on her arms as she pushed through the mesquites, trying to find a place to hide. Then she broke free of the branches and nearly fell as she stumbled down the muddy red bank into the arroyo. The winding, shallow creek was wide as a road, and the water came up to her knees. Her feet scared away a school of tiny, translucent minnows.

She tried to splash across to the other side, but the red mud sucked at her soles. Her left foot got stuck when she was halfway across. Her terror turned to frustrated anger as she tried to pull her foot free, only to lose her sandal in the mud.

The mesquites rattled, and the boys appeared on the bank.

"Hey, that creek's too small for a whale like you," laughed Jason.

Charlie's heart was pounding with rage.

These little boys need to be taught a lesson, don't they, Charlie? It was the little girl's voice from the ocean, whispering inside her head.

"Yeah, come on out of there," said one of the other boys. "We just wanna play with you."

"What if I don't want to play?" she retorted.

"Then we'll *make* you," Jason replied, not smiling.

Charlie could feel her shadow spreading beneath her, hiding under the red silt, darkening the water to the color of blood. She could feel the beating of the boys' hearts, and she knew that the cruel power they'd wielded in the pool was gone in this living water.

"Then I guess you'll have to come down here and get me, penis breath," she said. "Unless you're scared of the water."

The boys looked at each other, then hopped down the bank and splashed toward her.

"*You're* the only one who's gonna have penis breath," Jason threatened.

"Jason, did you ever think about what it's like to die?" she asked.

He frowned, confused. "No."

"That's too bad. You should've thought about it, 'cause now you're *dead*!"

The dark, silty clouds curling around the boys' ankles suddenly turned to hard, razor-sharp jaws that clamped deep into their flesh. They screamed as their legs were ground down into the watery maws like celery sucked into a garbage disposal. In seconds their bodies were liquefied and consumed. The slashed rags of their swim trunks and sneakers were all that remained.

Charlie stared at the bloody water and rags and started to shiver. Dear God, she hadn't really wanted *this*, had she?

Her sandal bobbed to the surface.

Run back to the clubhouse as fast as you can, the voice told her. *Tell them you came out here to play hide-and-seek with Jason and his little friends. Two men grabbed the boys, but you got away because you were hiding.*

She grabbed the sandal, shoved it onto her foot, scrambled up the bank, and ran through the brush. Oh God, what had she done, what had she done? By the time she made it back to the gate, she was crying and screaming for help at the top of her lungs. It felt good to scream. A half-dozen people crowded around her, and she haltingly told them what the voice had said to tell. Someone ran to fetch Mr. Wilson and the club manager.

They wrapped her in a beach towel, and Mr. Wilson

sat with her and tried to soothe her with kind words and a soda from the snack bar. Charlie drank it, even though she felt sick to her stomach. Her lower belly hurt, too, a weird crampy ache she'd never felt before.

The police arrived and searched the arroyo. Soon, the officers came back with the boys' bloody trunks and sneakers in plastic bags.

When she finally got back to the house, Charlie locked herself in the bathroom and drew a big tub of hot water.

She undressed and eased herself in, wishing that the tub was bigger so that she could get her whole body under the water. The dried mud melted away from her arms and legs, staining the water a brownish red.

Charlie . . .

Suddenly, there came a bright pain like someone had stabbed her lower belly with an ice pick. She doubled over, bile rising in her throat.

Her eyes widened when she realized she was bleeding. A thin tendril of blood began to spread through the water. The pain was so bad she thought she might faint.

You're a woman now, Charlie. Hurts, doesn't it?

"Please, make it stop," she whimpered.

You'd be hurting a lot worse right now if I hadn't been there today to save you from those boys. I won't take away the blood, but I can take away the pain, if you do something for me.

"Yes, anything," she gasped. It felt as if her womb was trying to turn itself inside out.

Tell your aunt and uncle that you don't want to go back to the club, not after what happened today. Tell them you're old enough to be at the house by yourself . . .

The Wilsons reluctantly agreed to let her stay at home, and the voice took her for long walks around the city. They visited all the playgrounds and parks in the city, and she learned about the best places for her shadow: the river, park ponds, drainage pipes, ditches, even the perpetually sodden ground around the public water fountains.

She also learned to spot the quiet men who lurked near the playgrounds. Sometimes they sat and fed the birds, sometimes they jogged or walked dogs, but they always watched the children. One afternoon, she hung around a merry-go-round until one of the men noticed her. Pretending she didn't see him, she walked off to a deserted alley.

The man followed her in. He offered her a soda, then tried to grab her. She let her shadow devour him in a puddle of fetid water beside a Dumpster.

After that, her shadow made her hunt in earnest. She walked all day, sometimes even skipping lunch when her shadow scented a pedophile or a new wet place. By early August, she'd trapped two more men. Hunting was easiest when she was on her period; when she was bleeding, her shadow spoke to her constantly, urging her on. When she wasn't near her period, the shadow spoke rarely, and only around water. When it wasn't there to reassure her, she worried about the hunt, and

lay awake at night, wondering if her soul was destined
for hell.

When school started, Charlie had to abandon her
daily walks for the dull routine of books and teachers
and bland cafeteria food. She was in junior high school
now; she'd hoped it would be better than elementary
school, but it was just bigger.

She sat in the back of the classrooms, as always. Almost everyone ignored her. Everyone except her
shadow.

It started to whisper ominous suggestions when she
was walking to classes:

*See that boy? He burned a litter of kittens alive.
He's going to the restroom; follow him in and let me
have him.*

*See that girl? She's been trying to poison her baby
brother, putting soap in his formula. She'll kill him
soon if you don't help me take her.*

Charlie knew she couldn't possibly do what her
shadow wanted, not at school. Parks and underpasses
were one thing; there was lots of space, lots of ways
to slip away unnoticed even if people screamed as
they were dying. But she was trapped at school. She'd
get caught for sure.

She tried to ignore her shadow's exhortations by
making up rhymes in her head while she was between
classes or by doing anagrams and palindromes in
class when the teachers got boring. But when her
math class had a young substitute teacher named Mr.
Berling, the shadow became unbearable.

Mr. Berling was young and smiled a lot. He explained

things a whole lot better than their regular teacher, and Charlie liked him.

He touches little girls, the shadow told her. *Takes them out to see the horsies on his father's farm and feels them up in the stable.*

"Able was I ere I saw Elba," Charlie muttered under her breath. Her hands were shaking so bad she couldn't write.

He's scum, just like the rest of them. Follow him home, let him take you to the farm. He'll fit nicely in the horse trough.

"Stressed desserts." Charlie thought she was going to start crying.

"Charlie, are you okay?" asked Mr. Berling.

"I think I ate something bad at lunch," she stammered. "I think I need to go to the bathroom for a while."

"Please do," he agreed.

Charlie bolted from the classroom, ran downstairs to the girls' restroom in the basement. It was usually empty; Charlie prayed no one else would be in there.

She pushed through the door and found four girls clustered around a pack of Camels. Two were inexpertly puffing on cigarettes as the third showed the fourth how to work the childproof lighter. They all turned to stare at her when she came in.

Charlie, get out of here this instant! the shadow demanded. But it seemed to be growing weaker, recoiling from the smoke. With each breath she took, it slipped farther away.

"Can I try one of those?" she asked, stepping toward the group.

"I guess," said the girl with the pack. She pulled out a cigarette and handed it and the lighter to Charlie.

Charlie lit it and took an experimental drag, then immediately started to cough and gag. This was surely the foulest thing she'd had in her mouth since . . . since a time she didn't want to remember. Eyes streaming, she took another puff.

It was working, wind and fire canceling water and earth. Her shadow's indignant demands were faint, fading into the rhythmic drip of the leaky faucet.

Charlie soon learned that it only took two cigarettes a day to silence her shadow. She smoked them on the sly in the bathroom at school and in the backyard at home. When the shadow started to talk to her in her dreams, Charlie bought incense and started burning it in her room at night.

She knew she was vulnerable without her shadow. The sick men she'd hunted before were still around. And she had the awful suspicion that she was still attuned to them, and they were attracted to her. She needed a way to protect herself.

So when her aunt asked her what she wanted for her fifteenth birthday, she asked for martial arts lessons. Her uncle took her to Master Kim's Tae Kwon Do Dojang, bought her a white uniform and belt, and enrolled her for a class that started that very night.

Charlie had always hated PE classes, and although tae kwon do was several degrees harder than any sport she'd been made to try at school, she liked it instantly. Unlike running stairs or chasing balls, the kicks and strikes had a *point*, a real and practical purpose. Everything she learned was useful; getting into shape was just a happy side effect.

Another happy benefit of the class was David. He was a year older than Charlie, tall and cute but painfully shy. Charlie was attracted to him the moment she saw him. It took her weeks to swallow her own fear and talk to him after class, but once she did they became fast friends. Best friends, and as far as she could tell, each other's only friend. He already had his driver's license, so they often went out to see movies or go hiking in the low hills north of the city.

Six months after they started going out, Charlie knew that she loved David, even though he'd only hugged her briefly and had never tried to kiss her. He didn't say so, but she suspected it was because of her smoking. His favorite aunt had died of lung cancer, and he hated being around smoke. She cut back as much as she thought she could, and wished she could explain her habit to him. But she knew that her shadow, although it had gone silent, would not tolerate being exposed.

A year later, David got his red belt, and Charlie got her blue. They were both drenched in sweat by the end of their respective skills tests. Charlie took a quick shower and changed at the dojang, but David never liked showering in the men's room there, since Master Kim had not thought to provide separate stalls for the men.

"I feel way gross," he said as they climbed into his truck. "I probably stink, too. Sorry. Let's go back to my place and let me get cleaned up, and then you wanna go get some ice cream?"

"Sure." Charlie suddenly realized that she hadn't had a cigarette all day. She hadn't smoked that morning because she wanted her lungs clean for the test, and she'd forgotten to bring her pack with her for a puff in the ladies' room afterward.

"It's really cool that you've got your blue. Now you'll be able to spar with us in tournaments. I heard Master Kim on the phone the other day; he's arranging for all of us to go to Corpus Christi next month for the Tejas Invitational. That will totally kick butt; we'll get to go to the beach. I've never been swimming in the ocean before."

The ocean. Charlie's skin prickled with dread.

"I—I can't go," she muttered.

"What do you mean? You gotta go, this will be too cool to miss!"

"I can't." Dammit, why had she forgotten her cigarettes?

"Is it because you're nervous about competing? You shouldn't worry about that, you're really good. And you know how to intimidate people. I mean, you should see the look you get on your face when you hit the heavy bag—"

"Look, don't bug me about this!" she snapped. "I said I can't go, end of discussion!"

"Okay, okay, sorry."

They drove on in silence until they got to David's house. The place was empty; his father was probably off on a sales trip, and his mother was probably working another fourteen-hour nursing shift at the hospital. David didn't like to talk about his parents much.

She followed him into the house and to his bedroom.

David kept his room excruciatingly tidy; Charlie
doubted she'd even be able to find dust on the tops of
his bookshelves.

"You wanna just hang out here while I shower?"
he asked as he pulled fresh clothes out of his dresser.
"If you want a Coke or anything, just help yourself."

"Okay."

David padded off to the bathroom, and she sat
down on the edge of his bed, trying not to muss the
perfectly smooth green bedspread. She stared around
at the neat rows of kung fu movie posters on the
walls.

I wonder what David keeps under his bed.

Charlie's breath caught in her throat. Had that been
her own thought, or her shadow's?

"Are you there?" she whispered, aching for a cigarette. "Damn you, David's a good guy, there's nothing
bad under his bed."

Are you sure?

Charlie sat very still, muttering anagrams to herself
while she tried to ignore the dreadful curiosity building inside her. She could hear the hiss and spatter of
water from the shower.

*Are you afraid? If you don't look, you'll always
wonder.*

"Damn you." Charlie slid off the bed, got down on
her hands and knees, and peeked under the bed. She
pushed aside a baseball mitt and a pair of cleats and
saw a wide, flat cardboard box. She pulled it out and
opened it up. Inside was a stack of comic books in
plastic sleeves.

"See, it's just comics," she said, starting to rifle

through them. "Batman, and Nighthawk, and the Hulk, and . . . oh shit."

At the bottom was a Swedish magazine, unsleeved. She couldn't understand the words, but the pictures of naked prepubescent boys were clear enough. The center spread showed an elevenish boy giving a slightly older boy a blow job. And tucked inside the back cover were three Polaroids of a naked boy in different poses on David's bed. On the same green bedspread she'd tried not to wrinkle.

Charlie felt completely and utterly numb. Defeated. She put everything back exactly the way she'd found it and reassumed her perch on the bed. A few minutes later, David came in, freshly dressed and toweling off his short brown hair.

"You're right, I shouldn't be nervous about Corpus Christi," she announced. "I changed my mind; I'll go to the tournament."

His face broke into a broad grin, and he leaned over and gave her a quick hug. "That's great! We'll have a terrific time, I bet."

In her mind, Charlie could see David, the only real friend she'd ever had, being torn apart in the waves. Her shadow felt smug, satisfied.

Was her whole life going to be like this?

Despite her depression, Charlie did well at the tournament, placed tenth in her belt class out of a field of seventy competitors. David did even better, placing third. In fact, most of Master Kim's students did quite well, so he took all eight of them out for pizza that night, and drove them to the beach in his big van the next morning.

The sky was overcast, and though it was a hot day, the strong, salt-greasy wind from the ocean carried a chilly bite.

"Watch out for undertow!" Master Kim admonished as they piled out of the van in their flip-flops and big T-shirts. "It take you down like *that*." He hit his palm with his fist for emphasis. "And watch out for what lifeguard say. If he yell 'shark,' get out of water, fast as you can."

Charlie walked across the sand and set down her beach bag. She pulled out the single-edged razor blade she'd hidden in the folds of her towel. Hiding it in her hand, she kicked off her flip-flops and headed out to meet the waves.

David had run ahead of her and was already paddling around, happy as an otter. The water was dark, a gray like decaying headstones. Then Charlie waded out away from the others until she was in chest-deep.

He's in over his head, her shadow whispered. *Let me have him.*

"No."

For a moment, nothing happened as her shadow considered this new rebellion. Then Charlie felt a sharp cramp, deep in her womb.

Give him to me. The shadow's little-girl voice was ominous.

The cramp got worse, and bile rose in Charlie's throat. "No."

I saved you! the shadow shrieked inside her head. *Without me, you'd be less than nothing, and* this *is how you repay me?*

"Maybe I *am* nothing. But it's better than what *you* are."

I'm your God, and don't you forget that.

The cramping became a wrenching pain in her stomach and intestines, and she cried out.

"Charlie?" David called, paddling toward her. "Are you okay?"

"I'm fine, please don't come over here," she managed to call back.

You'll do as I say. And today we're going to start with that little boyfucker over there.

"You haven't proved to me that he's done more than look, and even if he has, I won't let you. Not today."

She began to slit her left wrist with the razor blade. Her blood was invisible in the dark water. "I'd rather die than live like this. You're not getting my permission to kill, never ever again. You asked me what I wanted, and now I want you to *go away*."

The shadow shrieked inside her head, the pain almost unbearable. A big, sandpapery shape bumped up against her body. Sharp jaws clamped down on her bleeding wrist.

It yanked her down beneath the waves and shoved her into the sandy bottom. Through the cloudy water, she could see the pearly dead eyes of the big shark holding her down. The shark's wide, razored mouth was inches from her face.

Give. Me. The. Boy.

Charlie kicked against the shark, churning up the sand, sharp shells and rocks cutting her legs. With her free hand, she beat against the shark's snout, but the huge fish wouldn't budge. Her eyes burned, and her lungs screamed for air.

She saw movement in the corner of her eye. David was diving down toward her.

"No!" she tried to scream, but all that came out was her last bit of air in a long string of bubbles.

The shark released her and rose to meet David. She pushed off the bottom, trying to reach them, but she'd gone too long without a breath. She blacked out.

Charlie came to on a stretcher on the sand. Her left arm was splinted and wrapped in bloody gauze. Master Kim and two paramedics hovered over her. Kim's face was grave.

"Where's David?" she whispered.

"I'm right here." He pushed through the crowd and knelt beside her. There wasn't a scratch on him. "Everything's gonna be okay."

Her shadow seemed to be gone. But the shark's attack crushed bones in her wrist and forearm and severed a couple of tendons. The doctors said she'd need more surgeries and it would be at least a year before she regained full use of her hand. She felt weaker than she ever had before.

David came to visit her in the hospital the next day. He could barely sit still, and his eyes glowed with fever.

"It told me that I could save you, just by wanting to," he said after the nurse left.

"It?" Charlie felt a deep chill.

"Yeah. It's like . . . it's incredible. I can kick more ass than Bruce Lee and Batman combined! I just have to be near water, and no one can stop me."

"Oh God, David . . ." Charlie trailed off as it all sank in.

Her best friend seemed not to hear her. "I'm gonna

go away, maybe to New York or Los Angeles. I just thought you should know, 'cause we're buddies and all. I don't need school, I don't need Master Kim. Now I can do *anything I want*."

"David, no, please, don't do this, listen to me—"

"Sorry, Charlie, I gotta cruise." He planted a quick, hard kiss on her forehead.

And then he was gone.

Charlie lay in bed, listening to her heart pound. Between the beats, she thought she could hear the shadow's little-girl laughter.

Grave Matters

Pal and I looked at each other; clearly the shadow was some sort of devil. Whether it was the kind we could deal with was another matter entirely.

Charlie crushed her smoldering cigarette stub in her lunch plate and lit up another. "I thought that would be the last I'd ever see of David, you know? And it was, until about six weeks ago. I was on night patrol near the fence when he popped up out of nowhere. He looks so sketchy now, I barely recognized him."

"What did he want?" I asked.

"He told me how he and the shadow had gone to L.A. for a while but they came back here—how did he put it?—because 'the darkness was coming' or something like that. And even though the shadow's a lot stronger now, it and David got stuck here like everyone else. He told me that he and the shadow are helping Miko. Before, when she popped out people's souls, their bodies might live on for a little while but then they'd die. The shadow gave him the power to turn them into zombies that she could control. They'll stay alive for months if you give them food and water. And so Miko let him and the shadow do pretty much what they wanted—I guess the shadow mostly wants living bodies to eat—as long as she got enough zombies to do what she wanted."

"But why did he come to you that night?"

Charlie shrugged. "Why *that* night? I dunno. But what he wanted was for me to join him and come back to the shadow. He said that he'd been going into abandoned houses and stealing money and gold and stuff that people had left behind, and he had millions of dollars in cash stashed away. He said that I'd always been his best buddy and he wanted to share the loot with me. And if I helped them, he'd make sure I got out alive, and once we got out we'd buy a mansion in Beverly Hills and have movie stars over for parties and all kinds of other crap."

"What did you say to him?"

Charlie looked indignant. "What do you *think* I said to him? I told him to go to hell and walked away. No way I was going back to the shadow. No way I was helping Miko. Not *ever*."

"Do you know where they are now?"

She nodded. "Civic League Park. There's a water lily garden there. Big ponds. The shadow's living in one of them, and David's in the gardener's hut."

I ate some peanuts and pondered everything she'd told us. "If we could cut off Miko's meat puppet supply, well, that *would* be a wedge we could use against her. But I need your help. If we're going to stop David and the shadow, I need to know that you're not going to back out at the last minute. I need to know you won't decide to give up and surrender to Miko like the major did."

Now the girl looked downright angry. "I put those

zombies out of their misery for you, didn't I? I've been doing horrible stuff like that for more than a year. If I were in the army, I'd have done my tour by now, but it ain't over, and I ain't giving up. I used to think I was weak, but I *know* I'm a strong person now. And if you need proof, just look at all the *other* people who gave up. And *I'm* still here."

She paused, then continued, speaking more softly. "Do y'all know where I should be right now? I should be at my aunt's house, visiting on summer break from NYU. I got my acceptance letter right before everything went crazy here. But I can't ever see her again. She and my uncle and everybody else in my family are dead. Because of the shadow, and because of Miko. I'll *never* give myself up to a monster ever again."

"Okay, then." I sat back in my chair. "Come upstairs with us. I need to get a little more information, and then we can figure out what our next move is."

My father was quick to answer his mirror. I was beginning to wonder if he ever left his workshop. He looked grave after I told him about Miko taking Cooper and the Warlock hostage.

"I hoped that you might be able to avoid a direct confrontation with her, but it seems she has left you no choice," he said. "I have some information that I hope will help you. A soul harvester like Miko would find much better hunting in large cities. I did a series of forensic spells to try to discover why she came to a town as small as Cuchillo. And while much of the divination I gleaned was muddled, all of the spells turned up the name of a dead man: Henry Schleicher. I believe his bones have a tale to tell, and the information within his story may give you the means to defeat her."

"Is he a meat puppet, or is he in the ground?" I thought of the old man I'd seen in Miko's memories.

"His body has been laid to a Christian's proper rest, although I don't believe his soul has met a comfortable fate."

"How many graveyards are in this town?" I asked Charlie when I came back to my body.

"Well, there's a Jewish cemetery, I don't know exactly where, and a Catholic cemetery over by Sacred Heart, but the main cemetery is off Avenue N," she replied.

"Is the main cemetery very far away?"

"Just a couple of miles . . . why?"

"We've got a body to dig up."

Once we'd gathered some digging tools, hand-crank lanterns, and a couple of burlap sacks, and had gotten my shotgun and Charlie's AK-47 out of the dorm's weapons check, Pal flew us and the black kitten he'd claimed to the fifty-acre Fairmount Cemetery. We landed in the courtyard beside the cemetery office, and I broke into the building to rifle through the filing cabinet. The graveyard was laid out in different numbered blocks, and after a bit of hunting I discovered that he was buried in no. 84, the section reserved for World War II veterans.

The sun was starting to fade below the horizon as we finally found his plot. His marble headstone had a purple heart symbol etched on it, and the date said he'd died nearly a decade before at the age of seventy-four.

"We need to get back before it gets really dark; this place isn't very—"

"Defensible. I *know*. So let's get to digging." I turned to Pal. "Unless you know a spell for this kind of thing?"

Pal cocked his head thoughtfully. "You know, I think I do."

He began to play a new calliope tune. A few seconds later, the ground began to shake, and a crack formed in the earth covering Henry Schleicher's grave. The soil bubbled and foamed as if it had been turned to liquid, and suddenly the plain black casket bobbed to the surface. The soil went still and firm again beneath it, and the casket settled slightly.

"That's hella slick," I told him.

He took a bow.

I hefted the pick and used it to crack open the lid. The corpse inside was little more than a skeleton in a stained army uniform; short strands of white hair still adorned the parchmentlike scalp adhering to the top of the skull.

I touched one of Henry's desiccated fingers; instantly, my mind was filled with his nightmares and memories of his death, still painful and bright even after ten years in the dry darkness:

—*Miko pulled me tight, her breath hot and ragged in my ear. As I gasped for air, I felt a strange tugging in my chest, my testicles, my mind. Something deep inside started to peel free. "Oh yes, please, yes . . ." she whispered. My soul tore away. Her body convulsed against mine, and she let out a hoarse, animal groan of delight.*—

—*I knelt beside an eighteen-year-old soldier with a*

chest full of shrapnel, and I couldn't stop the bleeding. I could hear the Zero making another pass over the island. The kid was dying, no matter what I did. The plane was zooming closer, and I knew we had to get to cover.—

I shoved his memories aside and regained enough focus to jerk my hand away, breathing hard. "He's the guy, all right."

Using one of the burlap sacks as a mitt, I reached back in, grabbed the skeleton's closest wrist, and pulled. There was a crack as the bones came loose at the elbow. I pulled the half arm into the bag and tied it off.

"I've got what I came for." I heaved the casket lid closed. "Can you put him back where we found him, Pal?"

"Certainly."

Izanamiko No Oni

Once we got back to campus, we checked in our weapons and went up to the eighth floor.

"Guys, I need to try to find some useful memories in Henry's bones," I told Charlie and Pal as I picked up my mouthpiece. "My gut's telling me that there's something here we can use against Miko. But the imprints are so strong . . . the old guy went through some horrible things. The Goad might slip out and take over my body while I'm under and try to do some serious damage."

Charlie stared at me. "Are you possessed by an evil spirit or something?"

"Yeah." I winced. "Forgot to mention that part. Sorry." I sat down in the restraint chair. "Anyway, I need you guys to strap me back in this thing." I popped the mouthpiece in. "Please leave my jaw and my flesh hand free."

They did as I asked.

"Pal, put his bone in my hand; take it away if I have a seizure or lose consciousness or anything like that."

"I will."

He put the bone in my outstretched hand; immediately I was hit with Henry's primary death-memory. I bit down on the mouthpiece and tried to ride it out, tried to catch the memory-threads I could feel drifting below it—

The girl stood at the new releases shelf, and God almighty, she was a looker. She wore tight worn-out cutoffs that barely covered up enough to keep her from getting arrested, and she was barefoot. The first three buttons of her black silk blouse were open, and I could see her breasts swaying free under the fabric. Thick hair, as shiny and black as her blouse, hung nearly to her waist. I wondered if her hair would feel like silk.—

I pushed that thread away and moved on to the next.

The girl had the spooky, unnatural grin I'd seen on the faces of shell-shocked soldiers who'd cracked to the point of endlessly giggling at the horrors they'd seen. Her eyes were glassy, and I wondered if she was sick, or on drugs.

"I came to apologize, Henry." Her words came out in a breathless rush as she stepped toward the cash register. "I was a bitch, wasn't I? Shouldn't be bitchy to a nice old man like you. So very nice."

The scent of her rose perfume was thick in the air, but under it was the faint stink of sulfur and scorched metal.

"I mean, I can't be mad about what happened, can I?" she said. "America fixed Japan up so nice afterward, and put in bases to protect us. My own father was a GI, and if not for the bomb . . . I wouldn't even be here, and I should be glad to be alive, huh, Henry?"

I was sure the girl was utterly out of her mind. "What do you want from me?" I stammered, starting to inch toward the telephone mounted a few yards away on the wall.

"I want what everybody wants . . . that special

someone who'll make me . . . complete. I feel so alone, and I think you do, too. Are you the man I'm looking for? I said yesterday that you're a part of things, but I've got to make sure . . ."

She lunged forward and pinned me to the wall. I struggled and hollered for help, but her arms were iron. She pressed her body against mine. I couldn't help but thrill at the feel of her silky hair tickling my neck, her hard nipples brushing my chest.

"Sh, I'm not going to hurt you. Just relax."

She started to kiss me, and her right hand slid down my belly to rest over my fly. I squeezed my eyes shut. Trapped between terror and lust, I could do nothing but moan as she unzipped my pants and pulled my johnson free.

When she went down on me, a blue shower of sparks exploded behind my eyes. Oh dear God in Heaven, my wife, Violet, had never done this, never would have done it if I'd begged and pleaded, oh dear God!

"Who . . . who are you?" I gasped.

I felt the buzz of the girl's muffled laugh, and she bobbed faster and faster against me to match the slamming of my heart, and suddenly I was afraid I was about to have a heart attack, but at my age maybe this wouldn't be a bad way to go, and I came, a hot, sweet explosion that rocked my whole body—

The vision was yanked away along with the bone in my hand. Pal and Charlie peered at me, concerned. My shirt was damp with perspiration, and I was panting like I'd been running a marathon.

"Are you all right?" Pal asked. "You started crying out."

"I'm fine," I replied, my voice hoarse. "I think I'm getting closer to something useful."

I wiggled my fingers at my familiar. Pal blinked at me uncertainly and put the bone into my hand, and I went right back into the memory:

The girl pulled away, and I slid down the wall to lie in a sweaty heap. When I finally realized I hadn't, in fact, had a stroke or heart attack, I opened my eyes and fumbled my pants back on.

She was gone, but a book entitled The Myths of Japan *lay on the floor a few yards away. She'd taped a note to the front cover: "Can you guess my name?"*

Trembling, I crawled to the book and opened it at the page she'd marked. I began to read about Izanami, mother of the gods, who became ruler of the under-world after she'd burned to death giving birth to Kagu-tsuchi, the god of fire.

The memory faded, and I grabbed the one closest to it:

My best friend's chest exploded in a crimson spray. The young soldier fell twitching in the sandy mud. I helplessly tried to do something, anything, for him with the pathetic canvas medical kit. My buddy's eyes rolled up into his head as he let out an awful wet noise. Then he was dead.

I dropped the kit and stared over the palm log at the Japanese machine-gun nest. The Japs were still fir-ing, black smoke snaking from the slits in the bone-pale concrete bunker. I looked down at the sticky blood on my hands, at the black flies that were al-ready crawling over my buddy's wounds.

My field of vision started to twitch in time with my

pounding heart, and bile rose hot in my throat. Those filthy yellow cockroaches were gonna pay for this. I grabbed my M1 rifle and a grenade and vaulted over the log. Screaming at the top of my lungs, I pounded across the clearing. I felt lances of fire slash my shoulder, my thigh, as I pulled the grenade pin and hurled it into one of the black slits.

The percussive gust nearly knocked me down, but as soon as the orange bloom of fire died I kicked open the door and fired a half-dozen rounds into the bunker. When no one returned fire, I jumped down inside.

A half-dozen Japs lay sprawled on the concrete floor, faces and bodies torn apart by shrapnel. Then I heard a ragged moan and saw one of them start rolling around. The kid was maybe sixteen or seventeen, his face a blood-speckled mask of shock. His close-cut hair looked like the down of a black duckling.

In two strides I was on the Japanese soldier and bashed his face in with the butt of my rifle.

"Ah, truly the deed of a mighty warrior!" came a laugh behind me.

I whirled around, but found my arms were paralyzed, my rifle useless.

One of the corpses rose, and in the dimness I first thought it was a man dressed all in black. But when it stepped into a shaft of sunlight, I saw it was a naked woman, her whole body charred almost beyond recognition, cooked flesh peeling from the bones of her face and hands. Her eyes were bright amber, live coals glowing in the ruin of her face.

She raised a hand, and my dog tags slithered up my chest to my throat. The chain jerked tight, then broke, leaving a stinging track on my neck. The tags flew into her open palm.

"Henry Schleicher, corporal," she read aloud. "You please me. You've sent many souls to my realm today. Now you'll drop your weapon and please me more.*"*

My hands released the rifle and I staggered backward to fall against a pile of bodies in the corner. To my utter horror, I realized I had an erection, and the woman was coming for me, her grin baring rows of gray shark's teeth—

The vision mercifully ended as Pal snatched the bone from my hand. My throat and jaw ached, and tears stung my eyes.

"Are you *sure* you're okay?" Charlie asked.

"You were screaming," Pal added.

"Think I'm gonna be sick," I croaked. "Get me out of this."

They untied me and I lurched into the bathroom to throw up. I washed my face, brushed my teeth, calmed myself down, and went back into the room.

"Okay. Let's try this again, guys." I sat back down on the chair.

"You're sure?" Charlie asked.

I shook my head. "Not really. But this is still the only idea I've got."

Once they strapped me back in, Pal put Henry's remains in my hand and I slipped into the next memory:

"Can you guess my name?"

My heart froze. The girl stood beside my bed. Her slim body was shoehorned into torn, faded jeans, a black T-shirt, and tall boots. She'd cut off all her hair, buzz-cut it nearly to the scalp.

"How'd you get in here?" I stammered, blushing at

the hard-on straining against the elastic waistband of my pajamas. I crossed my hands in front of my fly.

"What, you won't even guess? You're no fun," she pouted. "Anyhow, I'm Miko, and I'll be your demon for the evening."

"How'd you get in here?" I repeated.

She nodded toward the open window. "Climbed your ivy. Same as when I came for your wife."

It took a moment for the implication of her words to sink in. "You . . . you killed Violet."

Another nod. "She was distracting. Not very satisfying, though; I had to kill an old man in a nursing home today, just to make sure I'd be halfway sane when I came here tonight."

I couldn't keep from staring at the gun on the table. There was no way I could get to it before Miko did.

She followed my gaze. "Is that for me, Henry? You can't kill me, you know . . . thanks to dear ol' mom, I have no soul. What'd my mother look like when she raped you, Henry? Burned or wormy or what?"

"Your moth—Oh dear God." The room started swimming before my eyes.

"She looks like a big smoke cloud now. She and my brother were fighting over the souls in the war, and Kagu-tsuchi tricked her into being at Hiroshima when Little Boy blew," the girl continued. "Did you know that the mother's responsible for giving her child a soul? Kind of an automatic thing, usually, but since mine's the queen of the dead, she gave me a jones for murder, instead. Mother likes 'em young, and so she made sure I'd send plenty of kids her way."

She sat down on the edge of the bed and gave me a grim smile. "I guess you could say my soul is on lay-

away; I get it as soon as I've made up for what my brother took from my mother. Kagu-tsuchi gets the souls of people who burn to death, and at Hiroshima and Nagasaki that was pretty much everyone. Mother was very angry about losing the souls, not to mention being vaporized, so I have to match the A-bomb body count: 236,962 people. And since I can't use fire, bombs and guns are out, so I pretty much have to take lives one by one. So far I've only managed to send off 538. At this rate, I won't be done for another twenty thousand years."

She rubbed her face. "I wish you guys had just nuked *one* city, *a much* smaller *city. I'd be lying if I told you killing wasn't a kick, but I'm ready to do something else for a change, you know?"*

"Why . . . why are you telling me this?" I asked.

"Because you can get me out of this. You're my father, and if you willingly give me your soul, I'm freed from my birth curse."

She seemed absolutely, horrifyingly sincere, but I reminded myself she had to be insane, or some sicko getting her kicks at my expense.

"Why should I believe this crazy story of yours?" I demanded nervously. "All that was just a dream I had, and you're just playing with my head. I . . . I can't possibly be your father."

She dug into her pocket, pulled out a silver chain, and flipped it through the air. "Catch."

I caught the chain. Two dog tags lay in my palm, gleaming like razor blades. They bore my name, rank, and serial number. The metal was flecked with brownish gunk that might have been blood or rust or both. I turned the tags over and saw the crude American eagle

I'd etched with my pocket knife in a fit of barracks boredom. My heart dropped to the soles of my feet.

"Where did you get this?"

"Mother likes to play games. She gave me a box full of hundreds of dog tags a few decades ago, and told me one of them belonged to my father. I've blown a lot of old men, Henry, and you're the only one who tasted of my mother's poison."

Her mother's poison.

Miko met his mortified stare. "I'd always expected my father would be a man who was responsible in some important way, maybe Oppenheimer or the pilot of the Enola Gay or somebody, but it was just you," she said quietly. "You didn't ask for this, but neither did I. And if you don't give me your soul, nearly a quarter of a million people are going to get something they didn't ask for, either."

She stood up and went to the window.

"Do I have a choice?" I stammered.

"You have all the choice in the world. Your soul's no good to me if I have to take it by force. If you want to give me and everybody else a chance at a normal life, you'll meet me tomorrow at midnight on top of Mount Nebo. Otherwise, you can just stay here, and I won't bother you again. By the taste of you, I'd say you'll live to an even riper old age, maybe even see a whole century."

She swung a leg over the windowsill. "I guess it all depends on whether you're still willing to die for your country or not."

And then she was gone.

The memory ended, but another curled around its tail; I followed the new thread:

I opened the top drawer of the bureau, took out the tray that held all my old medals and ribbons, and stared down at them. The tray told me that I'd been a hero once, and like my daddy always told me, heroes took care of business, never shied away from what had to be done.

I felt cold deep in my bones. If Miko had been telling me the truth, I had to deal with her, had to stop her from killing anyone else. But how could I stop a demon?

I went downstairs and reread the Japanese mythology book, pored over the entries on Izanami's other deadly child, the god of fire. If the gods truly feuded as Miko claimed they did, then Kagu-tsuchi wouldn't want his little sister to complete her task, would he? If all this was real, then I ought to be able to contact the god of fire, somehow.

I went to my bedroom and arranged my medals in a big glass ashtray. I carried it down to the kitchen, set it on the counter, cracked open a bottle of brandy I'd been saving for company, and sloshed the liquor over the decorations. Part of my brain hollered at me for wasting good booze and ruining family heirlooms, but the rest reminded me that I had no real blood relatives left to inherit my treasures . . . except Miko, if she was telling the truth. And if she was, then contacting the god was a hell of a lot more important than a few medals.

"Okay, Kagu-tsuchi, if you're out there, tell me what to do," I muttered, then lit a match and threw it in the ashtray.

It blazed bright, and I stared into the flames. The Silver Star and Purple Heart began to blacken, and the ribbons crackled as they caught fire. The crack-ling got louder, and suddenly I heard a hissing voice inside my head:

"While the mother survived, the daughter shall die."

The fire grew hotter, brighter, and suddenly the ash-tray exploded. I stumbled back, momentarily blinded, eyebrows singed.

When the gray afterimage finally faded, I saw that the ashtray and medals were scorched slag, a black, bubbled mess melting into the countertop.

The memory faded into another one:

That night, I stood before the mirror, dressed in my old army uniform. The seat of my pants sagged and my belly bulged around the waistband, but the fit wasn't that bad, considering.

I slipped the shiny Smith & Wesson and a road flare into the left pocket of my jacket. Then I carefully slid a Mason jar filled with home-brew napalm into my right pocket. I'd made the jellied gasoline that after-noon by soaking packing peanuts in gas; I hoped I'd made enough, hoped the jar wouldn't leak.

I headed downstairs to my old Buick. It was a hot night, so I turned the AC up high as I drove. Mount Nebo was fifteen minutes outside town, hardly a mountain but certainly the largest bump in the flatland for miles. A local rancher had lived on Mount Nebo for a few decades, but five years ago his house had been hit by lightning and burned down, killing him and his family. Somebody back East had inherited the land, but nobody ever came out to do anything with it.

As I turned up the farm road toward Nebo, I saw the ruined chimney and walls silhouetted against the full moon. Below, I saw a flickering light, maybe a campfire? I parked the car off the road, clicked on my flashlight, and began to hike up the hill.

I had to pause midway to massage the rusty ache in my knees, and was wheezing badly by the time I reached the top. My dress shirt was sodden with sweat underneath my uniform jacket. When the blood stopped roaring in my ears, I realized I could hear Miko singing nearby, too softly for me to make out any words, but the sound sent an electric buzz through my chest and loins.

No. She was my enemy, and I had to stop her. I pulled out the Mason jar, unscrewed the lid with shaking hands, then hobbled around the weathered hunks of burned wood and cinder blocks to find Miko.

I turned a corner into what might have been a bedroom, and my breath caught in my throat. Miko was dancing naked on a red blanket surrounded by dozens of candles, from tiny white votives to slim tapers to enormous three-wick cylinders. The thin flames curled and flickered in the hot night breeze, and Miko's dance mimicked them, her body twisting and rippling, the light gleaming on her hair, her breasts, her taut arms and legs. Maybe she had more muscles than I'd been brought up to think a woman ought to have, but she was the most beautiful thing I'd ever seen. The words to her serpentine melody were Japanese, but I understood the message: Come to me.

I wanted more than anything to go to her, to touch that wonderful body, but I knew what I had to do. She was the enemy. Swallowing nervously, I pulled out the road flare and sparked it against a piece of cinder block.

Miko stopped singing and turned to me, eyes wide.

"No! Put that stuff down, you don't know what—" she began, rushing toward me.

Heart hammering, I slung the Mason jar at her. She knocked it away, but jellied gasoline splattered on her arm, her breasts, her face. She started screaming even before I threw the flare.

She virtually exploded. Her flesh seemed eager to burn. I watched, transfixed in horror, as her hair ignited like flash paper, her skin crisping and peeling, fat and muscle sizzling and popping under the burning napalm. Howling, she frantically beat at the flames spreading across her body. She stumbled backward into the candles and collapsed.

The air was thick with the smoke from her burning flesh. Bile rose in my throat as I watched her thrashing, scattering her candles, fighting the flames that had already destroyed her lovely eyes, her skin, her fingers. I wanted to turn away, but found I could not even shut my eyes.

Finally, her howling fell to a whimper, and then the whimper faded into the crackling of the dying flames. I realized I was crying, realized I could move again. I turned and staggered away, wishing I'd brought a handkerchief to cover my mouth and nose, wondering if I'd be able to keep from blowing out my brains when I got back to my empty house.

"Father, please don't leave me like this . . ."

Oh dear God.

I turned, and saw Miko's corpse stir in the ashes and congealing candle wax. Her face was that of Death, eyes and nose black holes, charred scalp peeling away from red bone. I wondered how she could still speak, how she could still be alive.

"Where are you?" She tried to raise herself up on an elbow, but couldn't. "Please, not like this . . . Kagutsuchi won't take me. Neither will my mother. No one will come for me. When my bones rot away I will still be trapped here."

She made a choking noise, and her whole body started to spasm. It took me a moment to realize she was sobbing.

Dear God, what had I done? Not even Satan himself deserved what I'd done to Miko. To my own daughter. Heroes didn't burn beautiful women alive, didn't damn them to an eternity of agony in a wasteland. I squeezed my eyes shut against the hot tears streaming down my face.

"Father, please . . ."

Heart hammering madly, I turned and made my way through the wreckage to Miko.

"What can I do?" I stammered.

"Take me in your arms."

Swallowing against a wave of nausea, knees creaking, I got down on the ground and lay down beside her. She slid a hand across my chest and wriggled close to me, her skin crackling with every movement.

I stared at the full moon overhead, my vision twitching with every beat of my heart.

She kissed my cheek, her lips dry and hard. A cold thrill coursed through my body. I felt my heart stutter, then cramp down. The pain was exquisite.

As my vision began to fade, I turned my head and

*saw fresh skin spreading across her face and body,
new eyes blooming open in her sockets.*

*Before the cold blackness engulfed me, I felt her
gently kiss my forehead. Her lips were soft as funeral
roses.*

"Thank you," was all she said.

I came out of the vision and released Henry's bones.
Clammy sweat drenched my clothing. The sun coming through the blinds was low and golden; I'd been
reliving the old man's memories for hours.

Pal blinked at me expectantly. "Did you discover
anything we can use against Miko?"

"Yeah," I replied. "We can kill her with fire. Or at
least hurt her really damn bad with it."

chapter twenty-eight

Shadowland

My journey into Henry's memories left me exhausted and shaky, and none of us thought that trying to stage an attack on either David or Miko after dark would be a good idea. So we decided to get up early and head out at dawn to try to cut off Miko's meat puppet supply.

But as Pal snoozed on the other bed, I lay awake, thinking of everything I'd seen that day. At least now I knew what we were dealing with. I hadn't thought a demon could become a devil by winning the soul of one of its unwilling creators, but clearly Miko had neatly exploited that particular supernatural loophole. And in the decade since, she'd managed to put herself on the road to becoming a brand-new death goddess.

Obviously she hadn't given up on taking souls, and twisting people into committing spiritual suicide wasn't any better than murder in my book. Then I reconsidered: perhaps she *had* stopped soul harvesting for a time, but returned to it with a vengeance a year ago. But why? How much of what she'd told Henry was actually true? It was impossible to tell.

After a few hours of sleep, Pal and I met Charlie at the cafeteria at 6 A.M. for a quick breakfast, and then we gathered our gear and weapons and the black kittens and flew out toward the Civic League Park near the center of town.

"The water lily garden is back behind those trees," Charlie said from her seat behind me, a little too loudly in my ear. She pointed toward a thicket of oaks beyond the sun-browned remains of a municipal golf course. "We should land before they see us."

"Okay," I replied. "How far can the shadow see and hear?"

"It can see people who are in the water with it, but if it's hunting on land it needs David's eyes and ears," she said. "It felt like it needed mine, anyway."

I scanned the ground beneath us; at the intersection beside the entrance to the golf course, there was an abandoned Sonic drive-in. *Pal, land us over there.*

Pal settled gently in the shade of the Sonic's covered parking area. Someone had long ago smashed most of the plastic menus at the individual order stations. I slid down to the weed-ridden pavement, and Charlie followed.

"So if we blind David, we've partly blinded the shadow?" I asked her as I pulled my black kitten off its climb up my brown dragonskin jacket. I tucked the little creature back into the sling I'd borrowed from the dorm's front desk. Even unbuttoned, the jacket was stiflingly hot, but the sun was strong and I didn't want to burn. The kitten seemed to sense that massive carnage was on the agenda, and it kept trying to crawl up around my neck.

Charlie looked startled, then distressed. "I guess so."

"Look, I know he's your friend, or used to be," I

said gently. "I know you don't really want to hurt him. Pal or I can temporarily blind him with a spell. But we have to take him out somehow, or we'll have a hard time here."

"I know," she said. She pulled the clip on her AK-47, checked her ammunition, then shoved it back into the receiver. "The shadow picked *me* because it knew I had evil in me. Maybe I didn't do much of a job fighting it, but I tried. I really did. But David . . . I don't think he's tried to get rid of it, ever. He's not at all bothered by what it tells him to do."

Charlie paused, looking furious, as if she might start crying. "He totally hid that side of himself from me. How . . . how can you be friends with somebody for years, hang out with them all the time, and not realize they have that kind of evil in them? The . . . the things he's doing now, they're *nasty*."

"You weren't a bad kid. David didn't sound like he was a bad kid, either," I told her, hoping my words would help. I sympathized with her and wanted her to feel better, but more important, I needed her focused for what was ahead. "Everyone has a nasty side. Devils find the kernels of evil in a person, turn on the heat, and pop them until the good's buried. But it can be found again."

I hoped what I was telling her was true, for the Warlock's and my own sake as much as hers and David's. "If we can destroy the shadow, I bet he'll come around."

"I brought this on him. On everyone," she said quietly. "I need to see this finished."

She wiped her eyes, adjusted her gun strap, and shook the tension out of her shoulders. "Okay. We got to do this. Listen: the shadow can move from puddle to pond to river if the waters are near each other. There's a half-dozen lily ponds down there in the garden—the shadow's in one of them, I think—but there's another natural pond nearby and past that, the river. The shadow will stick around if it thinks it's gonna get something to eat, but it can bug out of there in a hurry if it thinks it's threatened. It can probably use the meat puppets to transport itself—they're mostly water, and they can't say no. If the shadow goes to the river we've lost it for good, probably."

She took a deep breath. "So I guess that's a long way of saying, I think we probably have just one shot at it. And I'm kinda worried that if the first thing we do is blind David, the shadow will know something's up and just hightail it for the river."

I hadn't thought of that; I was still feeling pretty feverish, the heat and sun weren't helping, and my brain was more than a little addled.

"Well, that changes things," I replied. "Does David keep a lot of the meat puppets around?"

"I think so, yeah. I think he uses them as . . . toys." She loaded the word with a variety of unsavory implications. "And when he's done with them, he feeds them to the shadow."

"Hm." I pondered the problem.

"Might I suggest," Pal said to me, "that going in spells and guns ablaze might not be our best strategy? If we could find some way of catching the shadow off guard, that would give us a greater likelihood of succeeding here."

"Right," I replied, shrugging out of my backpack.

"Okay. Change of plan. Pal, shrink yourself down as much as possible." I started to pull the saddle pad and saddlebags off his back.

He blinked at me. "How small, exactly?"

I stacked his tack in a pile against the drive-in's pale brick wall and laid my shotgun and pack on top. "I want you to look like nothing more than a common wolf spider and ride on Charlie's shoulder. Can you do that?"

"I suppose so." He sang himself down until he was the size of a small tarantula. "Is this good?"

"Good enough, I think." I scooped him up and set him on Charlie's shoulder. He blended in reasonably well with her gray T-shirt; I doubted anyone would be able to spot him at a distance.

Charlie didn't look entirely happy to have Pal sitting on her. "What now?"

"Now we walk over to the gardens." I pulled my kitten out of my sling and handed it to her, then took the sling off and threw it onto the pile of gear. "You're going to tell David that I'm your prisoner, a gift for the shadow. You've changed your mind and you want to join them in their merry life of murder and plunder and zombie raising."

The girl stood there holding the kitten, staring at me as if I'd sprouted a second head that was reciting French existentialist poetry. "You . . . want me to hand you over to the shadow? Are you *nuts*?"

"Yes, I do, and no, I'm not crazy. I have a plan." I gave her my best Cooper-style, everything's-gonna-be-okay smile. "Convince them that you're serious about joining Team Shadow, and then follow my lead. Oh, and one other thing: if all of a sudden I look like I'm not myself? I'm probably not. Get away from me as fast as possible."

She stowed the kitten in her sling with its twin, and we followed the sidewalk to the Civic League Park. The front gates were rusted open. The path inside the park led us through displays of long-dead rosebushes down to a ravine shaded with hemlocks and live oaks. Once we'd crossed a limestone footbridge over a small natural pond filled with koi, we came out of the trees into the big bowl-shaped water lily garden. The air stank of human filth and rotting flesh. I put my hands on top of my head.

"Put your gun at my back," I whispered. Charlie did as I asked.

On the opposite rim, a small cottage shaded by oaks and pecan trees overlooked the garden, which was roughly the size of a couple of Olympic swimming pools set side by side. In it were eight rectangular, raised concrete water lily ponds with wide limestone rims. Most of the ponds were in varying stages of decay and algae-choked neglect with a few lilies bravely blooming here and there; one pond, however, was nothing but foul-looking sludge, black as crude oil.

A skinny young man of maybe nineteen or twenty with a shaved head was dragging something down the path from the cottage. He was wearing just a pair of muddy canvas sneakers and a ragged blue Superman T-shirt.

He heaved once more on his burden, and then I heard him snarl, "Get up, dammit!"

The burden twitched, and laboriously stood. It was another thin young man, completely naked but for a huge

American eagle tattoo on his chest. His mouth hanging slackly open, he took three tottering, marionette-like steps and then collapsed onto his knees.

Cursing, David hauled the meat puppet up and half carried, half dragged him toward the pond of black sludge.

"God," Charlie whispered. "He looks even worse than he did before."

David, intent on his task, didn't notice us. He hauled the puppet to the edge of the sludge pond, stood him up, and pushed him in. As soon as the puppet landed inside, the sludge heaved up around him and then ripped him to shreds as if the liquid were made of a million vicious blades. In seconds it was all over, and the sludge was still again, gleaming quiet and dark in the sun.

David was leaning forward on his knees, catching his breath, but he turned his head sharply toward the sludge as if it had said something to him, and then he stood up, squinting at us.

"Who's there?" he yelled.

"It's me," Charlie called back. "I . . . I thought about what you said, and you're right. It's stupid to be on the losing side. I want to join y'all. And I got a present for the shadow."

"Well, heyyy, how about that!" David grinned, looking as excited as a six-year-old on Christmas morning. His teeth were rotted gray stubs in his mouth, little tombstones in his bleeding gums. "I knew you'd come around! We got us some good times ahead, girlfriend. Why don't you and your present come on down and let me take a look?"

We slowly walked toward David, my hands still on

my head, Charlie's rifle at my back. As we got closer, I saw that his head wasn't shaved; the hair looked like it had mostly all fallen out except for some stray long greasy strands here and there. Even his eyebrows were gone. His eyes were a sickly yellow, and he didn't look or smell like he'd bathed in months. His face was blotched with acne, and his bald genitals were crusty, pitted with chancres.

"Well, ain't you a tasty-looking piece?" he asked me, his jaundiced eyes shining. "Too bad you're a girl, but you look like you got some muscle in your bustle, so we can play a little make-believe. I bet you're a whole lot more lively than what I got around here."

David snapped his fingers, and there was a mass rustling in the trees and brush ringing the top of the garden. At least thirty meat puppets in various stages of dress and undress emerged and stood at attention. Most of them appeared to be captured ROTC cadets, and they were armed with axes and baseball bats.

Hoo boy. This could go badly.

"My very own gimp squad." David laughed. "They do exactly what I tell 'em, but sometimes that gets a little boring, you know? So, hey, Charlie, thanks."

"Sh-she's for the shadow," Charlie stammered, looking horrified.

"Aw, the shadow don't mind sloppy seconds. That's the deal, I always get first dibs." Then his expression soured. "Well, *Miko* gets first dibs, but that ain't gonna have to go on too much longer, 'specially not now that you're here, Charlie."

He beamed at her. "Good times, I'm telling you! We'll bust on out of here with all the loot I got up at the house, drive to Vegas, live like gangstas!"

David suddenly turned toward the sludge pond like a dog that had been chain-jerked. "Aw. Seriously? . . . Fine."

He turned back to Charlie, petulant as a kid who'd just been denied an ice cream cone. "The shadow wants to see her. Get her up on that ledge over there."

Charlie poked me in the back with the barrel of her rifle, and I stepped toward the sludge pond, my heart hammering in my sweaty chest. At least with my jacket on over my bull-riding glove, David couldn't see my fire, and with a little luck the shadow wouldn't be able to sense it until it was too late.

Jessie . . . I heard the little-girl voice inside my head. It was just as creepy as Charlie had described. *Tell me what you want, Jessie.*

Licking my suddenly dry lips, I climbed up onto the pond's ledge and stared down into the shiny blackness. Tried to blank out my thoughts, in case it had stronger telepathy than Charlie had suggested. I started to replay the lyrics to Beastie Boys songs in my head, over and over, no sleeping till Brooklyn, it was sabotage.

Come on, you can tell me, the shadow wheedled. *I bet you don't like that Miko much, do you? I don't like her, either.*

Suddenly, I had an image in my head of myself killing David, taking his head right off with one of the puppets' axes, and taking his place. I wouldn't become a diseased wreck like him. I was strong, so much stronger than the boy, and the shadow and I could defeat Miko together. And then we could rescue my men and leave the town. I could have anything I wanted, and with the shadow's power, nobody could stop me.

It was a compelling vision, all right, and for two milliseconds I might have even believed it.

"I hate Miko with the white-hot passion of a thousand burning suns," I whispered, crouching down on the ledge. The surface of the sludge was bulging slightly; I knew the shadow was right there below me. "But you know what?"

I whipped off my glove and plunged my flaming hand into the sludge, and as the shadow shrieked inside my head, I pulled us both into my hellement.

I was standing in my old bedroom, and before me was what looked like an overturned five-gallon bucket of raspberry jelly, only it sure didn't smell like any fruit you'd want to eat. It didn't have any visible eyes or mouth or any other features, but the thing shuddered as if it were startled, disoriented.

"I hate slimy, parasitic little devils like you a whole lot more," I told it.

The jelly shrieked and whipped spiky pseudopods at my legs. I jumped backward onto the bed to dodge the swipe, rolled across the mattress, and landed on the other side. The jelly was sprouting pseudopods everywhere, the red tentacles shooting up to stick to the ceiling, the walls, lifting the boneless body up off the ground as the jelly separated in the middle, forming a toothy, noxious maw. Worse, the jelly was swelling, growing, apparently feeding off the dark energies that still irradiated the hellement.

"That was a nasty trick, bringing me here," the jelly said in its little-girl voice. "I'm going to kill you for it."

My sword and shield were by the dresser where I'd left them; I snatched them up barely in time to slash at a pair of pseudopods shooting at me from across the bed. The cut pseudopods retreated, whipping away, spraying me with ichor that sizzled painfully on my face and arms. The jelly was growing so quickly that in a few minutes it would surely suffocate me with its sheer bulk.

"If you kill me, how are you going to get out of here?" I yelled, trying to ignore the pain from my acid burns.

My question registered, and seemed to stymie it for just a minute. I quickly blinked through several gemviews with my ocularis, hoping I'd see something . . . and there it was: a pulsing heart in the middle of the gooey mass.

There was no time to waste. I launched myself back across the bed at the monster and rammed my left arm right into its soft body. Instantly my flesh was burning, my skin melting, and the creature was shrieking, whipping my back and arms with its pseudopods, and I knew I'd be dead in just a few seconds if I didn't kill it. Right before the nerves in my hand died, I felt my fingers close on its nasty little heart and I gave a hard jerk, pulling it free. The pseudopods went slack, and the jelly fell to the floor with a tremendous splat.

I staggered backward into the dresser. My left hand was nearly skeletal, and the blue-black heart slipped from my fingers onto the floor. The organ sprouted centipede legs and started to scurry back to the jelly mass, presumably to regenerate the monster. I took careful aim with my sword and speared it right to the floorboards. The heart spasmed around the blade, then began to disintegrate into a nasty gray liquid. The jelly body, too, was decaying to a pool of sour blood on the floor.

Once the burst of adrenaline subsided, I realized that my left arm was in tremendous pain, and the acidic ichor was continuing to eat its way through my flesh and bone. Time to leave. I hopped over the puddle and opened the red portal door with my good hand.

The return to my body was disorienting and unpleasant. I couldn't see; there was a thick, stinging liquid in my eyes. My face was wet and sticky, and there was blood and something else in my mouth. I spat it out, just as a dozen death-memories hit me, and I spent the next few minutes being violently ill.

When I'd purged most of the blood and the memories along with it, I wiped my eyes with my arm—thank God, I was still wearing my dragonskins—and blinked, trying to see.

I was sickened but not even remotely surprised to see the mangled corpse of a meat puppet at my feet. But I wasn't in the garden. I looked around; I'd run up into the trees, I supposed to find more puppets to kill. The garden below me was the scene of a massacre; it looked as though David had sent a half-dozen puppets after me at the sludge pond, but then I'd run around killing anything I could lay my hands on. No one was moving.

My heart dropped. Charlie. Where was Charlie? And then I saw her kneeling beside David. She looked like she was okay, or at least not badly injured. David's jaundiced eyes were staring wide, and I could see a dark pool of blood under his head.

The exhaustion hit me all at once, and I had to lean against the trunk of a nearby pecan tree to keep from keeling over. I got my second wind after a moment or

two, and I made my way down the path toward Charlie, my arms and legs shaking and muscles twitching
and fever at full burn.

"Charlie," I croaked. "Are you okay?"

She nodded, not replying. Tears were running down
her cheeks as she stared at David's body.

"Did I do that?" I asked.

She shook her head, then gently turned David's face
toward me so I could see the bullet wound in his tem-
ple. "I did, when he sicced the zombies on you."

"I—I'm sorry you didn't get to say something to
him, before, you know . . ." I trailed off, then
thought, *Pal, where the heck are you?*

"I'm over here, on this lily pad. I wasn't sure how
I could do any good; Charlie reached safety on her
own and attempting to stop the Goad rampaging in
your body seemed rather perilous even at my full
size."

*Well, embiggen yourself, already . . . looks like we've
got more corpse hauling to do.*

She wiped her face on the back of her hand. "It's
okay. What was I gonna say, anyhow? 'Sorry I brought
this evil into your life'? 'Sorry you liked the evil a
whole lot better'n you ever liked me'? 'Sorry you
turned out to be a real freak, and yet part of me still
loves you'? Shee-it. The bullet probably said everything that needed saying."

"Do you want to bury him?" I asked.

"No." She stood up slowly, still gazing down at his
body. "He used to be the best friend I've ever had . . .
but all these other guys? They were someone's best
friends, too. Someone's sons and maybe a few of them

were someone's daddies. Whatever we do for David, we do for all of them. And I ain't got the strength to dig all those graves, do you?"

"Tell her we can give all of them a proper burial," Pal said. "I know a spell we can use . . ."

chapter twenty-nine

Showdown

I was completely wrung out by the time we got back to campus. After a couple of cadets hosed the blood off me in the courtyard, it took my last bit of energy to go upstairs, take a hot shower, change into one of the stupid pizza shirts to sleep in, and collapse into the restraint chair. I was out before Pal finished strapping me in.

A pounding at the door woke me as the morning's first light was streaming through the blinds. The sound hurt my aching head.

Pal, get that, would you?

I forced open my blurry, sticky eyes and watched him open the door. Charlie was standing there in tiger-stripe fatigues, her AK-47 locked and loaded. She looked pale and scared and excited.

"Miko's super pissed that we cut off her supply," Charlie said. "We just got word from the scouts that there are thousands of meat puppets coming to attack campus; they'll be here in less than an hour. She had *way* more zombies in reserve than anyone knew. We've got the guns, but we're pretty severely outnumbered. I heard some people talking like maybe we don't have enough ammunition. Captain Flynn—he's in command now—is mobilizing everyone and having them report for battle."

While she spoke, Pal came over to me and undid my head restraints and pulled out the mouthpiece so I could reply.

"Am I supposed to report for battle, too?" I asked, trying to work the stiffness out of my jaw.

She shook her head. "Well, not here, anyway. Sara told me to tell you that whatever y'all are planning to do to attack Miko, y'all best get to doing it pretty soon. The only thing is, I can't come with y'all, I gotta stay here. Captain's orders." Her expression darkened. "And Sara said I'd just get myself killed, anyhow."

Charlie reached into her sling and pulled out two MREs sealed in tan plastic. She tossed them onto the bed. "That's y'all's food for today; they shut down the cafeteria and gave guns to all the cooks. I got you a vegetarian one, and him a meat one."

"Thanks," I said. "Did Sara happen to say where I'm supposed to find Miko?"

"Oh. Yeah. She says the cats say that Miko's base is in the Saguaro Hotel downtown. It's hard to miss; it's the tallest building in the whole city."

She shuffled her feet awkwardly. "Hey, I've got to go. I feel like I should give you a hug or something. But that might be kinda weird with you in that chair."

"Yeah, probably."

"So, um . . . bye? I hope I see you around later?"

"Me, too," I replied. "Fight good. Stay safe."

Charlie gave me a little wave, then hurried away toward the elevators. Pal freed me from the chair, and I stumbled into the bathroom to pee and splash some cold water on my face.

"I'm so not ready for this," I croaked to Pal as I rested my forehead against the cool edge of the sink. "I feel like I've been run over by a whole fleet of Greyhounds. And then set on fire. God knows what other crap I got infected with yesterday."

Pal picked up his MRE. "Well, eat some food and take your medicine; perhaps that will help you feel a bit better?"

"I guess it can't hurt." I found my Leatherman tool and opened up the veggie MRE, spreading the contents on the cot. The thought of eating cold cheese tortellini for breakfast made my stomach churn, but the package also had chunky peanut butter and crackers and, even better, a chocolate Soldier Fuel bar. I ate the energy bar with a bottle of water and took my antibiotics and ibuprofen. Then waited to see if the food and medicine would stay down.

To my joy, they did.

"I took the liberty of charm-cleaning and drying your clothing after you fell asleep," Pal told me as he licked clean the inside of his packet of pot roast. "The hose-down left the leather quite damp, and your T-shirt seemed . . . unsanitary."

"Thanks, Pal." I stretched, trying to unwind my knotted back muscles. "Well, let me get dressed, and let's do this thing."

I couldn't bear the thought of another day in the hot riding helmet, so I had Pal clean it and then I traded it to a girl down the hall for her straw cowboy hat. She seemed happy to have something solid to wear into the impending battle. Evidently, combat and tactical helmets were in relatively short supply on campus.

Once we were airborne, our destination was dead easy to find; it was the tallest structure in the city by at least twenty floors. Furthermore, the pale brick tower had the letters SAGUARO HOTEL spelled out in tall steel letters on top of its red, Mission-style hipped tile roof. I was pretty sure anyone within fifteen miles could spot the building.

Once we got closer, I could see a crowd milling at the base of the hotel.

"Jesus, she didn't even send all the puppets she's got to campus," I marveled to Pal. Miko had certainly made serious headway on her two hundred thousand souls during her reign in Cuchillo.

I spotted an alleyway a block from the hotel that was clear of puppets. "Land us over there, behind that diner."

Pal descended quickly but landed gently beside a green Dumpster. "How are we going to get through that crowd?"

"My shotgun and your charm," I replied. "But maybe we won't have to use either. Miko did seem like she wanted a face-to-face with me."

Pal trotted out of the alleyway into the street in front of the hotel, expecting a fight. But the festering mob of meat puppets simply shambled aside as I rode Pal toward the stark white columns and broad marble steps of the hotel. There had to be a thousand bodies in the stinking brown sea parting before us. My skull was pounding again, the heat and hard West Texas sun nearly unbearable. I tipped my straw cowboy hat forward in a futile attempt to get some of the weak breeze on the back of my head.

And in a blink, Miko was suddenly *there* on the steps, Cooper and the Warlock strung up naked and sunburned on rough-hewn mesquite crosses to either side of her. As a small mercy, their limbs had been tied, not nailed, to the twisted branches. Their heads hung forward, insensible, as their chests shuddered to pull in shallow breaths.

The devil kitten in my saddlebag was purring loudly. *You ready for this?* I asked Pal.

"Ready for a slow, bloody, excruciating death followed by eternal damnation? Of *course*. What fun."

Ignoring his sarcasm, I drew my pistol-grip Mossberg shotgun and racked a cartridge into the chamber.

"Give 'em back, Miko!" My voice was tight, shaky, a mouse's outraged squeak at a lion.

She smiled at me, and all at once her beauty and power hit me like a velvet sledgehammer. If I'd been standing I would have fallen to my knees. I hoped I wasn't getting wet; Pal would know and it would be a sprinkle of embarrassment on top of the disaster sundae I'd brought to our table.

"You know what I want," she whispered, her voice floating easily over the distance between us. "Give yourself to me, and your men shall go free."

A tiny part of me—the part that was exhausted, weary of fighting, weary of running—wondered if giving my body and soul to her would really be such a bad thing. It was the same part that had entertained the shadow's vision of my future with it. I kicked that part of myself in the ass and chased it from my mind.

I swung my leg over Pal's vertebral crest and slid

down to the pavement. *Stick close behind me. I won't last long against her, and I don't want the kitten out of range.*

"Consider me your glue," Pal replied.

"What do you want me for?" I slowly approached Miko, the shotgun still gripped in my hand. It would be completely useless against her, but I didn't want her to know I knew that.

She laughed. "I always knew you would make a far better partner than the shadow, and you proved that beyond any doubt yesterday. Losing my puppets is . . . inconvenient, but I have more than enough to break down the last resistance. It's time to move on from here."

"What do you need a partner for?" I was still moving toward her; another twenty steps and I'd be able to light her up even if I couldn't get my hand to stop shaking. "I mean, not that I'm not flattered and stuff, but it seems like you do okay on your own."

Another laugh. "Oh, I do, but running a paradise takes a certain amount of focus and time, and it's nice to have someone who can be relied upon for both work and recreation."

I never thought the word "recreation" could sound quite as salacious as she made it sound.

"Paradise?" I was genuinely puzzled. She didn't sound as though she was speaking with irony or sarcasm. "What paradise?"

"In here." She pointed at her heart. "I am an entirely benevolent goddess to those who submit their souls to me. They receive the gift of living the afterlife of their dreams. If I have to take a soul by force, well . . . that soul gets to watch everyone else having a good time."

"That sounds real nice." I was in range. I dropped the shotgun and before it had hit the pavement I'd yanked off my glove and let loose with a blast of incendiary ectoplasm—

—which fizzled into nothing as she made the smallest of gestures with her left hand.

And then she grabbed my claw with her right, sending me down to my knees on the marble steps, flooding my body with pain.

"Now, that *wasn't* very nice," she said softly. "Or very smart. Did you seriously think I'd still be vulnerable to something as common as fire? *That* curse hasn't bound me since I won my soul."

Miko shook her head at me. "A shame you weren't just a little more intelligent. I guess it's true . . . good help *is* hard to find."

She reached down to touch my face with her left hand, and I knew that she meant to take my soul, and I couldn't speak or move and in my panic I did the only thing I could think to do and retreated into my hellement.

I found myself standing in the bedroom, the floor still sticky with the remains of the jelly.

I'm about to die, I thought. When Miko figured out I'd run from her, she'd tear my body apart and that would be the end of me.

I held my breath, waited for the inevitable.

And waited.

And waited.

I scratched my scalp. Was I dead? Shouldn't I have

felt my death, somehow? And if I *was* dead, was I stuck here in the hellement forever?

There was only one way to find out. I went to the red portal door. Turned the handle.

And found myself sprawled on my back, the marble stairs digging painfully into my hips and spine, Pal's paws cradling my head, his face peering down into mine. I felt my hand flame up again; at least it was stretched out away from my body so I wasn't in danger of burning myself.

"Oh, thank Goddess. I thought you were dead," he said. Then his eyes turned toward my flames. "My goodness."

The black claw was burning away in my flames, crumbling painlessly to ash.

"What happened?" I asked. "Where's Miko?"

"It was very peculiar," Pal said. "She touched you, then screamed, shoved you away, and disappeared. The meat puppets all fell down; wherever she went, she's no longer controlling them."

"Whoa." I finally figured out what had just happened. "She popped the Goad spirit out of me instead of my soul. Guess she didn't much like the taste of it."

"I imagine not."

"Help me up; we gotta get the guys down from those crosses."

They were both unconscious; the Warlock still bore the gash on his forehead and other injuries from his beating, but it looked like Miko or one of her puppets had worked Cooper over even worse. He had knotty, purplish bruises everywhere.

Pal and I cut the ropes binding them to the mesquite

logs and carried them into the cool of the lavish, 1920s Renaissance palace–style hotel lobby. Nobody was in there except for a couple of meat puppets dying quietly on the shiny chessboard floor. We put Cooper and the Warlock on a couple of the wide leather couches and between the two of us were able to work enough healing magic to bring them out of their comas.

"Wow, you're a sight for sunburned eyes." Cooper gave me a lopsided smile, then winced as he sat up. "Where's Miko?"

"She's gone. She tried to take my soul, and got my devil instead. So the Virtii and the cats were right, and I didn't really have to do anything but show up."

"Huh. Why didn't we think of that?" the Warlock murmured.

"More to the point, why didn't Sara or anyone else just tell us that?" I sounded whiny, even to myself, but dammit, after everything I'd been through, I felt I'd earned a good whine.

"Miko's a mind reader," Cooper said. "So it wasn't gonna work if you knew about it."

"Have you seen my brother Randall here?" I asked Cooper.

He nodded, then looked like he wished he hadn't moved his head quite so vigorously. "I think so, yeah. Everybody's in the penthouse on the top floors. She's got the Talents chained up, broadcasting her antimagic spell. Some of 'em are in bad shape. We should get up there and get 'em free."

Thankfully, the old wire-cage elevator still worked. Pal and I helped the guys into the lift car. As we stood there, I realized the guys weren't meeting my or each other's eyes. Glad as they were to be free of Miko's torment, I got the feeling they weren't so happy to see *me*. Crap.

We stepped out onto the thick maroon carpet of the twenty-fifth floor, and almost immediately encountered the first real, live, soul-intact human in the building: a startled-looking Hispanic woman in stained, pale blue hospital scrubs who was clutching a pair of plastic IV bags. She was in her late twenties, and something about the curve of her jaw and the set of her shoulders seemed familiar.

"Are you Sofia Ray?" I asked her.

Her eyes grew big. "Yes. Who are you people?"

"I met your father at his store; he asked me to find you."

"Papa is still alive?" she breathed.

"He was when we left his place a couple of days ago," I replied. God, had we been in this godforsaken town for only days? Quick math told me we had, and I continued: "Miko seems to be gone now, so if you could show us where she's keeping her prisoners . . . ?"

Sofia led us down the hall into a big room that was set up with hospital cots outfitted with restraints; I counted thirty Talents strapped down to the cots, IVs dripping into veins and catheter tubes draining nethers. Some wore hospital gowns, others were mostly naked under sheets. Fine silver chains connected their feet, forming an unbroken circle of trance-bound spellcasters.

"Well, here's the source of our antimagic, antifire field," Cooper said.

"Interesting," Pal said behind me. "They're networked together like computers. That would be rather clever if it weren't a completely horrible thing to do to people."

"Lynn!" Sofia called. "Lynn, get up, help finally came!"

A woman who at first glance seemed to be part of the circle popped awake on a nearby cot and threw off her sheet. She was also dressed in scrubs, and wore a nurse's sensible white shoes. Her expression turned from surprise to joy and then to fear when she saw Pal, who hadn't shrunk himself down much for the elevator.

"Don't be afraid of my spider," I said quickly. "He looks scary, but he's good."

Cooper was touching the nearest length of silver chain, frowning. "I've heard of thrall circles like these. Someone here is acting as the pacemaker, and the others are just echoing the spell he or she is casting. If we can wake the pacemaker up, the others should come out of it, too. But if we break the chain before then, the shock could kill some of them."

Closing his eyes, he limped around the circle, holding his hands toward the enthralled Talents. And then stopped, right in front of a sandy-haired young man who looked to be five or six years older than me. "This one."

"Wait a minute," I said, stepping toward the young man. "I think that's my brother. How does he need to be awakened?"

"Gently, if possible," Cooper replied. "Shock to the system and all that fun stuff if you jerk him right out of the spell."

I went to the side of his bed and looked down at him. His face was puffy from all the IV fluids and drugs he'd been filled with, but he did look a whole lot like our father. And me.

"Randall," I called, not too loudly. "Randall, wake up."

He made a slight moan and stirred in his trance-sleep. I started patting his hand, and spoke just a little louder: "C'mon, dude, wake up. We gotta go home. You want to see your dad, don't you? Wanna take me to see Magus Shimmer?"

"Mugus shummur . . ." he slurred. His eyes fluttered open, rolled, seemed to focus on me.

"Whoa. Sis." His voice was a hoarse croak. He smiled at me. "I dreamed you'd come. What took ya so long?"

Sofia and Lynn helped us unhook the rest of the Talents, and after Pal and Cooper performed a healing spell on Randall, my brother was alert and almost hyper.

"Yeah, I can totally get us out of here," he told me. "This town is full of seams; I couldn't get 'em myself, not while Miko had me anyway. I played along with her after she ambushed my team; figured I could maybe get the drop on her, but I just didn't luck out. Man, I could use a burger. Fries, too. Fries would be *great* right now. There's this cool diner up in Dallas I should take y'all to. Hey, you're an opener, right?"

"What?" I asked, his sudden conversational switchback confusing me momentarily.

"An opener. Good at opening portals?"

"Oh. Yeah. I think so."

"Awesome-sauce." Randall grinned at me. "We are

totally out of here. Dad's got a really cool place, you're gonna *love* it."

"I need to take Sofia back to her dad's place," I said. "I promised him I would."

"Sure, whatevs," Randall said. "Gonna take a while to get everybody healed up and back on their feet, anyhow."

Sofia was afraid to ride Pal at first, but I finally convinced her to climb on behind me. The flight back to Rudy Ray's Roadstop was uneventful, and toward the end of it, Sofia seemed to be enjoying herself. Flying way up high in the open air is exhilarating if it doesn't give you a heart attack.

We touched down in the shade of the gas pumps, and I had just helped Sofia down onto the pavement when I heard the store's front door whish open.

"S-Sofia?" old Rudy stammered as he stumbled into the parking lot. He looked like he'd just awakened. "Is that really you?"

"Papa!" She broke into a broad smile and ran over to him. They caught each other in a strong hug.

Tears ran down Rudy's craggy face. "Thank God, thank God, thank God you're okay. I was so scairt I'd lost you forever."

He looked at me, blinking away the water. "Thank you, miss. I don't know how you done it, and I cain't ever repay you for this . . ."

"It's okay," I said, simultaneously touched by their joy and feeling a bit like a voyeur. "I don't need to be repaid, I just . . . want y'all to be happy."

I looked at Rudy and his daughter and thought of all

the meat puppets I'd seen since I got to Cuchillo. Remembered Henry's death. Remembered what Charlie said when she refused to bury David. And I made a decision.

We can't leave this town, I thought to Pal. *I have to go find Miko.*

"What? Why on Earth do you want to do that? You defeated her."

No, I didn't. Not really, I replied. *The Goad's not nearly strong enough to kill something like her. Having it in her drove her mad, yes, but maybe only for a little while. And then she'll go right back to mass murder, maybe do this to another town someplace. I can't let that happen.*

"But perhaps her madness is permanent," Pal countered. "Perhaps having a devil inside her is the one true weakness she had left."

Then that's just as bad, I replied. *Because that means I've just condemned thousands of immortal souls to hell. If it wouldn't have been right to abandon Cooper's brothers, then it surely isn't right to abandon the souls inside Miko.*

I looked Pal square in his eyes. "I'm not leaving until this thing is finished. Are you with me?"

He nodded. "I'm with you."